The Dobro® Workbook

by David Hamburger

Photo courtesy of Gibson Guitar Company

ISBN 0-7935-8040-4

7777 W. Bluemound Rd. P.O. Box 13819 Milwaukee, WI 53213

Visit Hal Leonard Online at
www.halleonard.com

Acknowledgments

Thanks to the following individuals for their help and support: Bruce Tovski for his excellent and unceasing efforts in engineering and producing the accompanying CD, Matt Weiner (bass) and Jim Henry (guitar) for their stellar backup work on the same, Bob Saidenberg, Peter Wallach, the Music Emporium, Michelle Allbeck, Andy Ellis, Luke and Gloria, Wayne Rooks, Hal Leonard Corporation, and all the folks at the Second Avenue bluegrass jams. Very special thanks to Stacy Phillips for writing *The Dobro Book*.

This book is dedicated to Fats Kaplin and Bill Barron.

About the Author

David Hamburger is a regular contributor to *Guitar Player* and *Acoustic Guitar* and is the author of *Electric Slide Guitar*. He has played Dobro, pedal steel, acoustic or electric guitar on dozens of independent recordings, and released his own solo CD, *King of the Brooklyn Delta*. For David's touring schedule, discography, and other late-breaking news, check out his website at www.songs.com/hamburski.

Table of Contents

Introduction

Unless someone mistakenly gave you this book for your birthday instead of bringing a dozen roses or sending you to Nazareth, Pennsylvania on an all-expenses-paid tour of, oh, I don't know, some guitar factory, you're probably reading this right now because you want to improve your lap-style resophonic slide playing. Have you come to the right place? Well, let's start with what I *can't* show you.

I can't teach you patience and determination, two relatively important ingredients in the sometimes difficult but generally enjoyable journey towards becoming a better musician. And inspiration—that impulse to take a weird left turn in your break, or to put two and two together and come up with thirty-seven—well, you're on your own in that regard, too. I can't even really show you some of the more tangible things like how to learn off of records or how to make discoveries by observing another musician perform or play at a jam. I might suggest ways to go about that, but I can't get inside your head to show you how that part of the learning process *feels*. Finally, I won't be showing you anyone's note-for-note solos, because I happen not to have the publishing rights to anything like that just lying around. But that's OK, because there are other places you can get that sort of thing.

So what can I show you? Well, I can show you some notes. To be more specific, I can show you which notes you might play, *how* you might play them, and when you might play which ones. Put another way, I can show you various *materials, techniques,* and *concepts. **Materials*** are more or less the facts of music—the scales musicians choose from, the tunes they play on. From these bedrock materials come more subjective, creative things like phrases, licks, and breaks. ***Techniques*** are essentially the mechanics of playing a particular instrument. How to execute slides, rolls, hammer-ons and pull-offs, melodic style patterns, right-hand fingerings, and bar moves—these are all technical concerns. You, yourself, have to ultimately train your hands to respond the way you want them to, to create the sounds you seek, but I can give you particular things to practice that will help you focus your brain and your muscles on one thing at a time. Finally, ***concepts*** are just that—ideas about music. You need to know what you're trying to do in order to work on it and get better at it. A concept can be very specific, like using call-and-response phrasing to create a break, or using syncopation to create a new roll. Or it can be something more general, like an approach to practicing more effectively.

The book is based on the demands of playing *bluegrass*—you can play any kind of music on the resophonic slide guitar, and I hope you take some of the ideas here and use them towards your own musical ends, bluegrass or otherwise, but bluegrass happens to be both technically demanding and possessed of a rich history of lap-style playing, which makes it a good point of departure for anyone interested in playing this instrument. I have tried to provide material that will work "in the real world," i.e., things that you could actually incorporate into your playing and really use. So while this is not a book of tunes *per se,* I have included arrangements of a handful of tunes from the the bluegrass repertoire, and many of the exercises are essentially sample breaks on those tunes. Some of the other exercises are really more like studies, designed to show you an idea, illuminate a concept, or give you a real workout executing a particular kind of move or pattern. These exercises are the musical equivalent of swinging two baseball bats while on deck before stepping up to the plate with just one—if you can get comfortable with a particularly difficult, demanding passage while practicing, the simpler things will come that much easier when you're on stage or in an impromptu jam.

Each chapter builds upon what has come before, technically and conceptually, as it introduces the next round of material. While I have tried to keep the theory to the necessary minimum, it will help if you have a basic understanding of major, minor, and blues scales as well as of major and minor chords.

Nearly every example has been recorded, so even if you don't read music, you should be able to put everything together using the tablature and the CD. I have tried to provide definitions of some of the more important musical terms as they crop up throughout the book, and if you want to sound suave you can pepper your conversation with these technical words the next time you're on the cocktail circuit.

The Technical Lowdown and a Note about the Recording

All of the examples on the accompanying CD were played by the author using a 1996 Dobro Model 27DX strung with John Pearse phosphor bronze resophonic guitar strings (.016-.059) and played with National metal fingerpicks, a National metal thumbpick, and a Shubb bar.

The short examples are played slowly, accompanied by a click track for reference. The longer examples are played up to tempo with a rhythm section. On the longer examples, you can use the balance control on your stereo to pan hard right, to hear just the example itself, or hard left, in order to play along with the rhythm track.

1 *All of the examples in this book are to be played in the standard High G tuning, G–B–D–G–B–D, low to high. The first track on the CD provides a series of notes to which you can tune up.*

A Word about "The Dobro™"

The Dobro was invented in the 1920s by the Dopyera brothers, four Czechoslovakian immigrants who settled in California. The unbelievably convoluted history of this family, their business, and their guitars has been documented elsewhere in greater and inevitably more accurate detail. For our purposes, the essential point of interest is that the Dopyeras participated in what was at the time a pressing effort to design an ever-louder acoustic guitar—one that could compete with the horns, drums, and other mayhem of the Jazz Age. What they came up with was the idea of inserting a "resonator" into the face of the guitar—essentially, a dish in the same shape as a speaker cone, designed to do the same thing as a speaker—to amplify sound. It being the 1920s, they covered these cones with highly decorative art-deco plates—the "hubcap," "pie plate," or shiny circular part that you see when you look at one of their guitars.

Hawaiian music was all the rage in the twenties, and this included the "Hawaiian style" of playing the guitar, which involved resting the guitar flat on one's lap, with the strings facing upwards, and fretting the strings with a solid metal bar or "steel." Again, the history of this stylistic development and the corresponding myth, lore, legend, and controversy surrounding it is available elsewhere. What matters for us is that the Dopyeras thus manufactured both regular or "Spanish-style" guitars, with ordinary round necks and low, frettable string action, and "Hawaiian-style" guitars. These Hawaiian-style guitars had square necks and raised action. They were never meant to be fretted without a slide, and the high action helped make for cleaner barring and even greater volume.

Now, watch carefully, because this is where things get complicated. By the 1930s and '40s, these Hawaiian-style resophonic guitars were being played in hillbilly and country-and-western bands. Then in the mid 1950s, a musician named Buck "Uncle Josh" Graves, a colleague and employee of bluegrass banjo innovator Earl Scruggs, took this hillbilly/Hawaiian approach and fused it with a combination of country blues licks and sparkling Scruggs-inspired banjo-style rolls to lay the foundation of the modern resophonic Hawaiian guitar sound in bluegrass.

Up until recently, the style invented by Graves, further refined and developed by Mike Auldridge and then carried on and broadened by Jerry Douglas and others, was referred to as "bluegrass Dobro." The specific brand name Dobro was used generically to refer to Hawaiian-style resophonic guitar played either on one's lap or on a strap with the strings facing upwards and played with a solid bar for a slide. One referred to someone as a "Dobro player," and to one's guitar as a "Dobro" regardless of the brand. (When I bought my first lap-style instrument—a Regal made in the 1930s for the Dobro company and as often as not sold under the Dobro name—I did not refer to myself as a "Regalist." Aside from whatever political problems that might cause in a king-fearing democracy like the United States, nobody would have known what I was talking about.)

At the time of this writing, however, this decades-old practice of using the specific brand name "Dobro" to refer generically to both a kind of instrument and a way of playing is rapidly disintegrating, and the search is on for a convenient way to replace this term in general usage. It sort of makes sense, at this point, because there are a number of fine guitar makers out there building resophonic Hawaiian or lap-style guitars who have nothing to do commercially with the Dobro company and who have every right to want their instruments to be referred to some other way. It also has a great deal to do with the Gibson instrument company buying the Original Musical Instrument Company or O.M.I., the descendant of the Dobro company, and with it the rights of the Dobro brand name. Gibson would like this brand name to be recognized as such and not bandied about in a generic way—much the way the good people at Kleenex would like you to use the term "facial tissue" when speaking of a rival company's product.

So, in subtitling this book "techniques, improvisational skills, and hot licks for lap-style resophonic slide guitar," I did so to make things clearer. Can you tell?

Some Essentials for Playing Lap-Style Resophonic Slide Guitar

Holding the Resophonic Guitar

In case you're not already aware, you can play lap-style resophonic guitar sitting *or* standing. If sitting, rest the body of the instrument on one leg and the neck on the other. Resting the body on both legs seems to be a natural impulse, yet that leaves the neck waving around in the breeze. You need to have the neck braced solidly on your leg so you can put pressure on the strings without the neck going anywhere. You may want to angle the neck slightly away from you rather than holding the instrument perfectly parallel to your body, as in the photograph.

If standing, round yourself up a good long strap. Most guitar straps won't be long enough, though you could conceivably lengthen one with a bandanna, a shoestring, a strand of linguine, etc. A few companies—like Webb Straps of Monroe, Va.—make straps designed specifically for playing Hawaiian-style standing up. The neck end of the strap has to attach at the headstock so you can bear down on the strings without the neck going anywhere. It's best to loop the strap between the second and third set of tuners, so the angle of the strap doesn't interfere with your barring hand's wrist.

A little pressure on the face of the resonator with your picking hand will help to stabilize things—it's common to rest the fleshy part of your palm somewhere on the side of the bridge closer to your body.

One big suggestion: if you're going to jam, perform, or otherwise play with other people while standing up, *practice* standing up. The angle of the instrument and the relative mobility of the neck when you're standing up is something you have to get used to compensating for. Stuff that you could nail sitting down will suddenly fall apart under your fingers when you try it standing up if you've never done it that way before the gig. End of sermon.

The Bar

Lap-style players obsess about their picks and their bars. For many years, the standard bar has been the Stevens Steel, a solid metal slide grooved on three sides to provide grips for your fingers. The grooves are what enable you to lift and drop the bar from and to the strings; this kind of control is the basis of the whole bluegrass hammer-on and pull-off style of lap-style playing.

More recently, the Shubb company and resophonic luthier Tim Scheerhorn, among others, have created a handful of variations on the classic Stevens design. Scheerhorn's bar has more mass, and the flared ends come to a sharper edge, which can help in executing hammer-ons and pull-offs. Shubb's #2 bar is in between the Stevens and the Scheerhorn—it has the flared ends of a Scheerhorn, but they're not cut as sharp and respond more like a Stevens would.

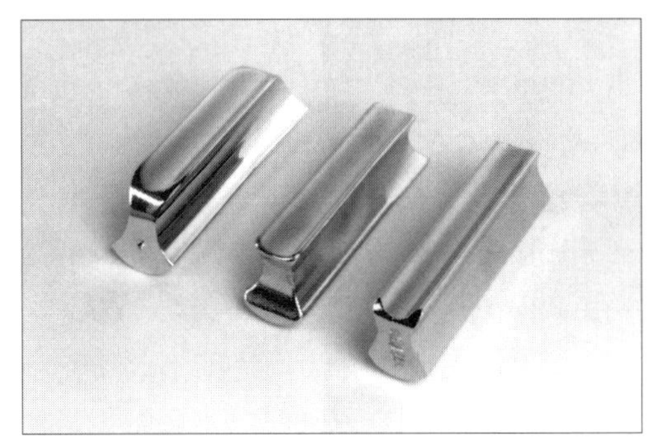

Scheerhorn, Shubb, and Stevens bars

As a general tip, try to keep the bar deep enough into your third joint, where your fingers meet your hand, so that the tip of the bar is securely *within* your fingertips, ending around the ball of your index finger on the top of the bar. This is particularly important for not losing the bar while playing slants or bar tilts or anything else that involves manipulating the bar beyond the simple straight-bar, resting-flat-on-the-strings position. For bar tilts, keeping the bar within your fingers like this allows you to mute the strings above the one you are playing, making for cleaner open-position playing whether ascending or descending the strings. The better grip you have, the more connected you will feel to the strings, to the instrument, and to the notes you are playing. Plus you won't drop the bar as much, and that's important if you want to look cool.

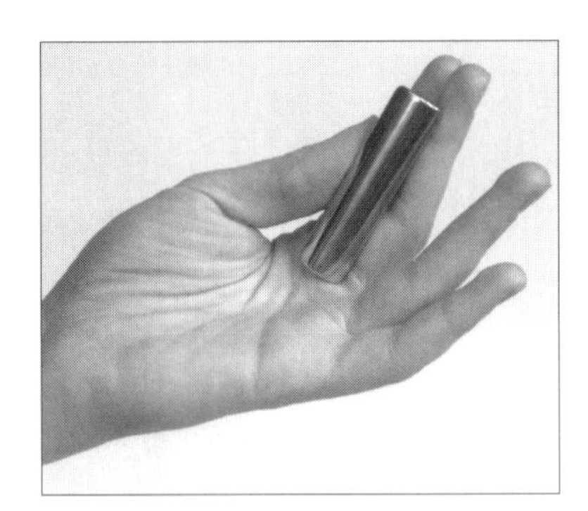

Holding the bar, palm up

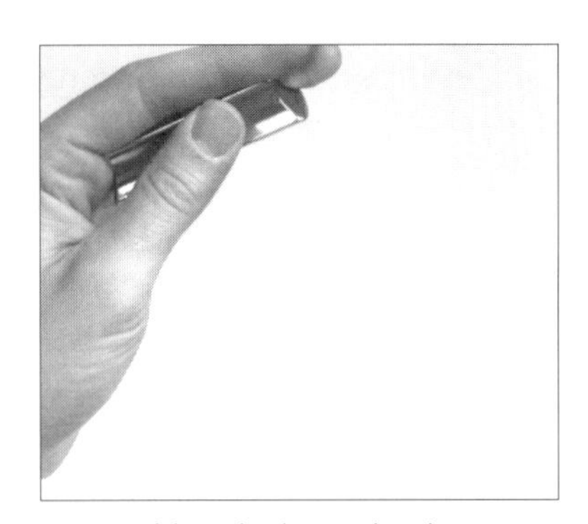

Holding the bar, palm down

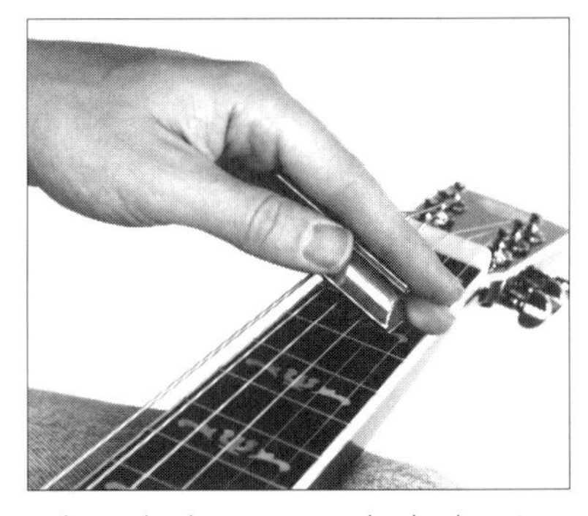

Tilting the bar, muting the high string

Picks

Picks are an even more obsessive topic than bars. Almost everybody plays with a thumbpick, either plastic or metal, and two metal fingerpicks—one for the index finger and one for the middle. Personally, I like my fingerpicks to curve to the contour of my fingertips. To shape them, I grip the base of the pick (the loop that goes around your finger) with a small set of pliers and use needle nose pliers to put a series of small bends into the pick part until it fits my finger. (I do this with the pick *off* of my finger, and keep slipping it on to test it, if that wasn't obvious...) The angle of the pick part relative to the string makes a big difference in the tone; I like to twist it slightly so that when I pick, the string can slide off the pick instead of coming sharply off right at the tip. It's kind of hard to explain, so do a little experimenting on your own until you get a sound and feel that *you* like. You might also do a little needle-nosing on the loops, the parts that wrap around your finger. The snugger you can get them to fit (without turning your fingertips purple), the less chance you'll catch them on the strings when you go to pick, making all kinds of stray sounds you weren't expecting.

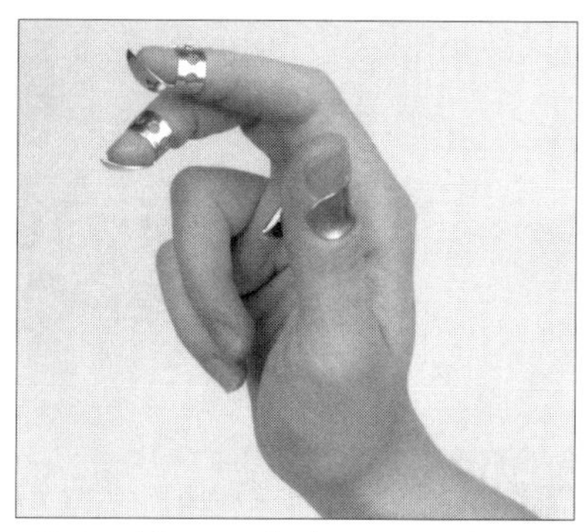

National fingerpicks, bent to perfection

Capos

Shubb, Leno, Sćheerhorn, and luthier Paul Beard, among others, make capos designed to work with lap-style guitars. I'm a fan of the Shubb, because it's the only one I know of that puts a solid support *between* the fretboard and the strings, thus eliminating any wobble of the strings to and fro as you put pressure on them while playing. Also, you can put it on and take it off with one hand, which is kind of convenient for live situations. However, it doesn't work on every instrument, particularly down by the nut or if the action is relatively high. Experiment to see what works best on your instrument.

Strings

A few different companies make string sets gauged specifically for playing lap style in High G (G–B–D–G–B–D) tuning. Generally, these gauges run from about a .016 for the high string down to about a .059 for the low string, with some variations. The biggest question is whether to use nickel or phosphor bronze wound strings. They provide very different tones, and the effect they have can really vary from instrument to instrument. Try a few different sets, and see what you like best on yours. I find that fingerpicks tend to particularly chew up those wound third strings, so I always buy a lot of extras in that gauge. That way, if the third string is starting to buzz on an otherwise still-OK set of strings, I can just replace the offending third string to get through a rehearsal or jam situation. (I love the sound of new strings, but I really loathe changing them!) GHS, John Pearse, and Paul Beard all make appropriately-gauged sets, or you can put together your own by buying single strings in the right gauges.

Basic Techniques in Open Position—Hammer-Ons, Pull-Offs, Slides, and Picking

This first chapter consists of exercises in the key of G in the open position. An exercise takes just one technical or conceptual element and isolates it, whether it's a left-hand technique like hammering on, a certain right-hand picking pattern, the location of a particular set of notes, or anything else. This way, you can focus on one thing at a time. Since much of this book is about playing and improvising in the open position favored by resophonic bluegrass players, this first chapter should help you sharpen your skills at hammering on, pulling off, and sliding, while focusing on which notes you have to choose from in the key of G.

The G Major Scale

Let's start with some scales. Now, I know "scales" sounds like piano lessons or something, and you're here for the hot licks, but hey, trust me. Scales are just a reference point, a way of talking about what notes work over what chords, among other things. I promise, we will be transcending the pedestrian scale in just a few short pages, but don't ignore them, because they'll be back later in other chapters. Get used to scales, let them become your friends, and they will serve you well. Really. I mean it.

Here's our first move: a G major scale in open position.

Fig. 1

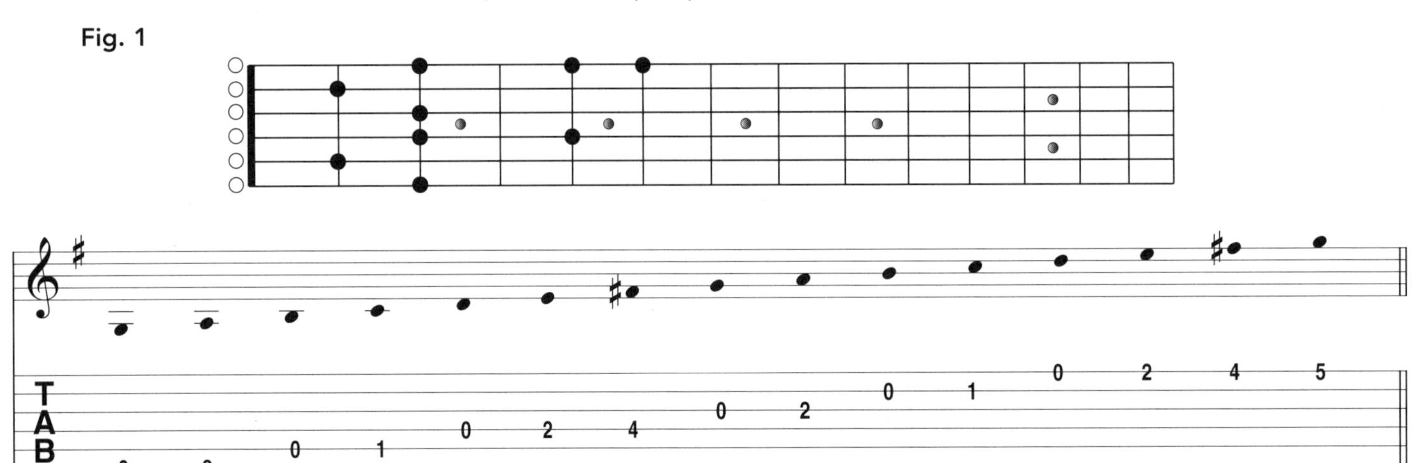

For now, don't agonize over the *articulation*—that is, whether you slide, don't slide, hammer on or whatever, in order to get each note. Just play each note and identify it by name if you can—G, A, B, etc. Even if you're working from the TAB, try saying the names of the notes to yourself as you go up. Work the names out using the open strings and counting frets. It sounds like I'm telling you to eat your peas and carrots, but really, if you start saying the names of the notes you're playing now—even penciling them in over the TAB if it helps—by the time you finish the last chapter, you may not be ready for the first Dobro chair at the symphony, but you'll be a good way down the road to knowing where the notes are on the fingerboard. (See the Appendix, "Finding the Notes on the Fingerboard," if you need more help with this.) End of lecture.

Hammer-Ons

Now, in real life, nine times out of ten, you're going to end up using less than the full seven-note G major scale when in the key of G. Leaving out the F♯s—the seventh degree of the scale—leaves us with two notes per string, which is very even and symmetrical, and conducive to the kind of shameless hot licks I *know* you picked up this book in the hopes of acquiring. So be it. Figure 2 shows this subset of the G scale. Try it out—it's a good warm-up for *hammering on.* "Hammering on" refers to playing a note by dropping the bar onto the string to play a note after first picking an open string.

Fig. 2

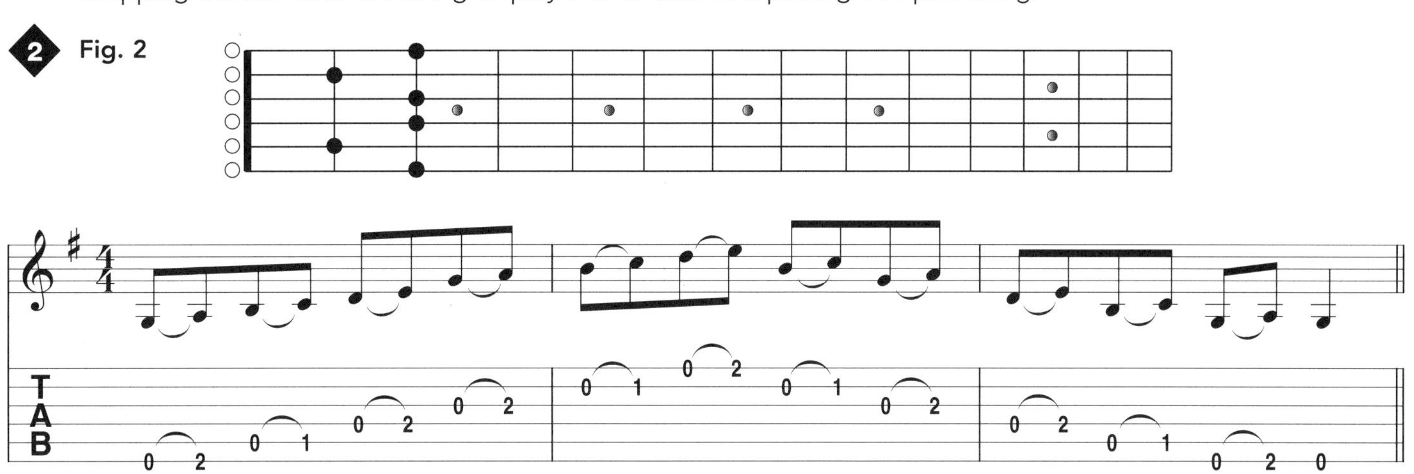

Listen to the recording and notice that all the notes are the same length, whether picked or hammered onto. There is a tendency to rush hammered notes because it seems like, if you don't do it quickly, the picked note will die away and you won't get any sound out of the hammer-on (the second note). But the sound is only partly coming from the vibration of the original note. The rest of the sound is coming from the impact of the bar on the string. If you drop the bar to the string in a single, sharp motion, it won't matter how long you wait after picking the original note.

Figure 3 is for drilling just on hammer-ons in this way. It is actually a right-hand exercise in disguise. Use the pattern indicated—thumb, index, thumb, middle. It may feel weird at first, using your fingers on the low strings and your thumb on the high strings, but it will strengthen your awareness of your fingers and your ability to pick any string with any finger, which will come in particularly handy in the later chapters on melodic style. Meanwhile, this exercise will also expand the possibilities of what falls under your fingers here in the open position.

Fig. 3

Working on Figure 4 will help you practice combining right-hand fluency with left-hand accuracy.

4 **Fig. 4**

Pull-Offs

Even more so than with hammer-ons, the sound of a *pull-off* comes more from the bar action of your left hand than from the vibration of the first note (the note you are pulling *off* from). "Pulling off" refers to playing an open string by removing the bar from that string after first playing a fretted note. As with hammer-ons, don't feel that you have to hurry to get the sound by doing the pull-off quickly. Try Figure 5, with a pull-off on every string:

5 **Fig. 5**

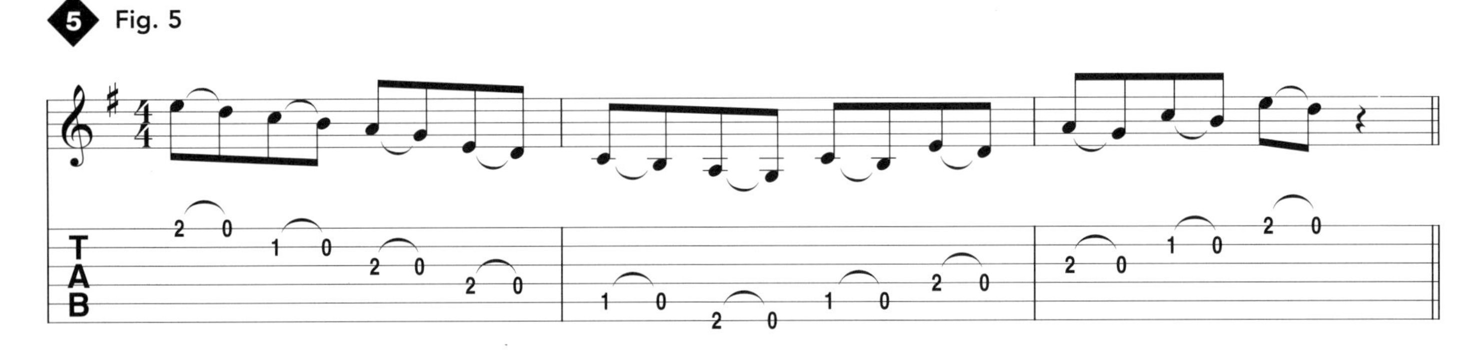

The most important thing about pull-offs with the bar is this: you don't *lift* the bar from the strings to make a pull-off, you go *into* the next string down. The order of events for a pull-off from, say, the second fret on the second string to the open second string, is this:

1. Pick the string with the bar over the second fret.

2. Pull the bar towards yourself and a little bit down into the fingerboard, until the string snaps out from under the tip of your bar, ringing open.

3. You should have landed on the third string, around the second fret. As soon as you do land, let your hand bounce up from the strings.

1.

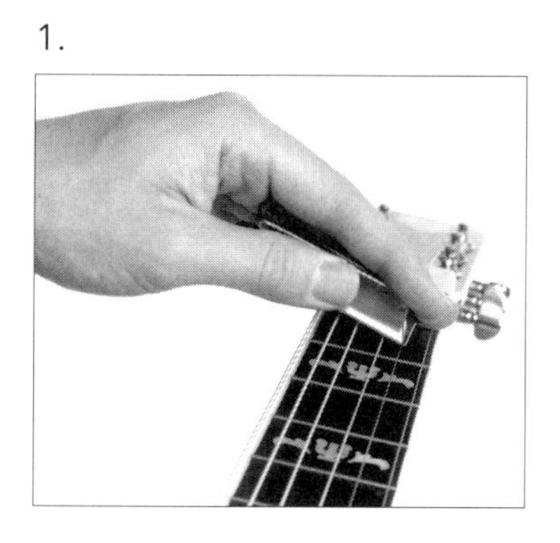

2.

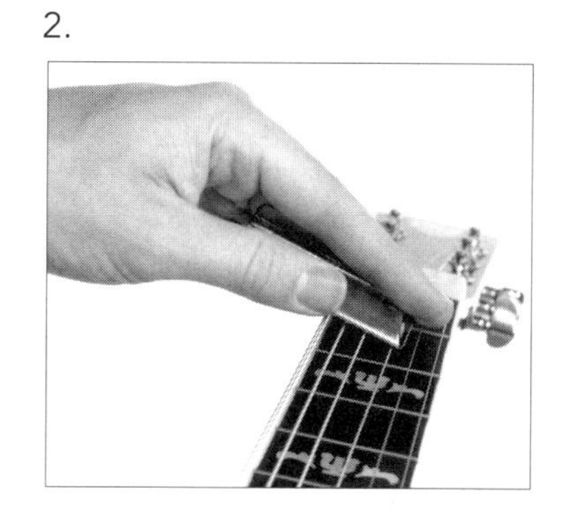

3.

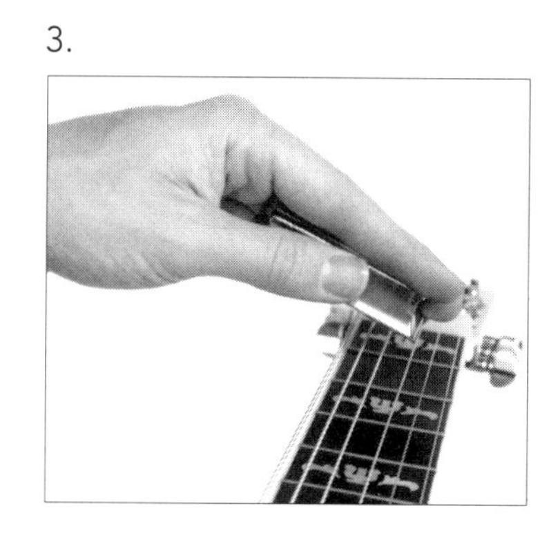

Each pull-off is a snap of the strings like this. Here's where that tip-of-the-bar-within-your-fingers stuff starts to come into play. The bounce on the next string depends upon your ring finger riding along the strings with the bar. In order not to get a great deal of extra string noise, your ring finger in the example above needs to hit the third string just before the bar does, and leave the string just after. Think of your ring finger as a damper that rides along with the bar, closer to the strings than the bar itself. It lands before the bar, and it leaves after, so that the string is only vibrating when the bar is touching it.

If this is more than you can think about right now, come back to it later. Your ears will tell you when you need to do things more quietly, and your hands will find a way to do it. You may find another way that works for you.

Figure 6 is more right-hand practice while you work on developing that left-hand snap:

6 **Fig. 6**

Figure 7 will get you moving across the strings with these pull-offs:

7 **Fig. 7**

Blues Notes in G

The subset of the major scale we've been using—R–2–3–4–5–6—is a very big deal in the key of G, in the open position. You're going to be using these notes for the rest of your resophonic life. But they're only half the equation. Take a swing at Figure 8:

Fig. 8

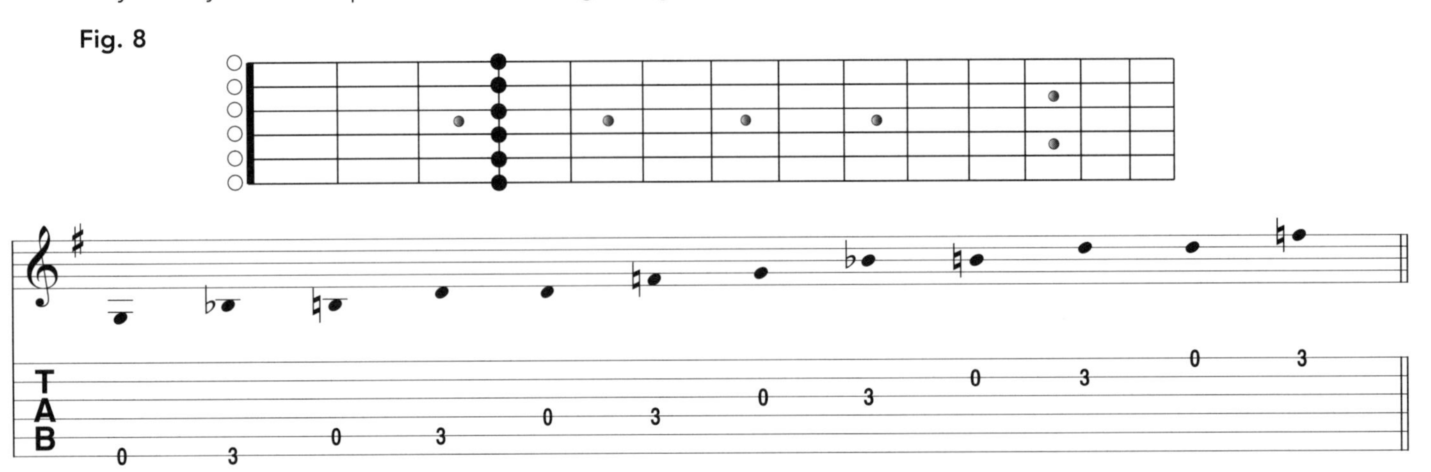

This scale is, loosely speaking, a collection of blues notes that work in the key of G. You can't quite call it a minor or minor pentatonic scale because you're still playing the open B strings, which are providing the major third of the G scale. But you end up with B♭ (the minor third, or ♭3) and F (the minor seventh, or ♭7) as well, so the whole scale gives you: R–♭3–3–5–5–♭7–R–♭3–3–5–5–♭7, from the bottom to the top. Every note is either open or at the third fret, with an even two notes per string—which, like the major scale subset we've already dealt with, facilitates the pursuit of the hot and the flashy in a big way.

You might go back and turn Figures 3–7 into blues scale exercises. Just replace any notes at the first or second fret with a note at the third fret. For instance, the first two measures of Figure 7 would become:

Fig. 9

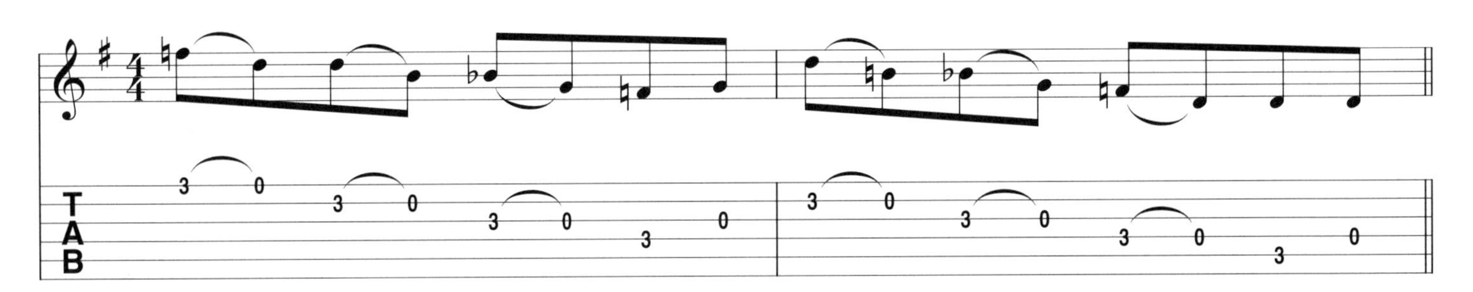

Figure 10 introduces the idea of *string-skipping*. Exercises like this, in which you make things more difficult than they really need to be, make playing more "normal" licks easier when you return to them. There are actually some relatively musical results to be had with this technique, too.

8 **Fig. 10**

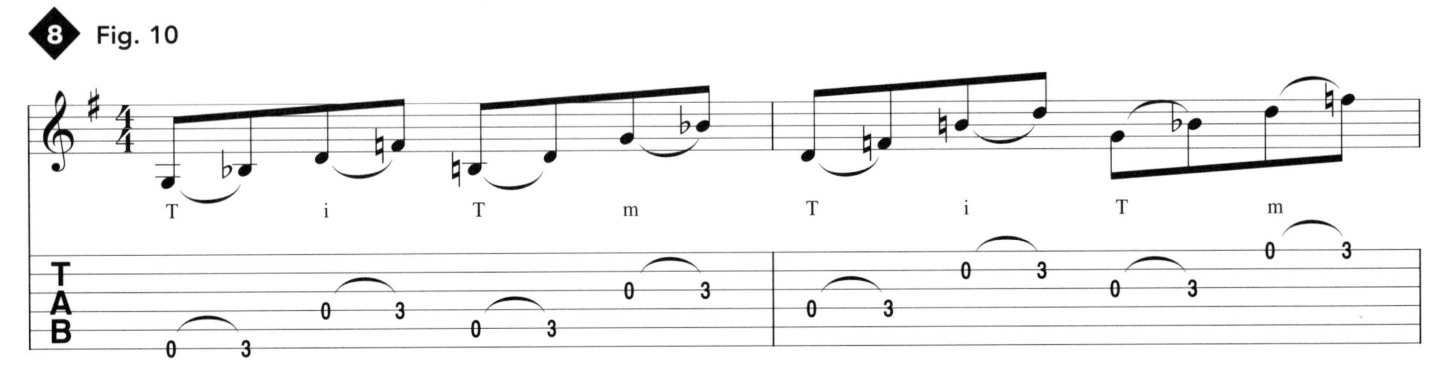

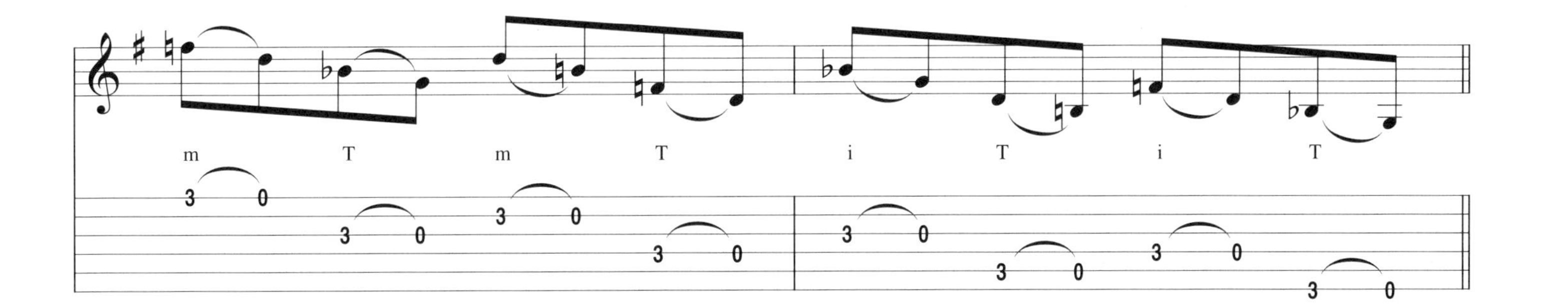

Combining Major and Blues Sounds

Ultimately, the sound of most bluegrass slide playing, as with bluegrass playing generally, is a fluid combination of major and blues sounds. Figure 11 gives you an organized way to practice integrating the G major and G blues sounds, while giving you yet another chance to work out your right and left hands doing hammer-ons.

9 **Fig. 11**

Figure 12 is another exercise in integration, this time using pull-offs:

10 **Fig. 12**

Combining Hammer-Ons and Pull-Offs

Before we leave this chapter and the nitty-gritty work of developing open-position technique, let's look at combining hammer-ons and pull-offs. So far we've looked at the two separately; now let's see what it takes to play them together.

Figure 13 is a gradually descending pattern using the blues scale in a typical bluegrass syncopation of three notes plus three notes plus two notes. We'll talk more about these syncopations and others in Chapter 3.

Fig. 13

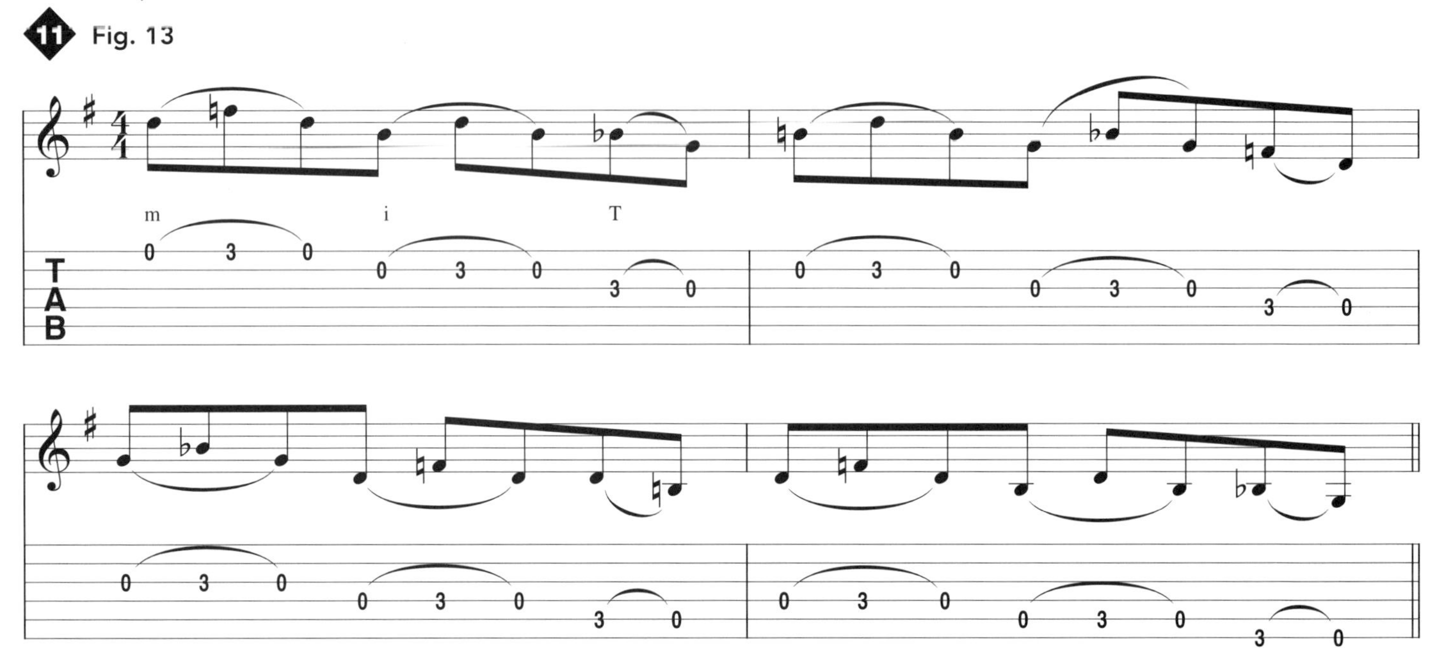

Try to keep both good hammer-on and pull-off technique in mind, and remember not to rush. If you have a metronome, do all of these exercises with it, and work them out as *slowly* as you can, to keep everything relaxed and evenly-spaced. Once you can get the hammer-ons and pull-offs to sound good by themselves, you'll be able to hammer on to a note and immediately pull off back to the open string, keeping it all sounding clean.

Figure 14 is an ascending syncopated pattern using the major scale:

Fig. 14

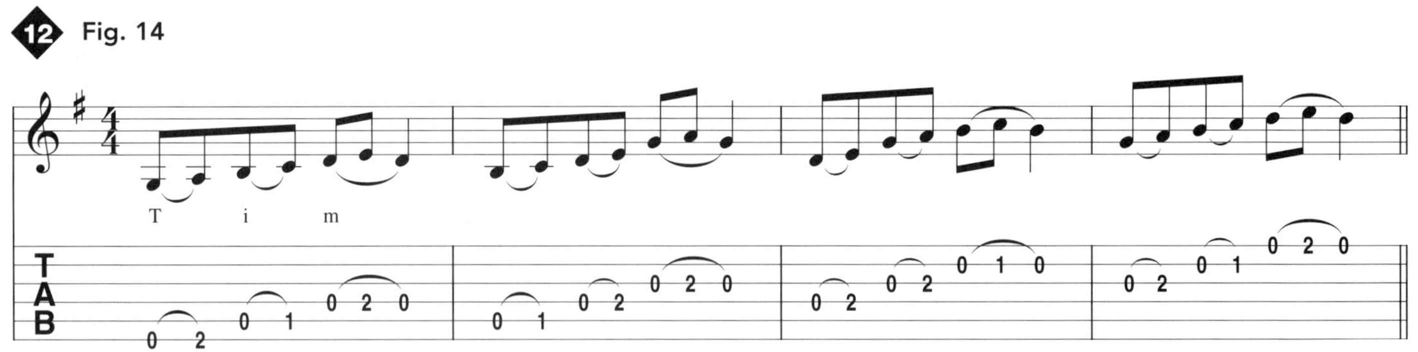

Slides

Finally, it's a good idea to be able to combine slides with hammer-ons and pull-offs. You can hammer on to a slide, and slide into a pull-off. Try Figure 15, in which you hammer on to a major note and slide to a blues note on each string:

Fig. 15

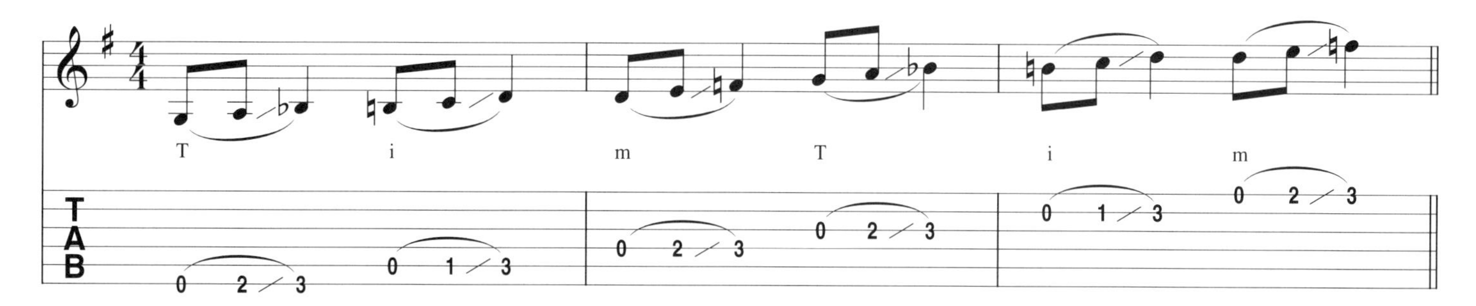

Figure 16 is just the opposite: on each string, pick the blues note, slide to the major note, and pull off to the open string.

Fig. 16

A big part of learning to play is learning to make up your own exercises. If you're working on a tune and you keep getting stuck somewhere, try to isolate what's tripping you up: is it the right hand, the left hand, or just knowing where the notes are?

Building Licks and Starting to Improvise

Now that you've gotten warmed up in the key of G, let's talk a little about improvising. Improvisation runs along a spectrum. At one end, the purest thing do to for a break is to play the melody. At the other end, you can simply use the chord progression as a framework, a place in which to play notes that match the chords but otherwise are entirely up to you. Both approaches have validity, but in most country- and blues-derived musics, the best improvisation tends to lie somewhere in between these two extremes.

Creating Your Own Vocabulary

There are many resources for learning the melodies to tunes. The focus in this book, however, will be on learning to create your own licks and vocabulary, beginning with some ideas that I can give you, with the intention that you will go on to work out some ideas of your own. This approach is meant to help you develop your chops, so that you can then make use of said chops selectively. Beware the temptation to flood the listener with notes! Many of these exercises emphasize phrasing and working off the melody, to help you practice creating similar dynamics in your own playing.

Listening to other people's breaks, knowing the melodies to the songs that you play, and having a fluency with the notes within the key of the song in question all contribute to your ability to make up music out of thin air, which is one of the most satisfying aspects of playing any instrument. Ultimately, to improvise is to create your own new melody in the space you are given.

Bridges & Hillbillies Return to Scene of "Crime"

Brooklyn, OH – Tex MacDonald and the Boerum Hillbillies made headlines last month when their star soloist, noted resophonic steeler Spider Bridges, was picked up by the Chops Police in a raid on a friendly jam session. Charged with playing too few notes on "Billy in the Lowground," Bridges spent a night in the county lockup, but in a brief hearing earlier this week the popular musician managed to beat the rap, on the grounds that the song was in C. (The judge, an amateur harmonica player who had once been stranded at a small town picking party with only an A♭ harmonica back in his law school days, let Bridges off with a warning.)

Tonight was the Hillbillies' first show since "the incident," and all eyes were on the slide star. Tex kicked off a new instrumental, "Pickin' Behind Bars," and after a blazing break, looked over and yelled "Take it, Spider!" But Bridges freaked out and stalled in first position with a look of panic on his face. Later, backstage, he just kept shaking his head. "I was fine playing the melody, I worked that part out and we rehearsed it. I was fine playing backup, I had learned the chords, too. But when my break came, I thought, 'Where do you begin?' I hadn't practiced *that*. So I froze."

Let's assume that, like Mr. Bridges, you need to be able to stand up there and take a break or solo on song X. Well, what do you know about song X? Let's say the break is eight measures long, and it's over the verse, which has a particular chord progression in a particular key. The song is usually done at a particular tempo. That's a pretty specific starting place—key, tempo, length, and style. With that list, we've already taken a big step towards creating order out of the void that is your eight-bar break. With that list in mind, we can talk about actually *practicing improvising*. You can practice playing the original melody to the song, and you can also practice running eighth notes through the song's chord progression. Certain kinds of licks will sound stylistically appropriate to the song, and others won't. You can work with a metronome or play along to a recording of the song to see what tempo you need to be able to play the song at. When you've done all these things, you can then make choices about how close to stick to the melody, where to depart from it, what licks to try out, and what position to play them in. Those kinds of choices are at the heart of making music. They are musical choices, and your personality will influence how you arrange those elements in your own playing.

Four-Note Units

Take the four groups of four eighth notes in Figure 1 out for a spin. Each one starts with a hammer-on from a different open string.

Fig. 1

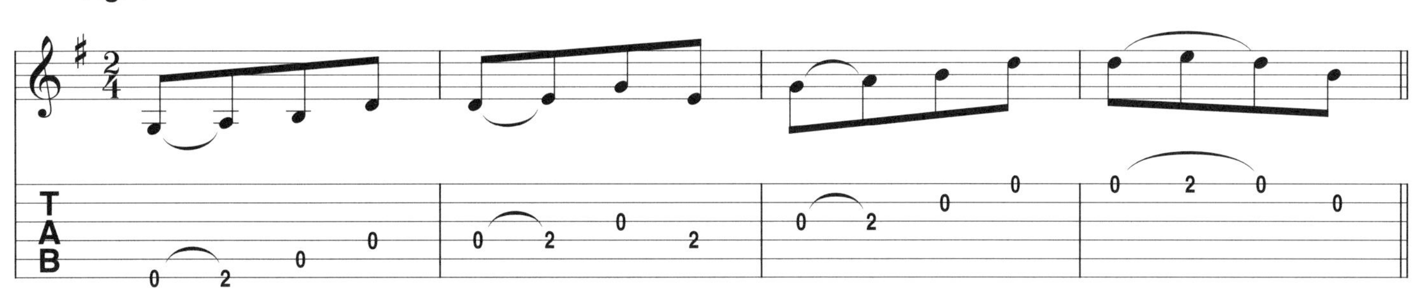

You can move around groups of notes like these as units, mixing and matching them to make up larger licks. Each one of the four-note units in Figure 1 is made up of notes just from the G major scale. Next, here are four more G major units. Each one starts with a pull-off to a different open string.

Fig. 2

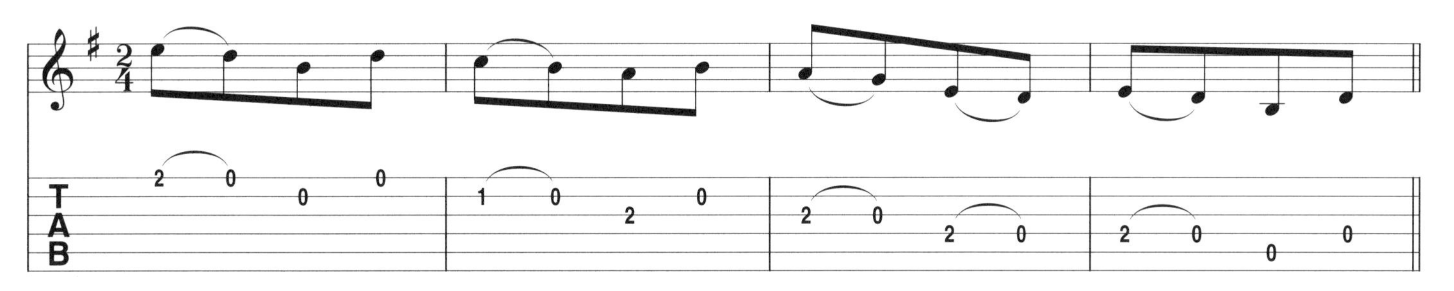

You could think of the following four units as blues versions of the ones in Figure 1:

Fig. 3

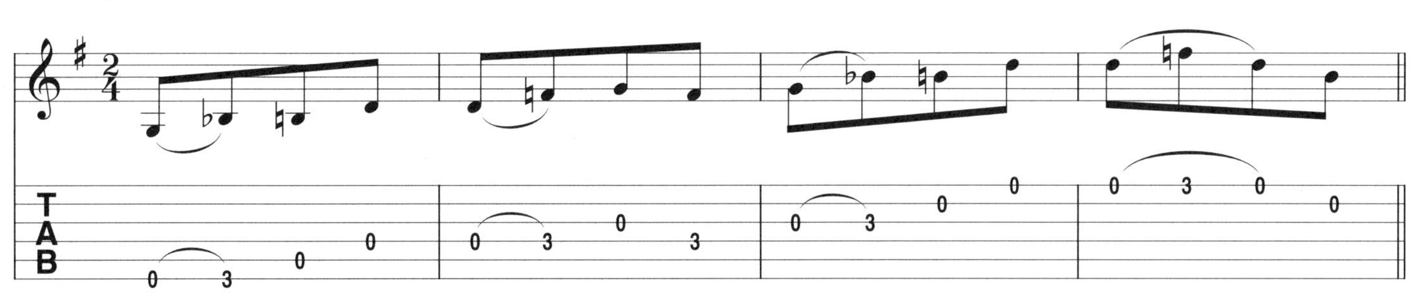

These four pull-off-based blues units have a logic of their own unrelated to the major pull-off units above:

Fig. 4

Combining Units to Create Licks

Now, just by combining any two four-note units, we can create a seemingly endless supply of one-measure eighth-note licks. Here are sixteen one-measure ideas to get your imagination fired up. Each and every one is simply a combination of two of the four-note units found in Figures 1 through 4. I swear it. You can go through and check.

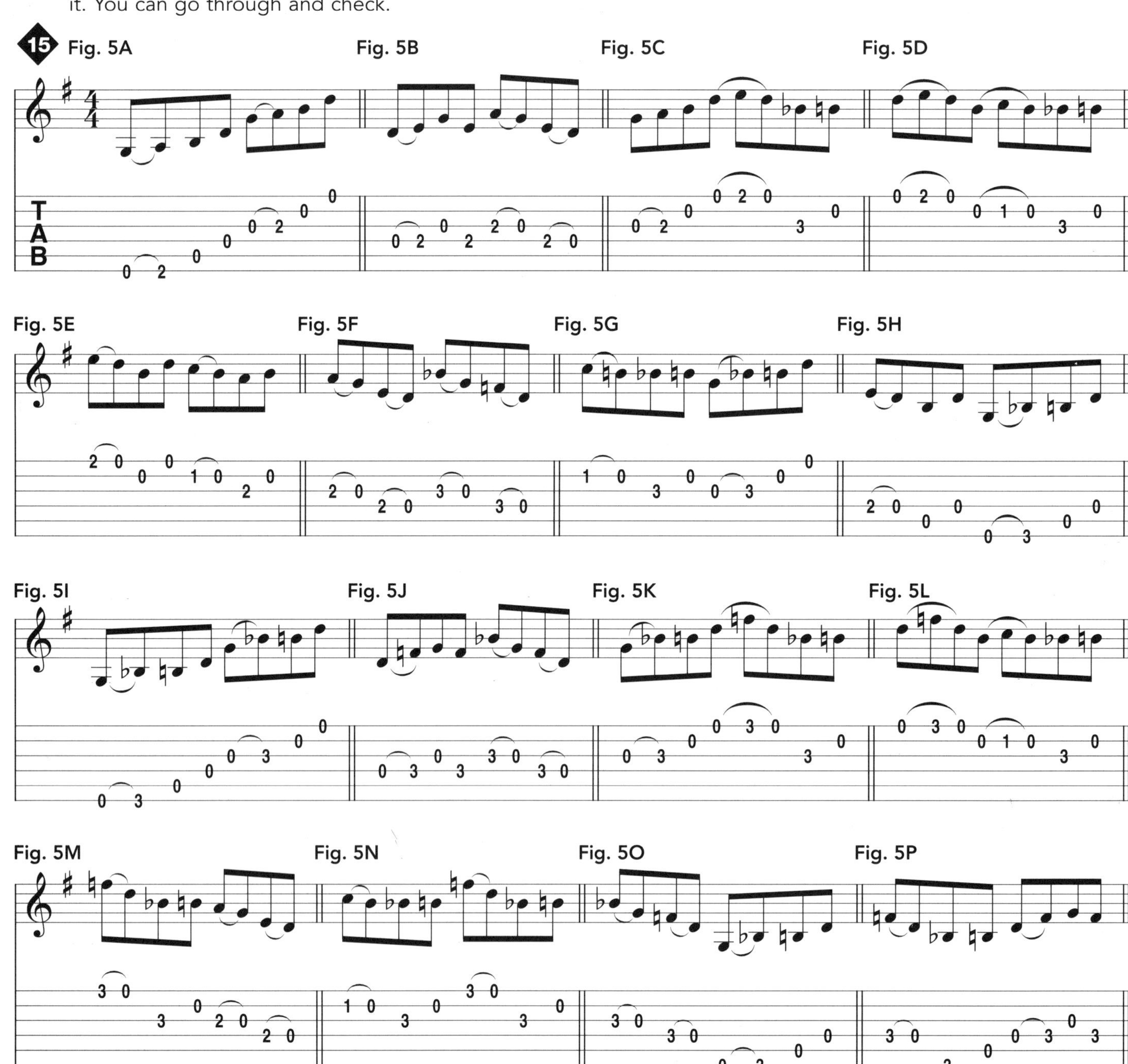

Isn't that cool? Now, to find *every* possibility, you'd want to start with each four-note unit and end it with *every other unit* just to see what the possibilities are. Then you'd pick out the ones you liked the best, and practice those. Then, when you felt you'd exhausted all the possibilities, you could go back and start again with some *new* four-note units. There are certainly more than the sixteen I've given you here.

Before we start working some of these licks into a tune or a break, let's go over a few of the typically "Dobro-istic" moves that will provide much of the idiomatic glue in your playing. It's easy to get wrapped up in practicing the jackhammer regularity of solid eighth notes and forget about all the funky, relaxed "twang-and-droing" that made you want to play the instrument in the first place.

Unison Slides

The first move is the *unison slide*. It's just what it says it is: you slide into a note and then play a unison, or the same pitch, on the next string. Figure 6 shows three typical unison slides; repeating Figure 6A makes a good "kickoff," similar to the way a fiddle player gets revved up to begin a break.

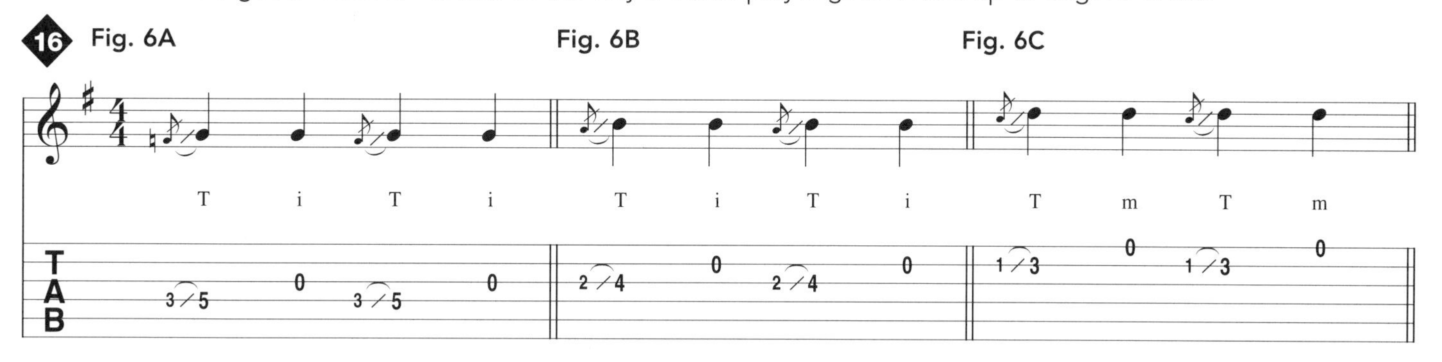

Figure 7 shows how the same unison slides can be worked into eighth-note licks:

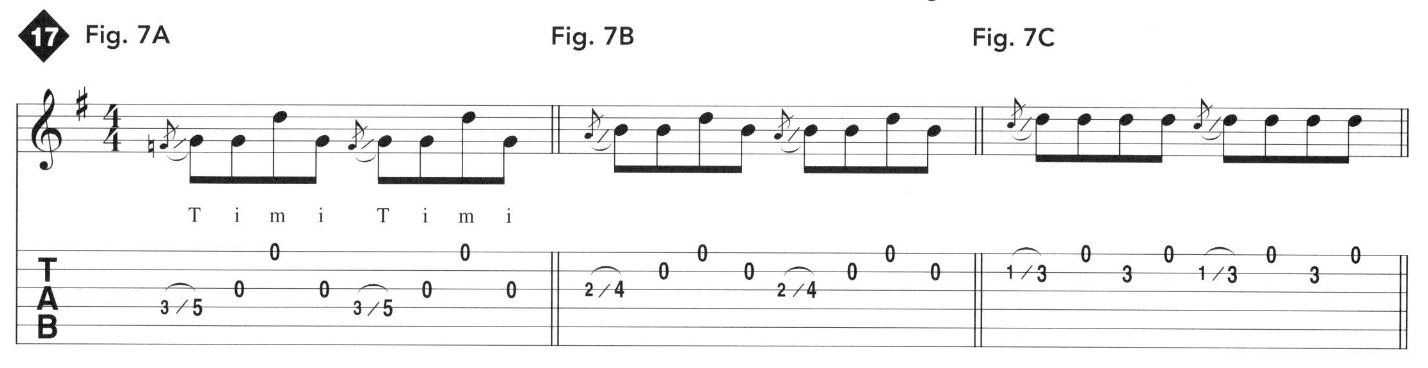

Double Stops

Double stops are two notes picked simultaneously. Figure 8 is a double-stop variation of Figure 7A. Notice the fingering: the only difference from the single-note version is the way you grab the first string with your middle finger. This string-skipping stretch may feel funny at first, but this move and those in the next example will get you used to it pretty quickly.

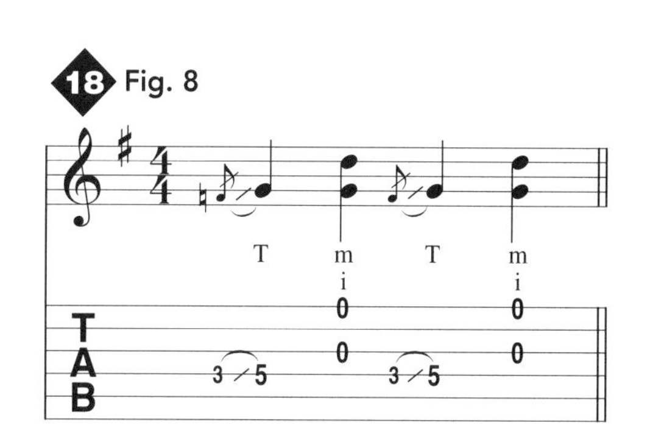

You can apply this same double-stop idea to moves without unison slides as well. Check out Figure 9, in which the first string is added in on four basic four-note units.

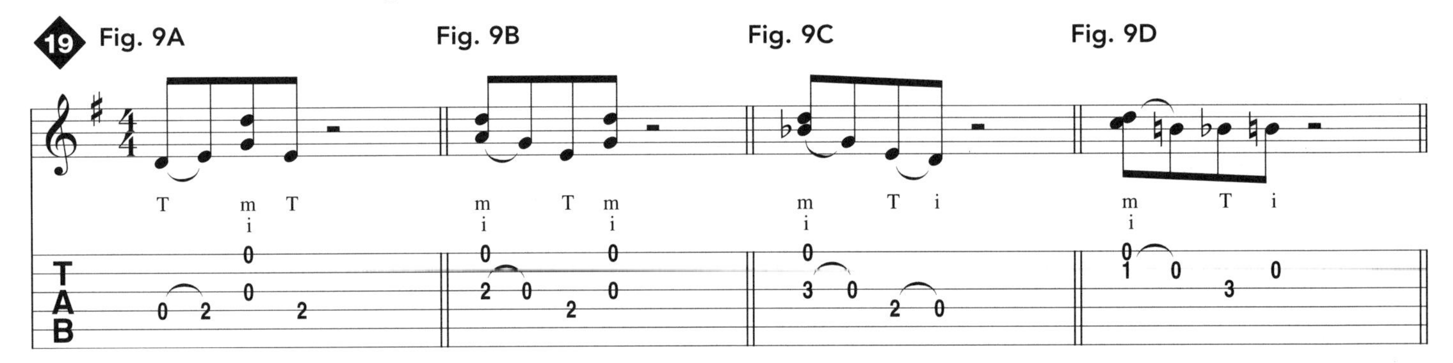

Call and Response

Call and response is an important part of blues and country music. Think about the classic blues song form, where the singer sings a line and is then answered by an instrumental lick in the space that follows. The vocal line is the "call" and the instrumental lick is the "response." You can hear this in bluegrass too, especially when the tune fits into the *form* of a twelve-bar blues, even though the performance style is different. Call and response creates a satisfying sense of structure in any kind of chord progression or style, and it helps you understand *phrasing,* which can be thought of as the art of knowing when and where to play, what to play, and how much or how little to play at a time.

Figure 10 shows how you can use a couple of simple double-stop licks as "call" phrases and "answer" them with some licks built from our vocabulary of eighth-note units.

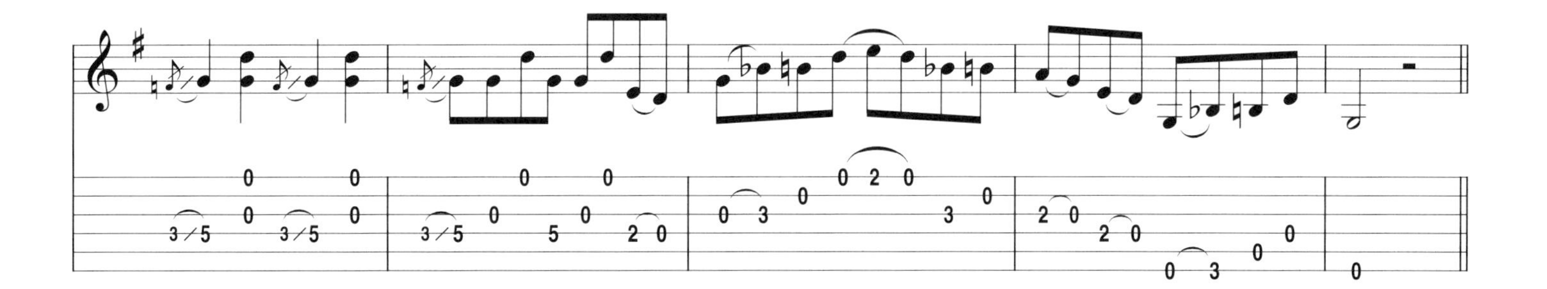

"New River Train"

Now let's apply this idea to an actual song. In Figure 11, the melody to the traditional song "New River Train" is played in a call-and-response style. Measures 1–2, 5–6, 9–10, and 13–14 are the original melody of the tune. Measures 3–4, 7–8, 11–12, and 15–16 would ordinarily be pauses in the tune's melody; here they are played as fills, with eighth-note licks sounding as the "response" to the "call"phrases of the original melody.

21 **Fig. 11**

À la "Nine Pound Hammer"

Some melodies don't lend themselves as easily to this approach. Figure 12 shows a melody similar to the verse of "Nine Pound Hammer":

Fig. 12

In this melody, each phrase is rhythmically in the form of a *pickup* into the downbeat. That is, you have a short phrase or lick leading up to more drawn-out notes on the downbeat, or the beginning of the next measure. In this case, you might make things more interesting by hot-rodding those pickups, leading up to every other measure with a cool eighth-note phrase. Check out Figure 13:

Fig. 13

Syncopations and Rolls

We spent some time in the last chapter working on creating a steady flow of eighth notes by combining basic units of half a measure each, or four eighth notes. Dividing everything up this way into neat little even-numbered amounts of notes makes it easier to string together new licks, but the sound can get tedious quickly. Much of the drive in bluegrass comes from *accenting*—or placing the emphasis on—notes other than the first and third beat of a measure. The symphony folks like to call such a shift in emphasis *syncopation*. Syncopation is about deliberately throwing things off balance, rhythmically, as they relate to the overall pulse established by the rest of the band. It would hardly be right to raise this subject without actually illustrating it, so...

Syncopated Rolls in G

Let's take a four-note roll, Figure 1A, and chop off the last note as in Figure 1B:

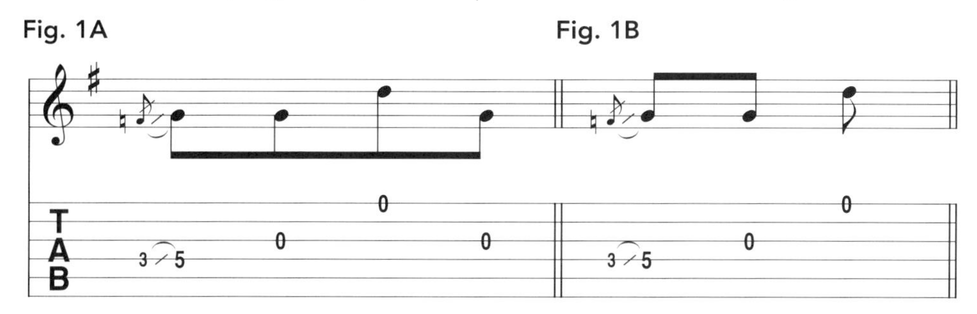

If we play this three-note phrase, repeat it, and wrap it up with a two-note pull-off, we get Figure 2.

Now we still have a measure-long flow of eighth notes, but it doesn't sit there as two four-note units—the weight is on 1, the "and" of 2, and 4. You can bring this out by really laying into the first, fourth, and seventh notes with your thumb:

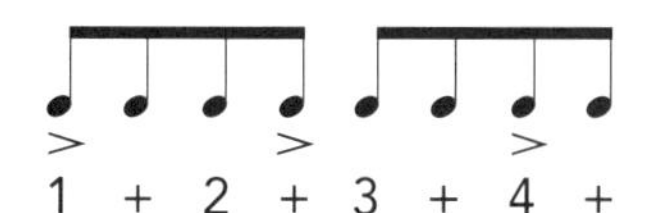

We'll call this a "3+3+2" syncopation, since it's made up of three notes plus three notes plus two notes. Here are a few more to try. Figure 3A reverses the last two notes of Figure 2, Figure 3B is the same idea as Figure 2 taken up one string, and Figure 3C illustrates that you don't have to begin with a roll for the syncopation to work.

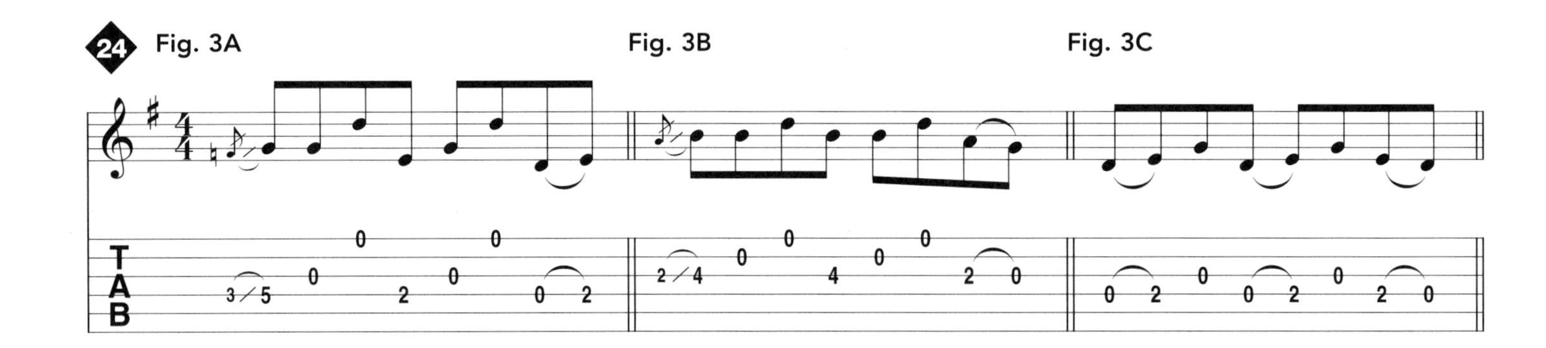

You can draw this idea out to a 3+3+3+3+4 syncopation. Think about it—it takes eight eighth notes to fill up one measure; you can use sixteen eighth notes to fill up two measures. Hipsters (and now you can be one too) like to call what happens during the third group of three notes "playing across the barline." What they mean is that the third roll doesn't end neatly at the end of the measure; it starts in the first measure and ends in the second, which creates a sense of suspense. The payoff comes when you hear the nice, neat four-note lick at the end of measure 2. Ahh... order has been restored, at least for the time being. Try the two licks in Figure 4, and experience it for yourself:

Nothing says you have to repeat your first phrase for syncopation to work. Check out Figure 5, which is still a kind of 3+3+2 idea:

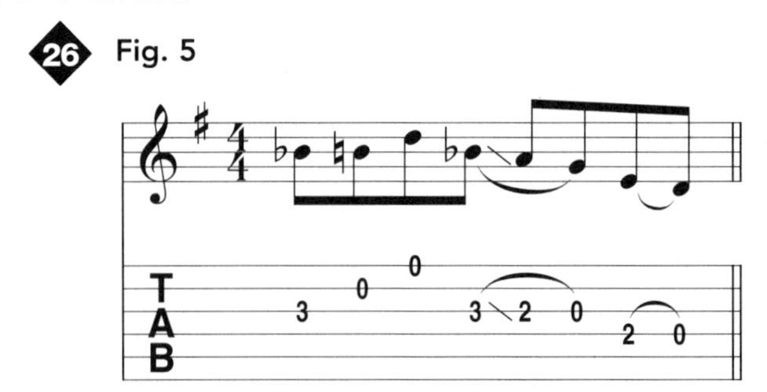

What we've really got in Figure 5, however, is a six-note phrase followed by a two-note wrap-up. What can we do with that? How about repeating a six-note phrase? Figure 6 shows the oh-so-groovy yet logical conclusion: a couple of 6+6+4 syncopations. (Once more, do the math—two bars = 16 eighth notes, 6+6+4=16.) Again, we have some across-the-bar action—both times, the second six-note phrase begins in measure 1 and concludes in measure 2. Try these two.

In Figure 7, another 6+6+4 lick, check out the pull-off from C at the fifth fret on the G string, one of my favorite sounds on the planet:

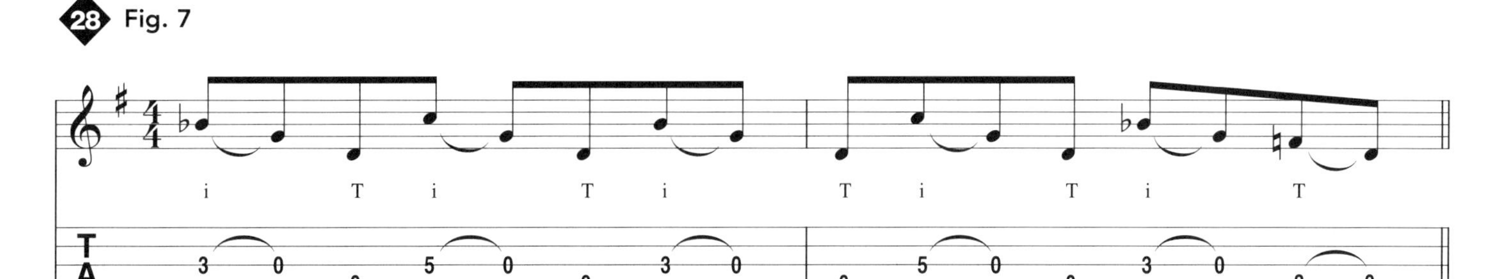

For Figure 8, keep the bar flat on the strings so you can play both the second and first strings cleanly. You need to really be sharp about the slides down from and back up to the third fret on the second string to make this 6+6+4 syncopation work. Work on playing it slowly first, and make sure that you can really hear the Ds and C♯s as distinct and separate notes.

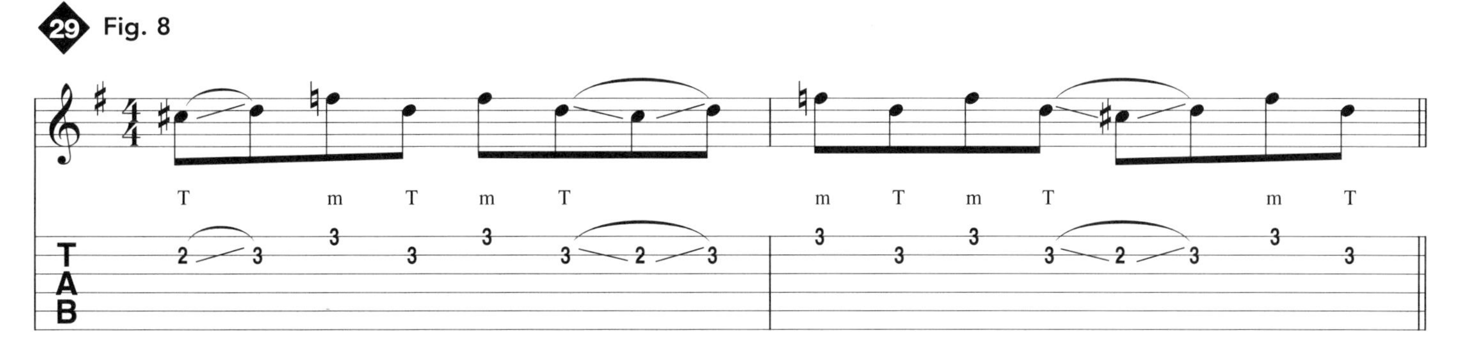

Look at where the accents, or strong beats, fall in these syncopations: on beats 1 and 4 in the first measure, and on beat 3 in the second measure.

You can have a lick like Figure 9, where some of the notes are quarter notes but the overall syncopation holds to the same accents as a 6+6+4 idea:

30 **Fig. 9**

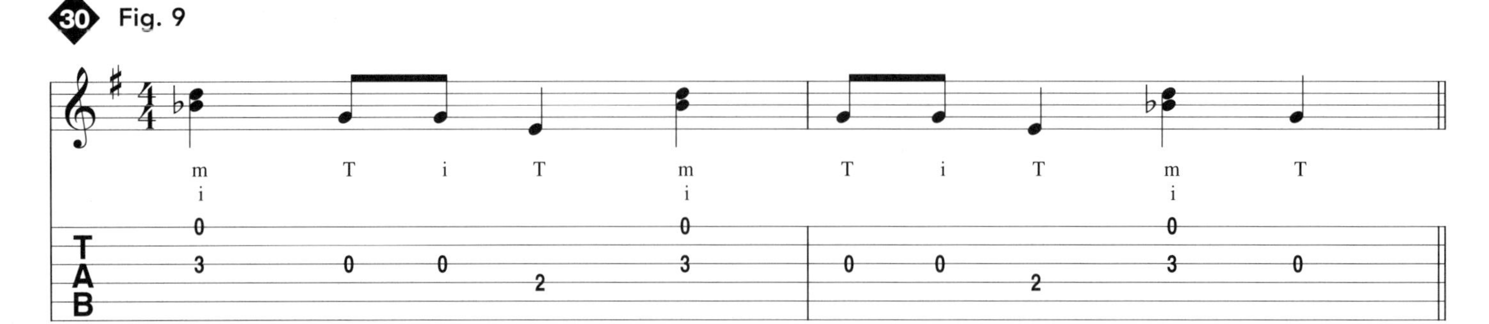

Syncopated Rolls over C

Syncopated rolls make for some good ways to deal with playing over a C chord while in the key of G. Let's begin with something banjo players and other pickers call a *reverse roll:* instead of rolling "up" the strings—thumb, index, middle—we're going to roll "backwards" or down the strings—middle, index, thumb. Starting off with one of our four-note units and then going into a series of reverse rolls gives us a new kind of sound, the 4+3+3+3+3 syncopation in Figure 10:

31 **Fig. 10**

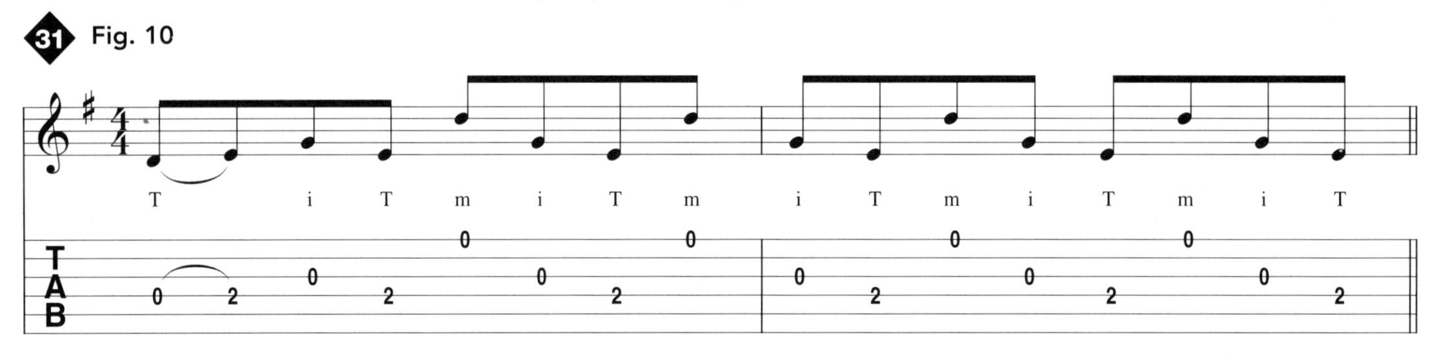

Heading up to the fifth fret, we can get things like Figure 11. Hold the bar flat across the bottom four strings:

32 **Fig. 11**

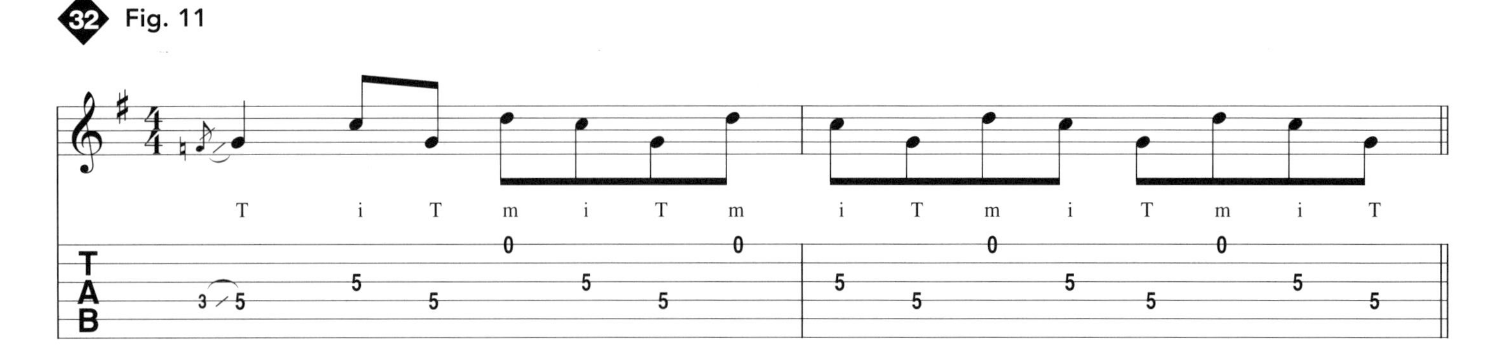

If you can get your middle finger to alternate between the first and second strings for every other roll, you can work out cool things like Figure 12:

33 **Fig. 12**

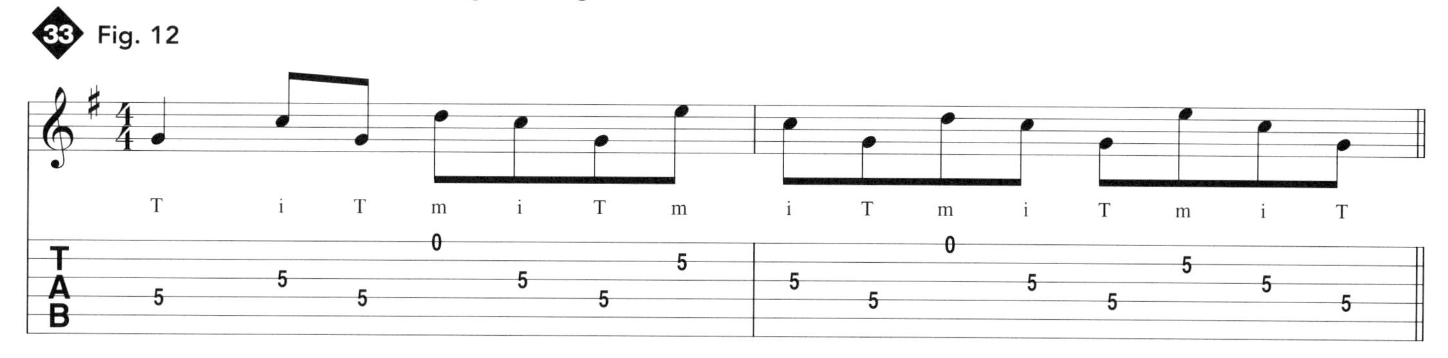

Figure 13 makes use of a simpler forward roll, which you have to keep shifting up a string and back. The syncopation is 6+6+4.

34 **Fig. 13**

If you want to really turn your fingers into spaghetti, you can try combining forward and reverse rolls, as in Figure 14:

35 **Fig. 14**

Syncopated Licks in the Closed Position

"Closed" being the opposite of "open," stringed-instrument players like to refer to "closed position," meaning "without using any open notes or strings." The advantage of closed-position playing is that any closed-position lick can be transposed to another key simply by moving to another fret position. For the moment, we're just going to stay at the fifth fret, with a few embellishments above and below, to see how we can maintain the momentum of syncopation on a C chord without using any open strings.

Figure 15 takes the forward rolls of Figure 13 to the next step. When you hit the high string the second time, tilt the bar so that it's only touching the high string when you make the quick slide up to the seventh fret and back.

36 **Fig. 15**

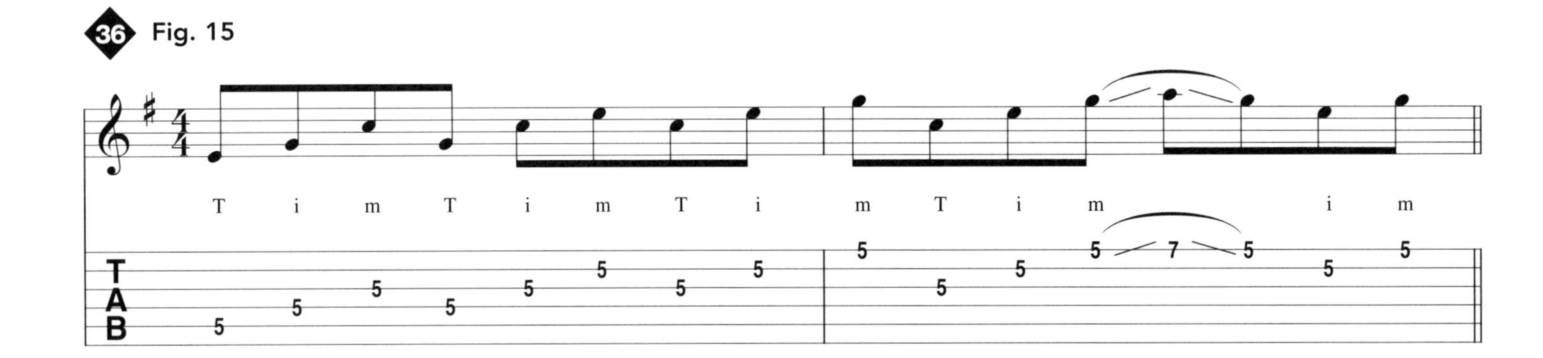

Figure 16 turns this same bar-tilt move into a six-note lick that is repeated. Slow it down to practice getting from the tilt to holding the bar flat across the strings and back to the tilt again.

37 **Fig. 16**

For the next lick, another 6+6+4 move, make sure that the slides from the fifth fret to the fourth and back on the B string are distinct. If you want to keep things incredibly clean, pull the tip of the bar back to just the B string when you're sliding, and use your left-hand fingertips to mute the high string.

38 **Fig. 17**

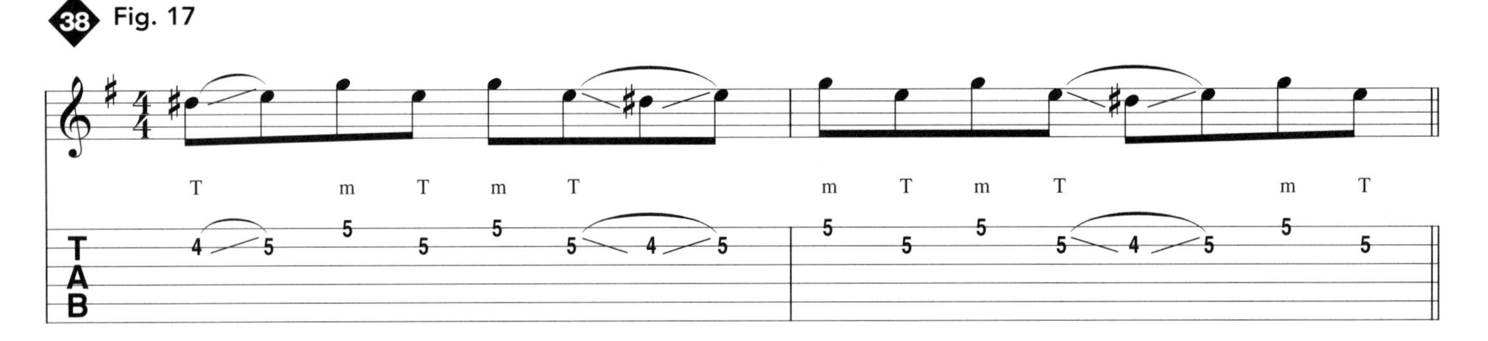

"Gowanus Valley Blues #2"

Let's see how some of these open- and closed-position rolls work in real life. "Gowanus Valley Blues #2" is a blues-based instrumental in the style of the Flatt and Scruggs banjo instrumentals from the 1950s. The chord progression breaks down like this:

G/// G/// G/// G///

C/// C/// G/// G///

C/// C/// G/// G///

D/// D/// D/// D///

D/// D/// G/// G///

Kind of a twenty-bar blues, if you will. Compared to an ordinary twelve-bar blues, it repeats the second line of four bars (C/// C/// G/// G///) and stretches out the turnaround on the D chord from two bars to six. The Gowanus Valley is of course that cool, lush oasis of vacant lots, abandoned storefronts, and derelict factory buildings that line the once-mighty Gowanus Canal in South Brooklyn, and while it's hardly the same as those rolling alluvial farmlands of fame in southern Mississippi, it's the closest thing we have in New York City to the Delta.

39 **Fig. 18**

Playing over C in Open Position

Let's go back to open position now for another look at playing over the C chord. Emphasizing the notes of a C chord within the G major scale is a good place to start; try these four units that emphasize C, E, and G—the root, third, and fifth of C major.

Fig. 19

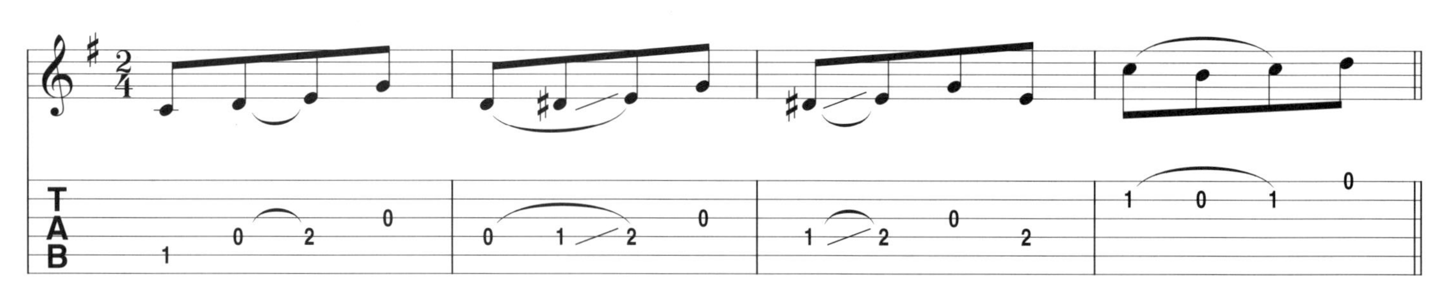

Combining these with a few select G major units gives us the following open-position licks to use over C.

Fig. 20A **Fig. 20B** **Fig. 20C** **Fig. 20D**

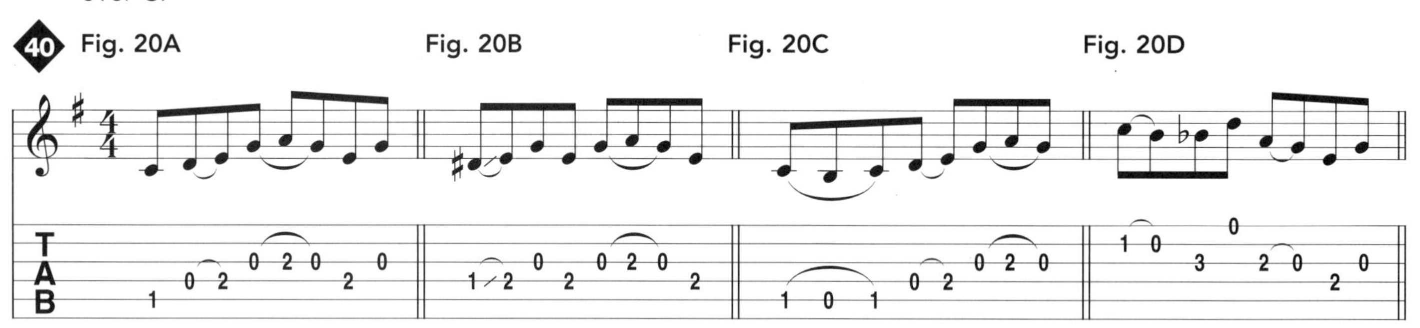

This approach can be particularly useful on fiddle tunes, where the chord changes sometimes are just *flying* by. If you're down in the open position in the key of G, it's helpful to know which notes to lean on to get the effect of playing on the C chord as it goes by. Sometimes you don't have the time (or the inclination) to go for a heavy-duty syncopated roll at the fifth fret.

"Bill Cheatham"

In the fiddle tune "Bill Cheatham," the chord changes do indeed fly by, particularly on the B section. The melody lies best using a combination of open position and fifth and seventh-fret chord positions, but once you're taking your break, of course, you can play wherever you like. Figure 21 is an arrangement of the melody.

Fig. 21

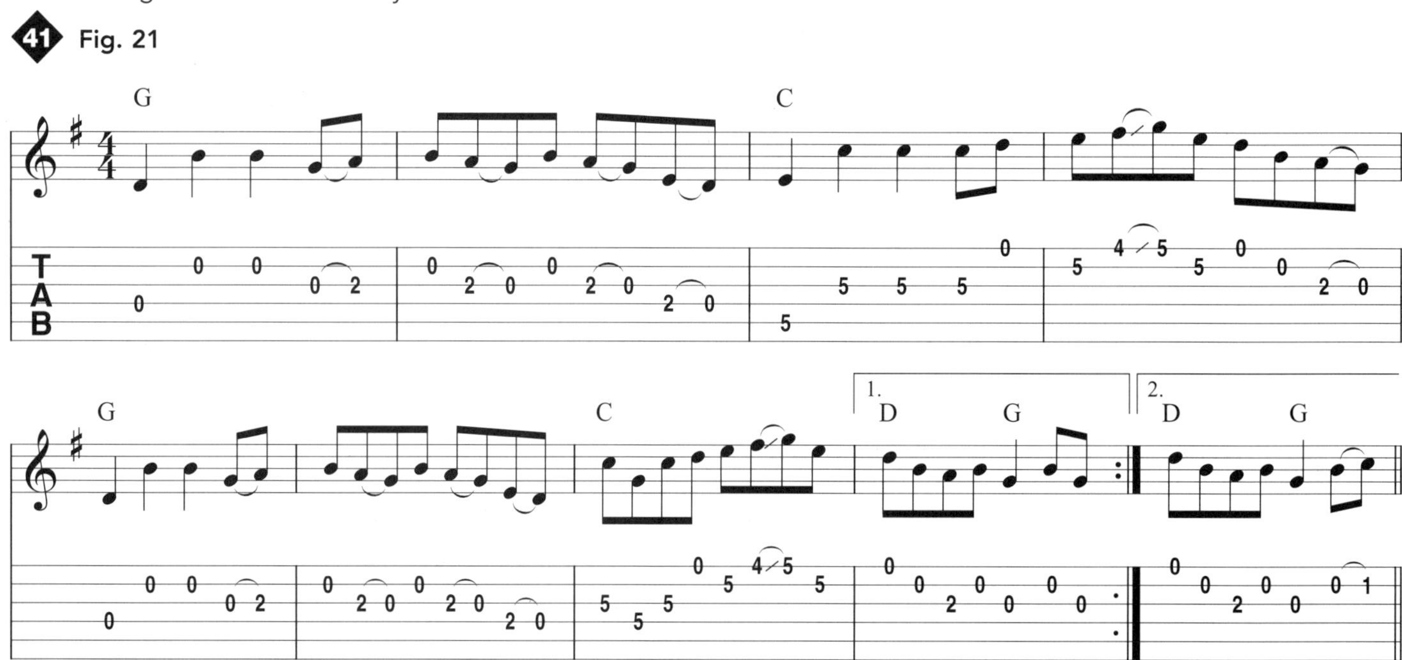

Now try out this break over "Bill Cheatham," which is an embellished version of the melody. In the A section, various rolls and licks are swapped in for the melody every other bar; measures 2, 4, 6, and 8 are still the original melody.

42 **Fig. 22**

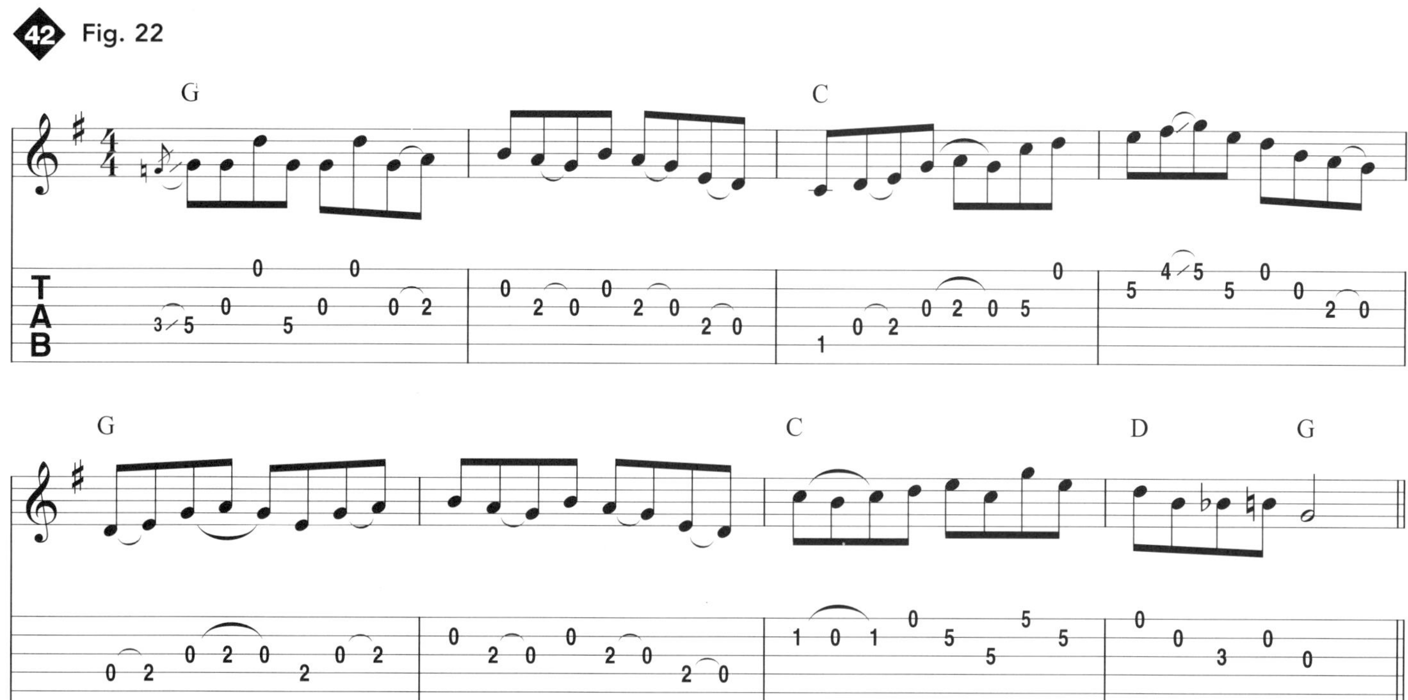

In this next example, the first four measures of the B section are an improvisation based on the chord progression, with a return to the original melody in the last four measures. Those first four measures of the B section thread through the chord changes without leaving the open position, by emphasizing notes from each chord at the moment that the chord is being played: G, B, and D over the G chord; C, E, and G over the C chord; and F♯, A, and C over the D(7) chord.

Fig. 23

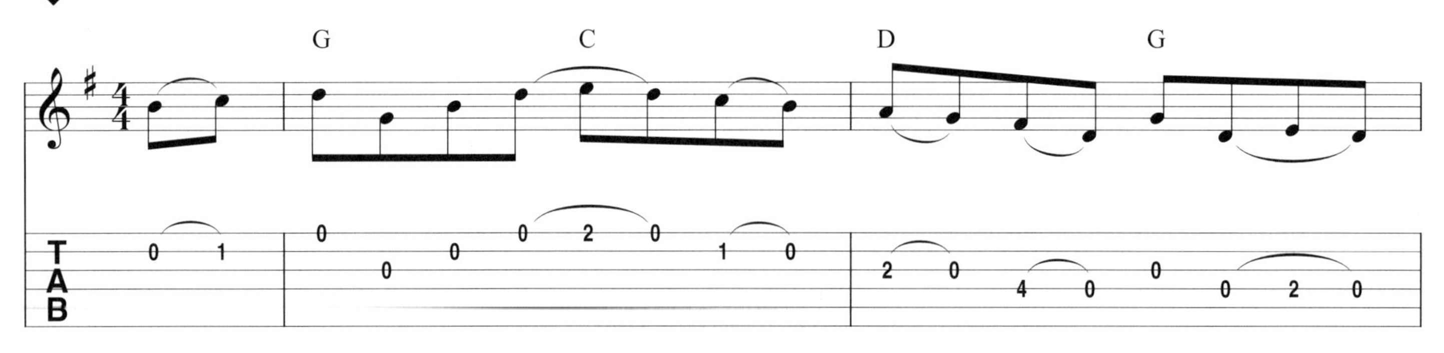

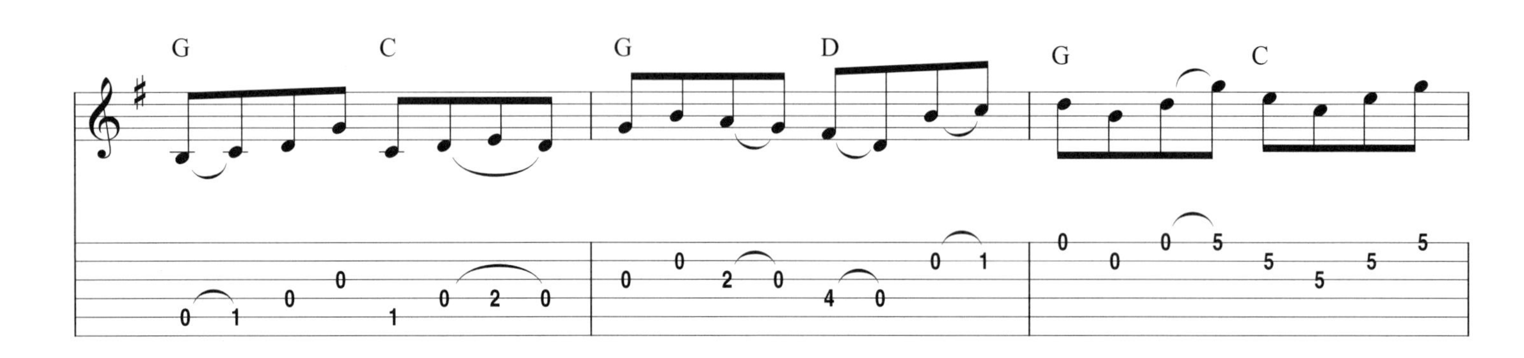

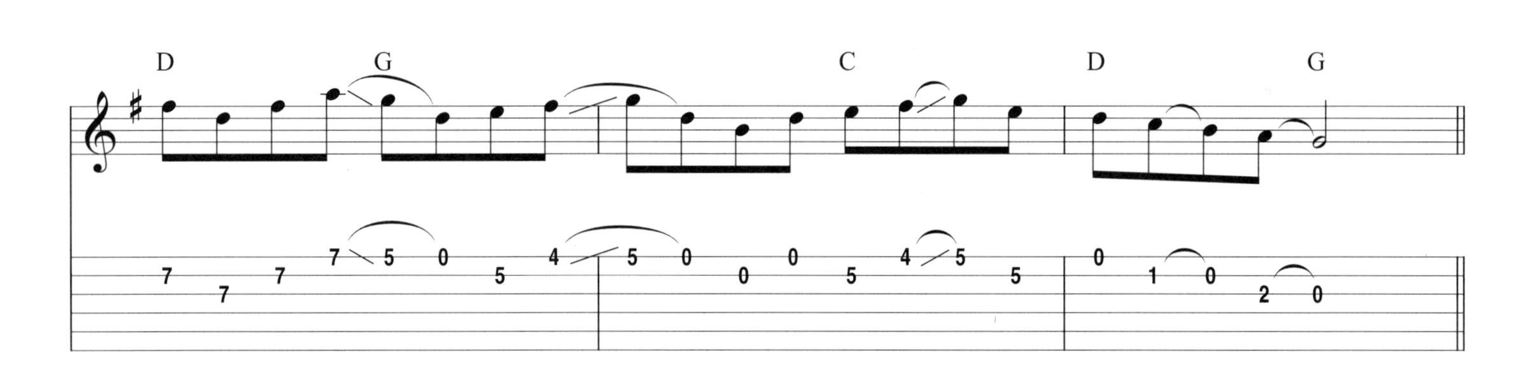

When actually performing this tune, you would of course still take the repeats of both the A and the B section, and you'd want to do something different each time, rather than play the same variation twice in a row for each section.

The Melodic Style

The "melodic style" of playing lap-style slide takes its name from a banjo style pioneered by Bill Keith in the 1960s. This approach is much easier to see than to describe, so let's begin with an example. Figure 1A is a typical G lick played in open position using hammer-ons and pull-offs. Figure 1B shows how you might play the same lick in the melodic style.

Fig. 1A **Fig. 1B**

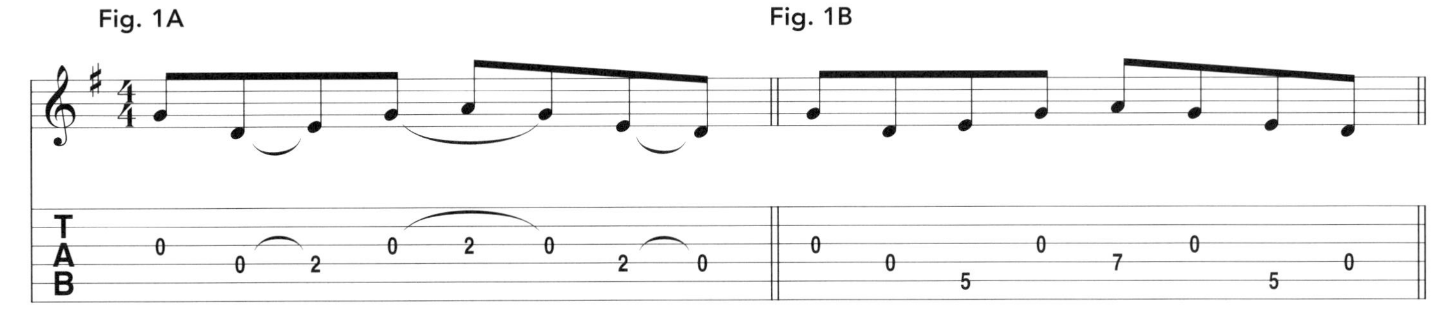

The basic idea is to replace fretted notes in the open position with the same notes played higher up the neck on lower strings. In the example above, the E at the second fret on the fourth string is replaced by the E at the fifth fret on the fifth string. The A at the second fret on the third string is replaced by the A at the seventh fret on the fourth string, and so on. Because successive notes are being played on different strings, each note can ring out for longer in the melodic style than it would if you were either hammering on or pulling off to the next note (and thus ending each note as you left it for the next). Licks and passages with this overlapping sound take on a sustained, shimmering quality, providing a change of pace from the straight-ahead drive of the open-position approach.

G Scales, Melodic Style

Musically, the tools for the melodic style are no different from what we've been using in the open position. Figure 2 is a basic G major scale arranged with melodic-style fingering:

Fig. 2

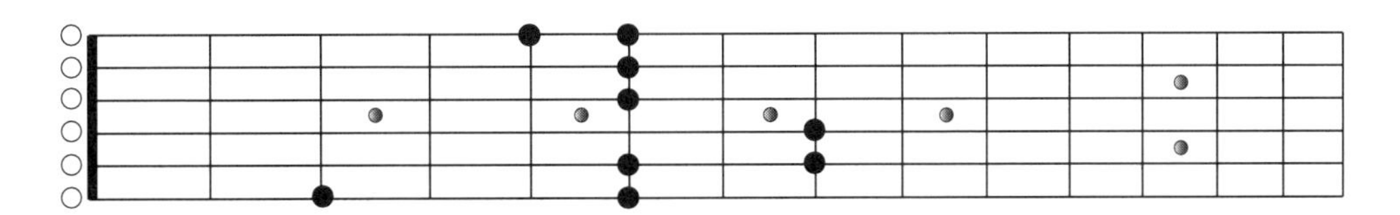

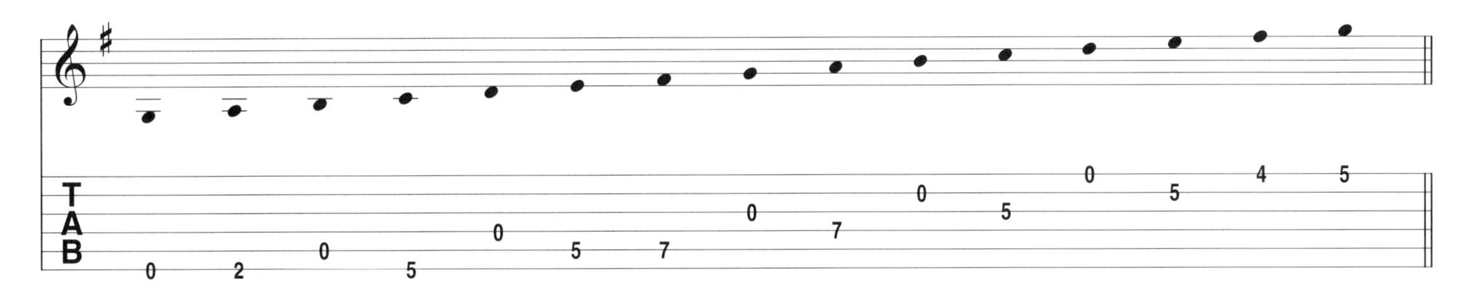

As in open position, we can drop the sevenths from the scale to play R–2–3–4–5–6, which still gives us the major sound but is simpler and more streamlined to play:

Fig. 3

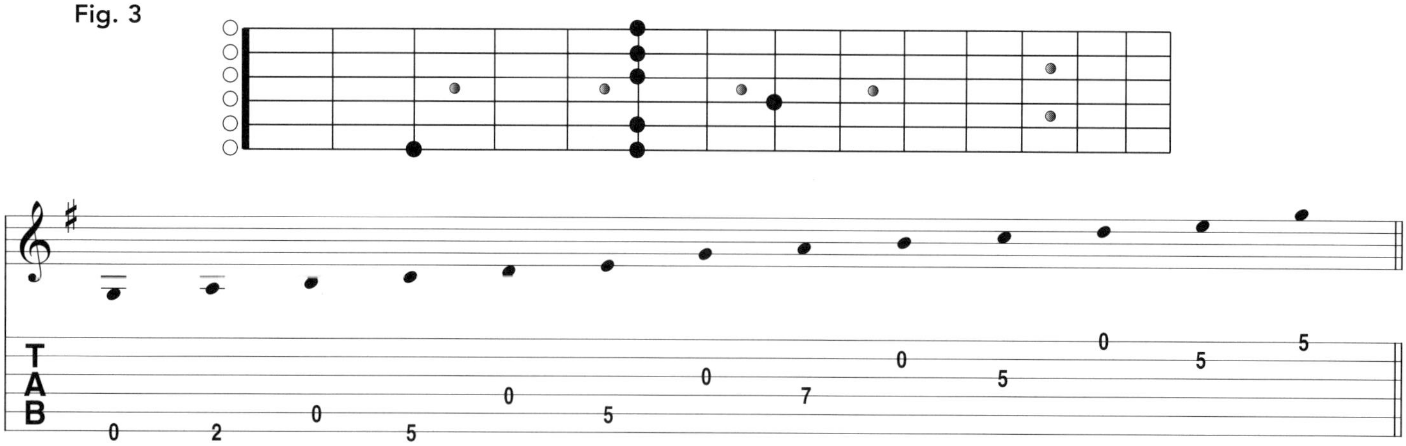

We can also find all the blues notes in the melodic style as well, as in Figure 4:

Fig. 4

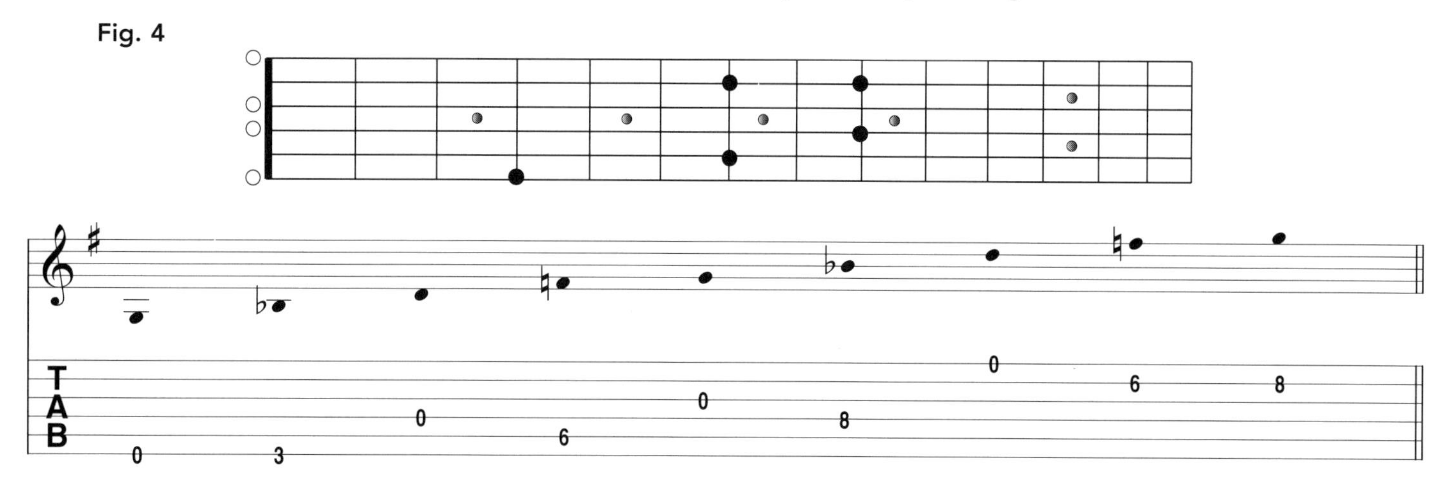

From Open Position to Melodic Style and Back

The following exercises are meant to help you get used to climbing from the open position up into the melodic zone around the fifth to seventh frets (in the key of G) and descending back into the open position. To really get the most from these exercises, here are Dave's Excellent Suggested Practical Guidelines—make of them what you will:

- First practice each measure separately. When you can keep repeating a measure in time without dropping any beats, work on the next measure the same way.
- When you can do each measure separately, combine them into pairs—first and second measure played together and played repeatedly in time, second and third measure played together, third and fourth played together, etc.
- Next, practice the exercise in its entirety. Pay attention to the right-hand fingerings; they are a real key to the melodic style, and these exercises are meant to get your right hand used to moving in these seemingly irregular patterns.
- Always remember to keep the bar tilted, using the tip of the bar to fret just the note that you're on.

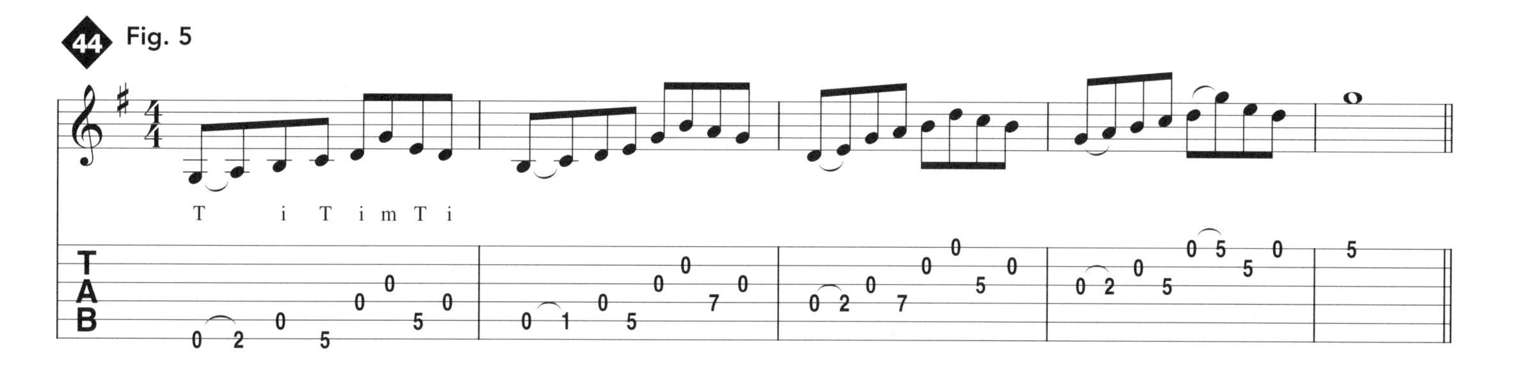

Fig. 6

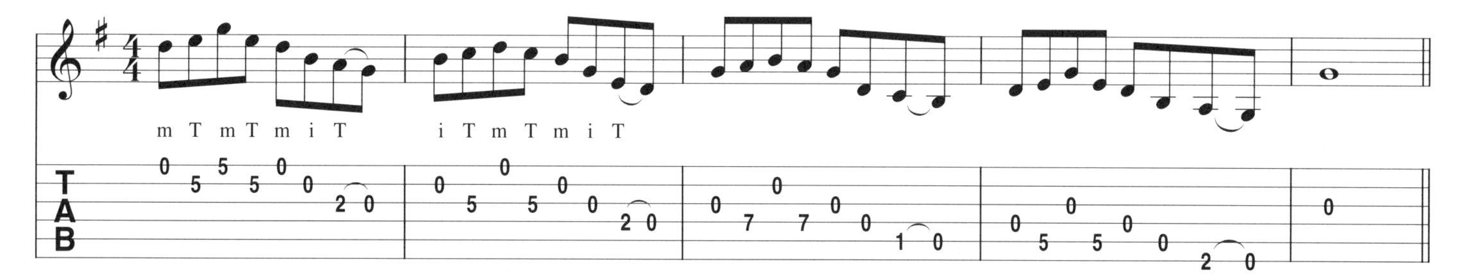

46 Fig. 7

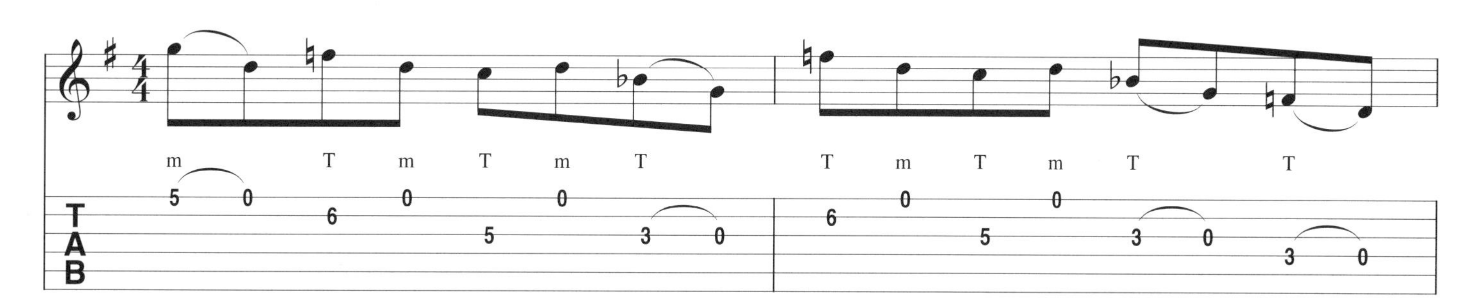

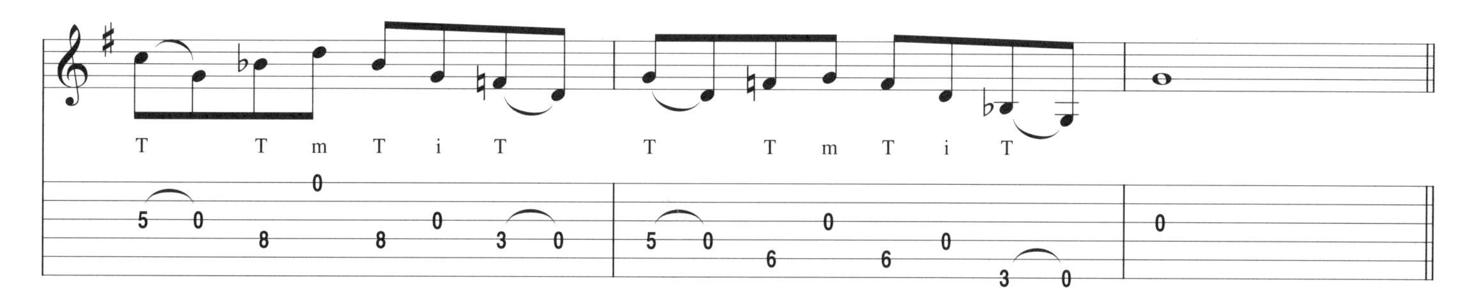

Fig. 8

Creating Licks in the Melodic Style

Working out some four-note units in the melodic style, just like we did in open position, will help you to work out breaks, improvise, and eventually arrange fiddle tunes and other melodies yourself, in the melodic style. Figure 9 consists of a handful of G major moves, each starting from a fretted note.

Fig. 9

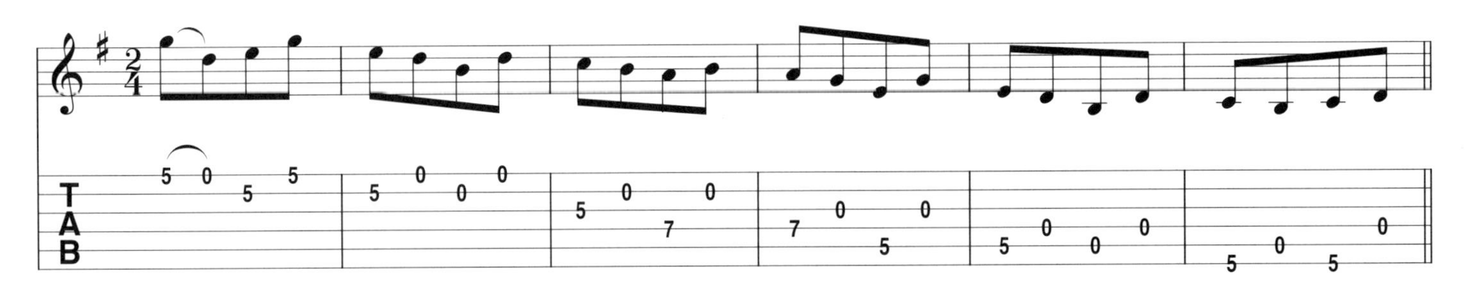

The G major units in Figure 10 all begin on an open note.

Fig. 10

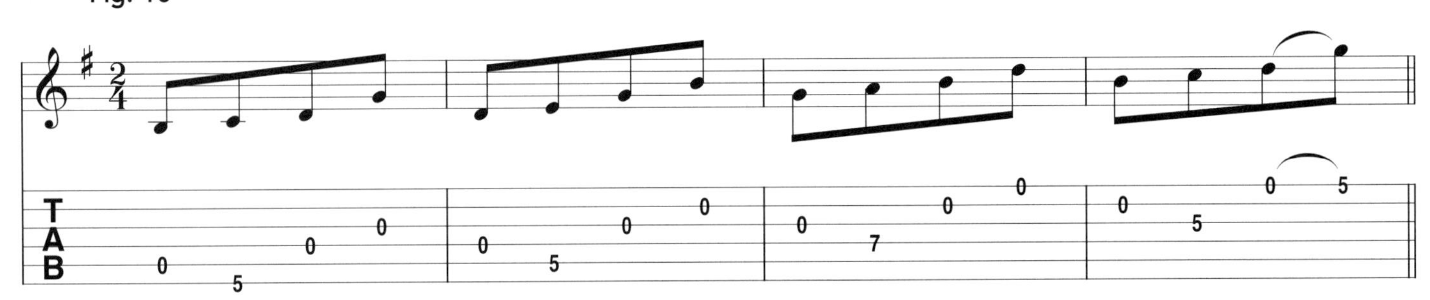

The units in Figure 11 are all drawn from the G blues scale and begin from a fretted note.

Fig. 11

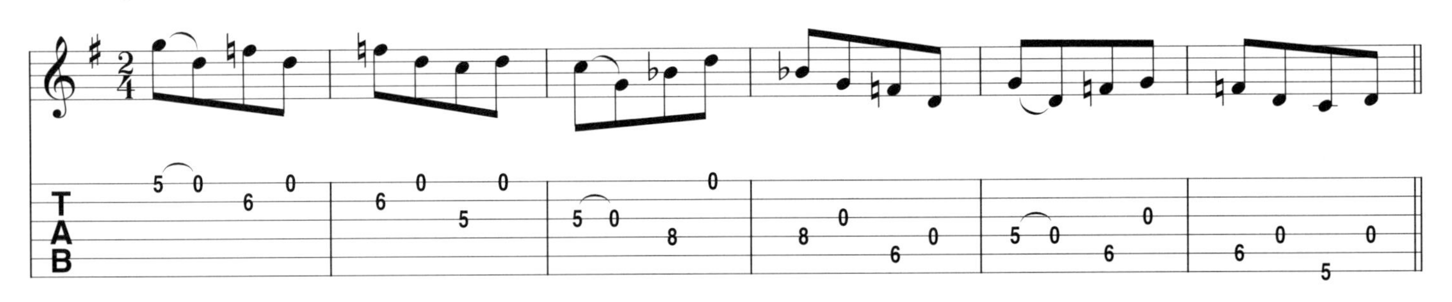

The G blues units in Figure 12 all start with an open note.

Fig. 12

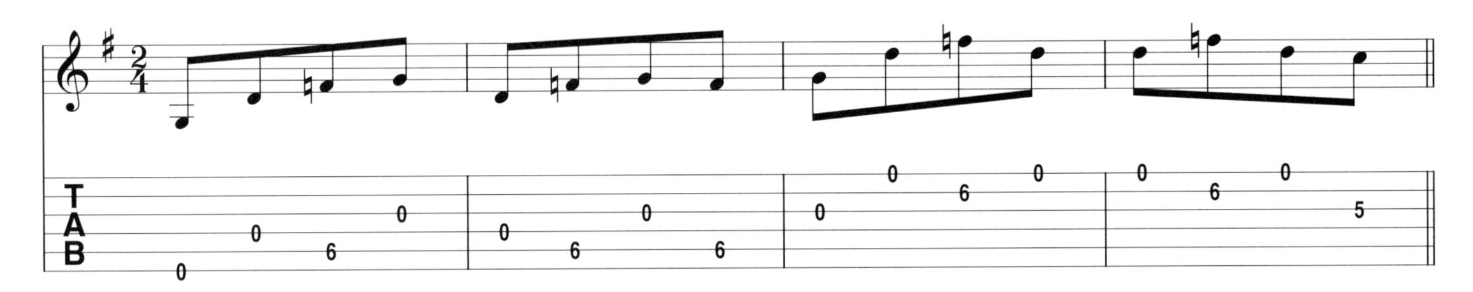

When you've started to get these units under your fingers, you can practice combining them into one-measure licks. I could insist that you figure some out for yourself first, but I'm not going to. Instead, I generously offer up the licks in Figure 13 for your enjoyment because, as an old teacher of mine used to say, that's just the kind of guy I am.

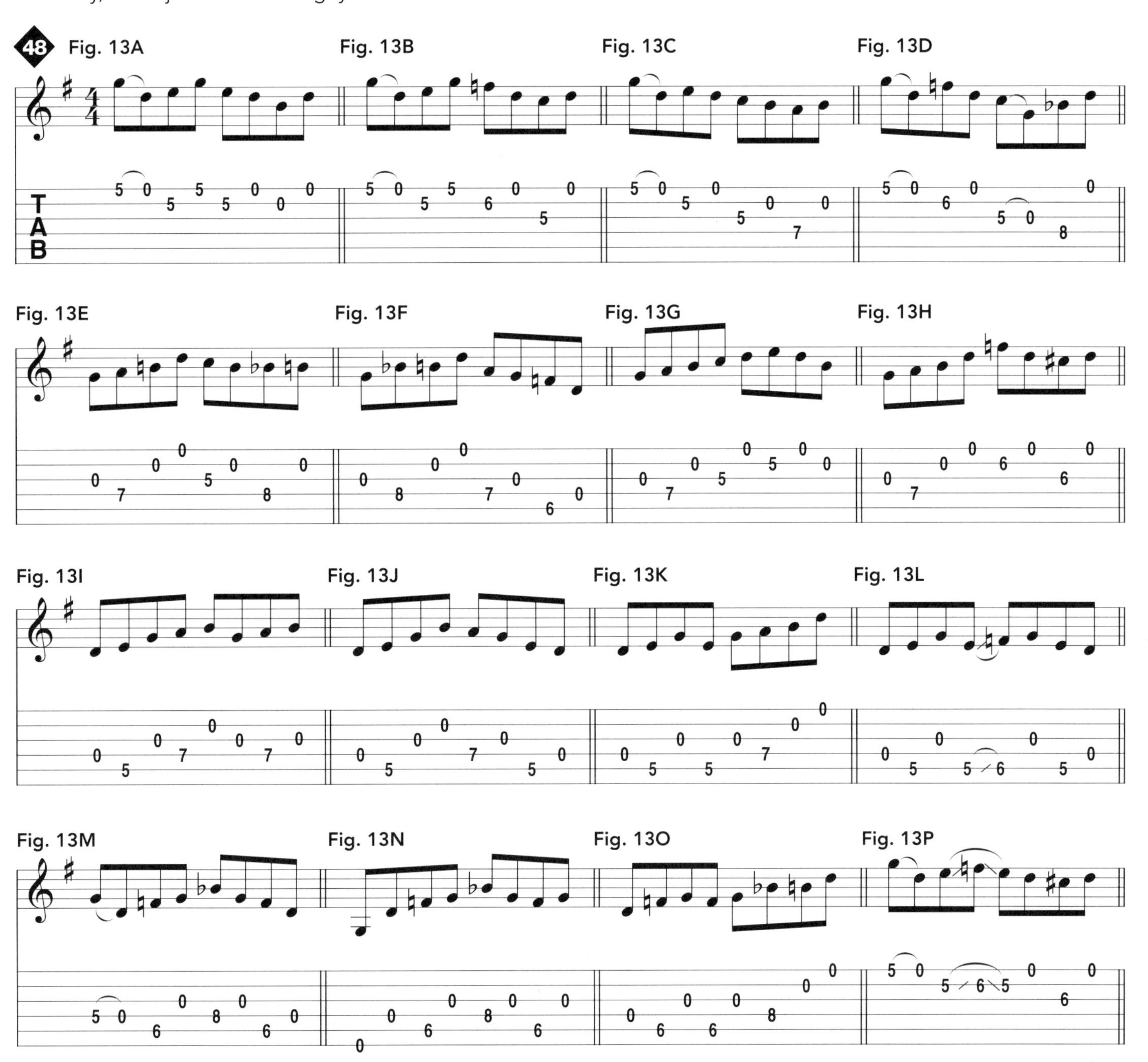

Of course, you're not really going to want to improvise using melodic-style licks at first. If you're playing some tune in G, and the tempo's really cruising along, and it's time for your break, the profound desire not to go down in flames in front of friends, peers, and the chief music critic from the resophonic desk of the *Daily Train Wreck* will lead you to whip out those ever-dependable open-position licks we spent so much time on in the first three chapters. And that's cool. However, if you're ever going to feel comfortable improvising in the melodic style, you're going to have to *practice* working some of those melodic moves and licks into your playing, so that they come more naturally to you under the pressure of performing.

"Sally Goodin"

Let's take the bluegrass mainstay "Sally Goodin" and look at some ways to practice improvising on it. We'll start with the tune itself, arranged in the melodic style.

> NOTE: This tune is usually played in A, so once you've worked some of these examples out, try capoing up two frets. Capoing in the melodic style can make things even more disorienting—when you're busy looking at the ninth fret, it's easy to forget whether the capo is even on the neck or not, back down there near the nut. So it's a good idea to practice with the capo on if you think you're going to be using it when you jam or perform on a particular tune. I've presented "Sally Goodin" uncapoed here to make it easier to compare with other material in the book based on similar "G shapes."

49 Fig. 14

Once you've got this down, the first thing you could try is throwing in a hot lick at the end of an A section as you play the melody. So the last two bars—measures 7–8—get replaced by a lick, as in Figure 15:

50 Fig. 15

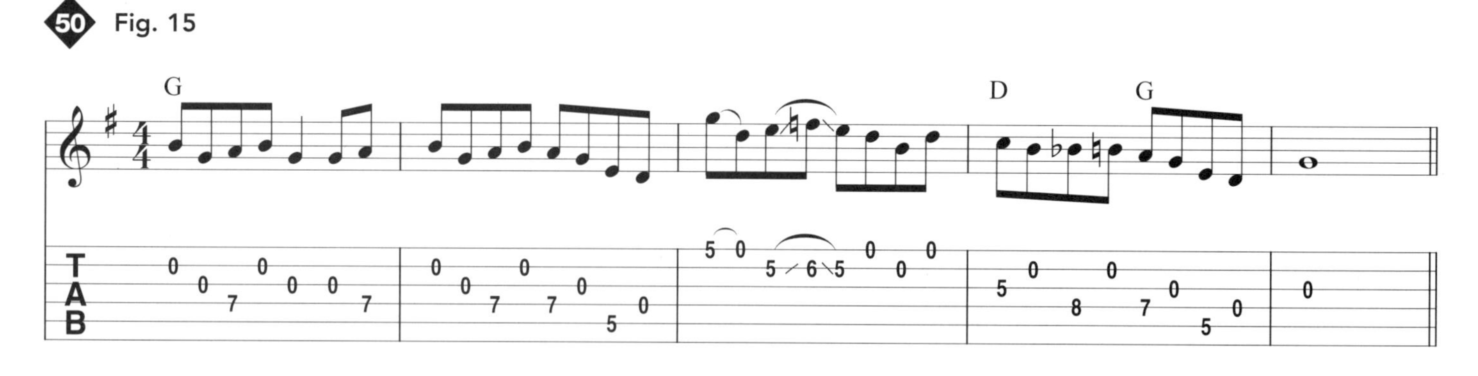

As we discussed earlier, in some ways your reflex will still be to go to the open position when you really want to tear it up. That's no problem as long as you can still get back to the melodic style and the melody of the tune when you want to. So why not practice that? Figure 16 is a call and response between the original melody and open-position licks. Measures 3–4 are a "response" made up of G major licks, while measures 7–8 are a "response" made up of G blues licks.

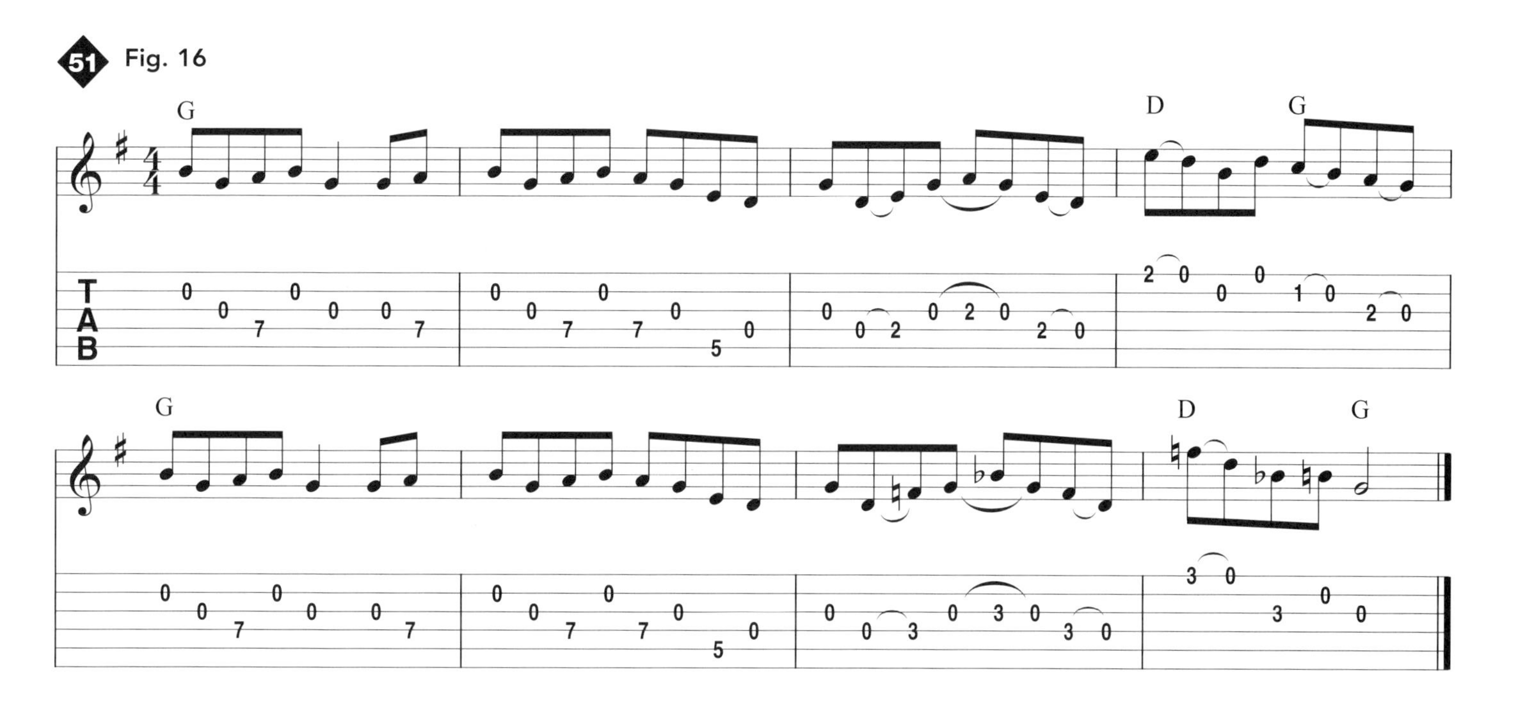

You can do syncopations in the melodic style just as we did in the open position. Rhythmically, the rules are the same. Before we do the next variation on "Sally Goodin," try out the four 6+6+4 syncopations in Figure 17.

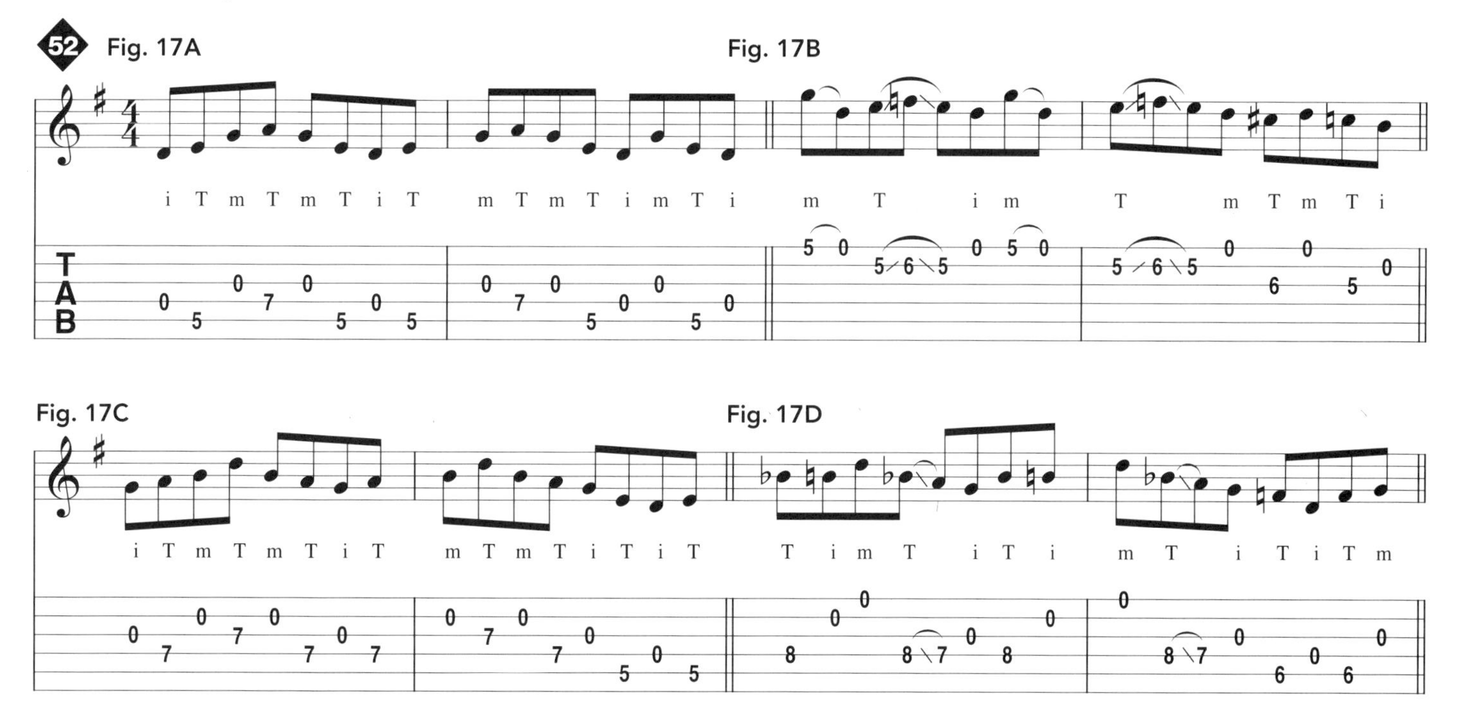

These licks are a great way to kick off the B section of "Sally Goodin." Try Figure 18, in which the syncopated licks in measures 1–2 and 5-6 are the call and the return to the melody in measures 3–4 and 7–8 are the response.

53 **Fig. 18**

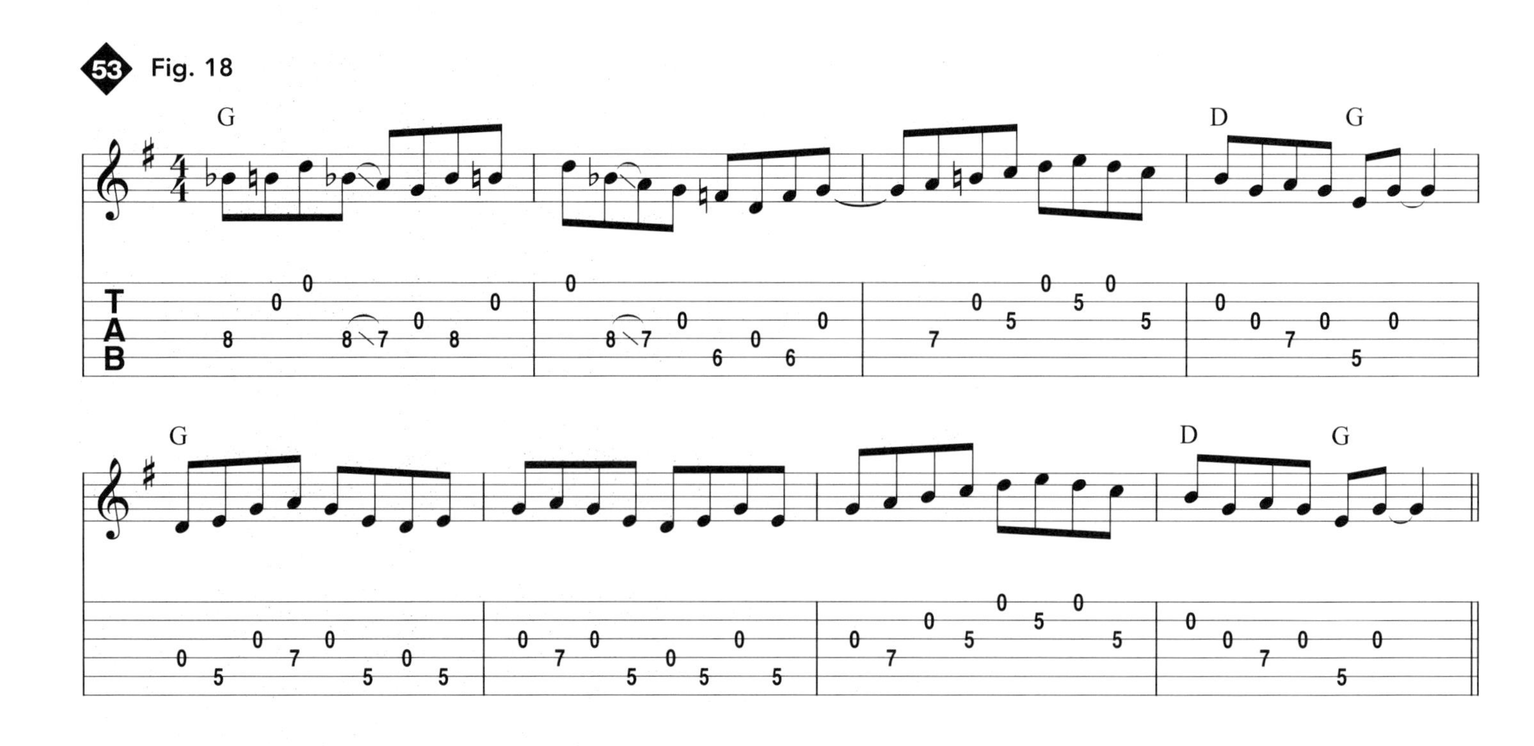

Finally, you could break the B section into two four-bar sections, as we did in some versions of "Bill Cheatham" in Chapter 3. In Figure 19, the first four bars of the B section stick to the melody; the response in measures 5–8 begins with a two-measure syncopated lick and wraps up with two measures of off-kilter bluesiness. This whole plan is then repeated, with different response licks, in the second eight measures.

54 **Fig. 19**

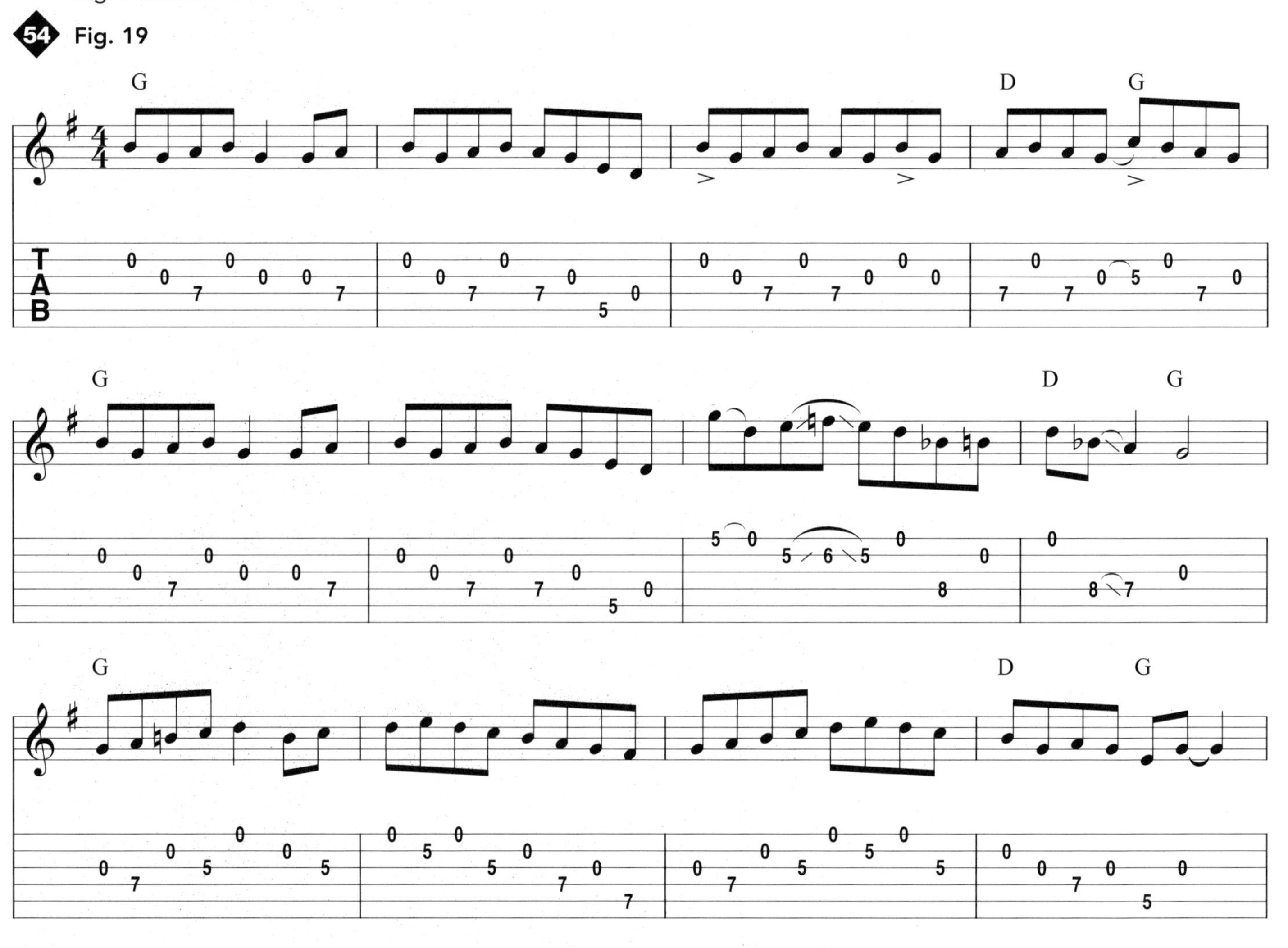

I would be remiss if I did not restate at this point that, of course, the ability to create an impenetrable wall of eighth notes is not exactly the *goal* of all this work. It *is* a very tangible way of developing your chops, and there are times when it's good to know you can keep up with everyone else on those ridiculously fast tunes. But you have to let your breaks breathe a little too. Most melodies have little pauses, resting points, and/or held notes, and that is something to be aware of in your breaks as well. There is a time and a place for furious eighth notes, and since they are impossible to nail down without some practice, these exercises are meant to help you work on that. But I hope you're catching the drift here with all the emphasis on working in and around the original melody. Try to stay aware of the phrasing of the original tune. If you're aware of the original melody, your break can follow some of the lilt and phrasing of that melody, whatever the style. Then when you do drop in those eighth notes, they serve as an embellishment, as coloring, as a moment that makes the listener go, "Whoa!" The reverse is equally effective. If you're racing along on a breakdown tune, churning out the notes, and you stop to hold one note, really drawing it out, that makes for an equally effective change of pace, as a break in the flow. It's *your* break—what do *you* want to create? Think about it, and try to come up with ways to practice *that.*

Playing over C and F

We're going to continue playing in the key of G but work on some melodic-style ways to play over the C and F chords that occur frequently when playing in G.

C Scales and Licks

First, here's one-and-a-half octaves of a C major scale in the melodic style.

Fig. 1

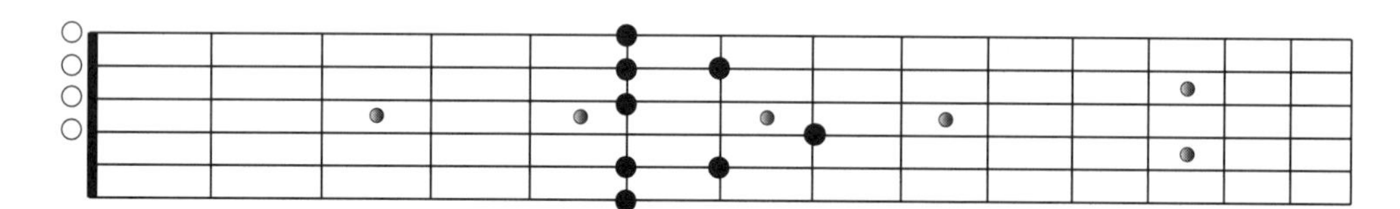

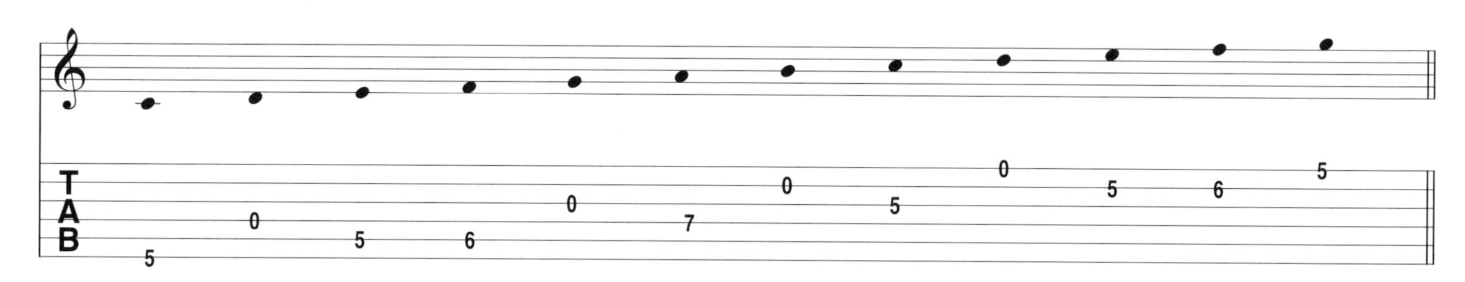

Leaving out the Fs makes for the more streamlined fingering in Figure 2. This will be the basis for most of the melodic C licks we work out.

Fig. 2

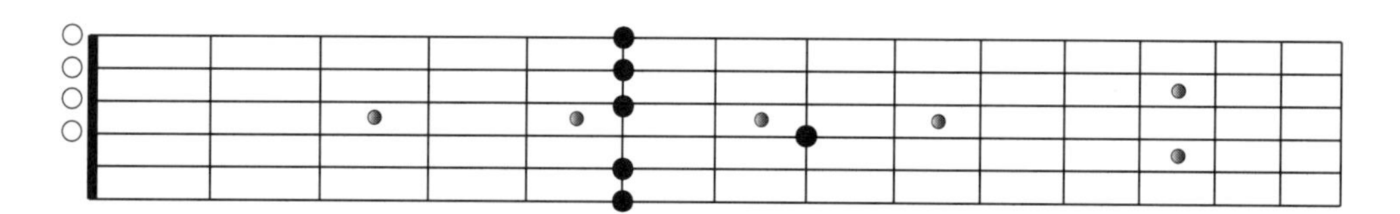

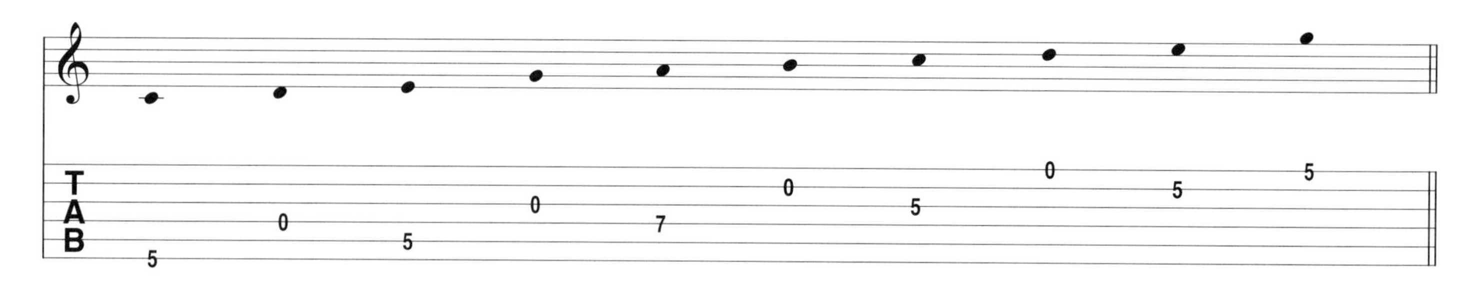

The approach in Figure 3 should be familiar by now: a series of four-note units suitable for mixing and matching, all based on just the C major pentatonic scale of C–D–E–G–A (R–2–3–5–6). Since all of these units also begin exclusively from a fretted note, I have simply organized them in terms of what string they begin on. Units beginning on the low string come first, then those beginning on the fifth fret, and so on.

There are certainly occasions for beginning a unit on an open string, and a few of these occur below. I have provided you with a handful of hot C licks to try out, served up with the usual recommendation that you take the time to pull these licks apart to see what makes them tick and assemble some of your own as well from the units above, or others that you come up with yourself.

Applications

The next set of exercises will give you practice integrating these new melodic-style C licks into various situations. First, try switching between G melodic and C melodic moves. Figure 5 shows a couple of ways to take a repeated riff on G and follow it up with a two-measure response in C.

56 **Fig. 5**

Figure 6 supposes you might be coming out of playing in G in the open position for a quick one-measure run in C before returning to G. The chord changes come fast and furious, so take it slowly at first.

57 **Fig. 6**

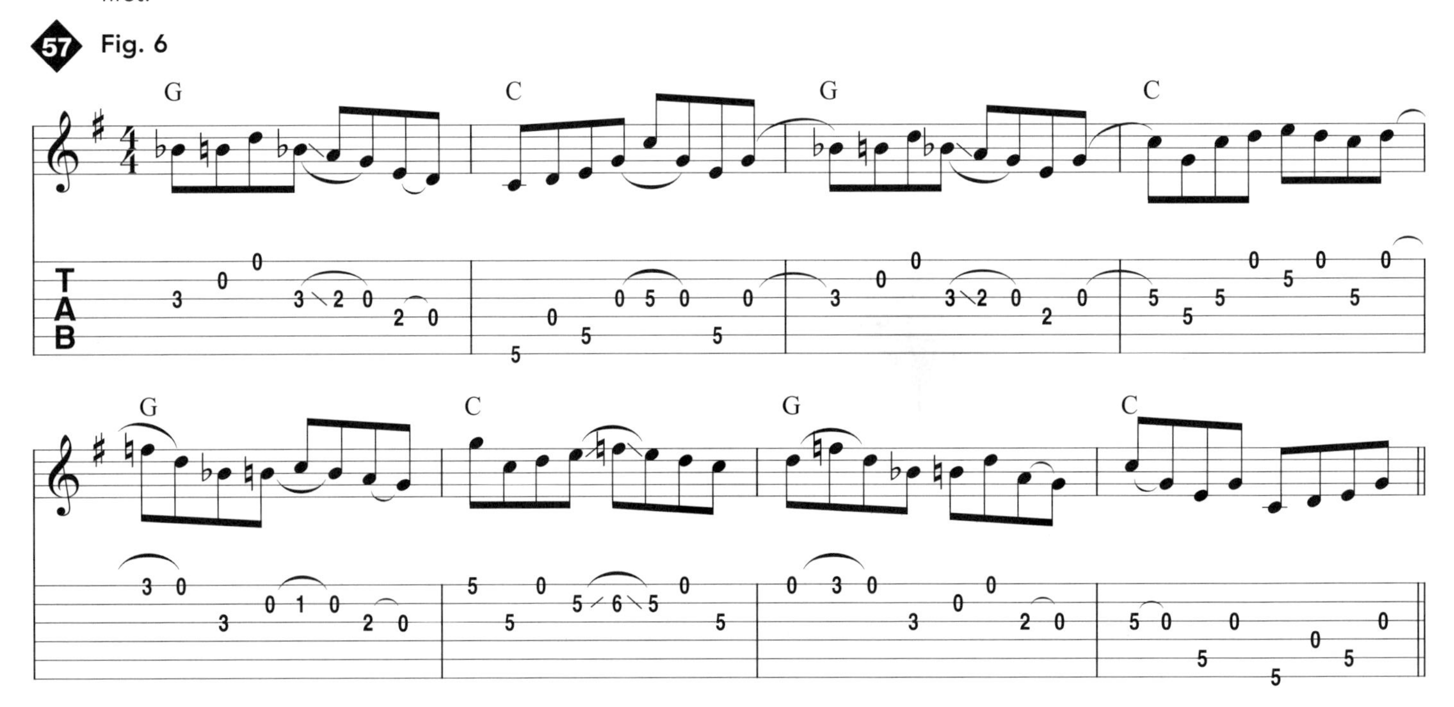

If you find yourself up in the bluesy stratosphere, playing at the eighth fret over C, you might want to drop in the occasional melodic move, as in Figure 7.

Fig. 7

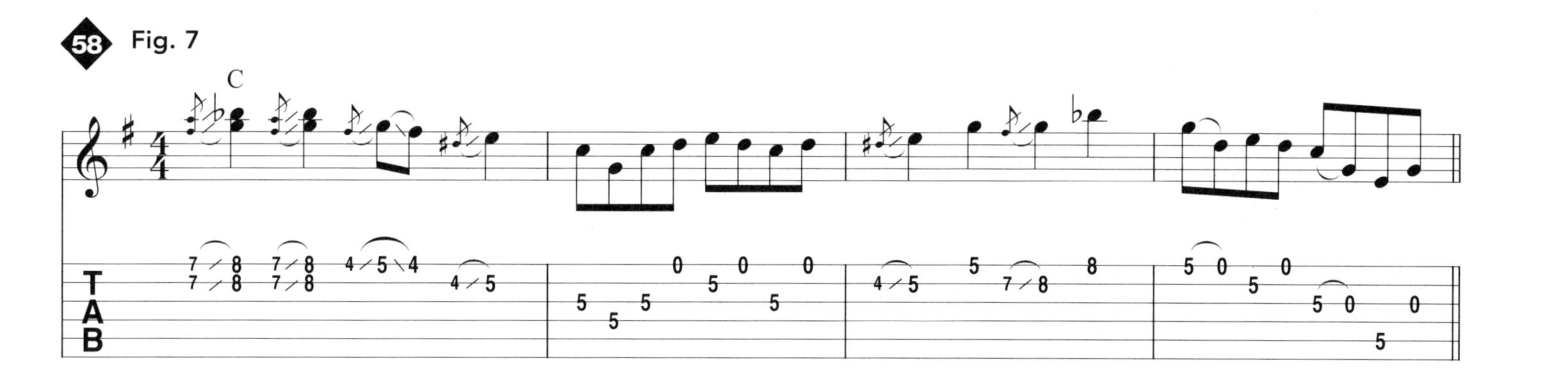

Sometimes you even need to be able to switch chords every two beats. In Figure 8, the first two beats of each bar are in G; the second two, in C.

Fig. 8

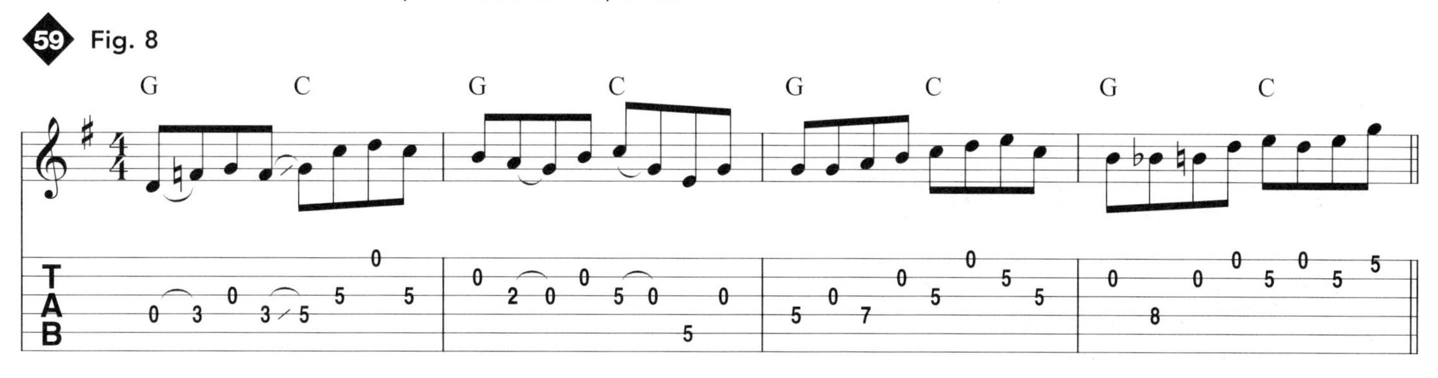

"Bill Cheatham" Revisited

Now, it would be mean to make you do all this work without getting to see how it works on a real live tune, wouldn't it? So let's revisit "Bill Cheatham" and see what kind of mayhem we can cook up playing it in a melodic context.

Our original setting of this tune in Chapter 3 actually had some melodic-style moments to begin with, usually when the melody went up to the C chord. To play "Bill Cheatham" completely in this style, substitute the two measures in Figure 9 for measures 1–2 and 5–6 in the original arrangement (on page 32).

Fig. 9

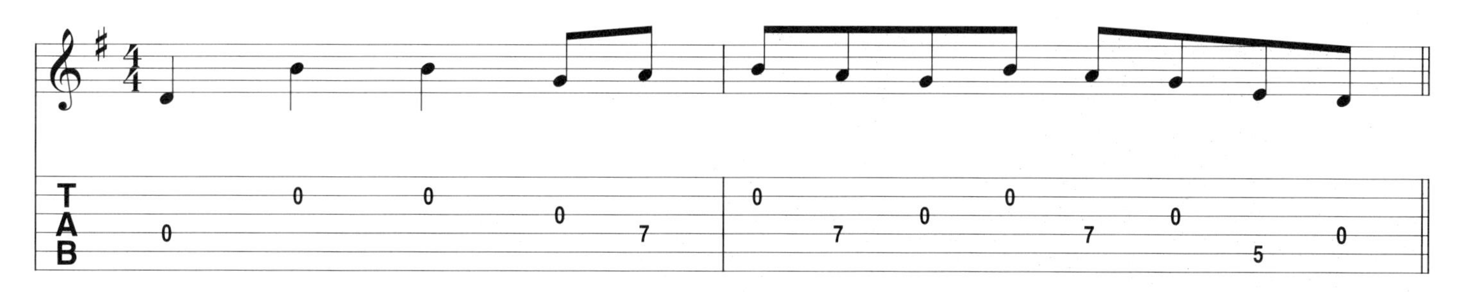

Now we can do a variation on this tune in which our excellent collection of licks in C will really pay off. In Figure 10, the melody in measures 1–2 and measures 5–6 is answered by combining two one-measure C licks together in measures 3–4 and again in measures 7–8.

60 Fig. 10

In this variation of the B section, the chord changes come every two beats. This variation goes to the second ending, and only measures 7–8 are from the original melody.

61 Fig. 11

F Scales and Licks

As with C, our primary concern about playing in F is being able to get around when an F chord shows up while we're playing in G. This happens most frequently on "modal" fiddle tunes. A modal fiddle tune is one where the melody is created from a mode, or scale, besides the major scale. Modal fiddle tunes in G are usually based around the G Mixolydian mode, or G–A–B–C–D–E–F–G. You can think of the Mixolydian mode, or scale, as being the same as a major scale, but with a ♭7.

Fig. 12

What all of this means is that the melody of a modal tune often implies a ♭VII chord, which in the key of G would be F. So if we're going to work out melodies and breaks on a G modal tune, it would be good to be able to get around in F.

To begin with, here is an F major scale played melodic-style in one and a half octaves:

Fig. 13

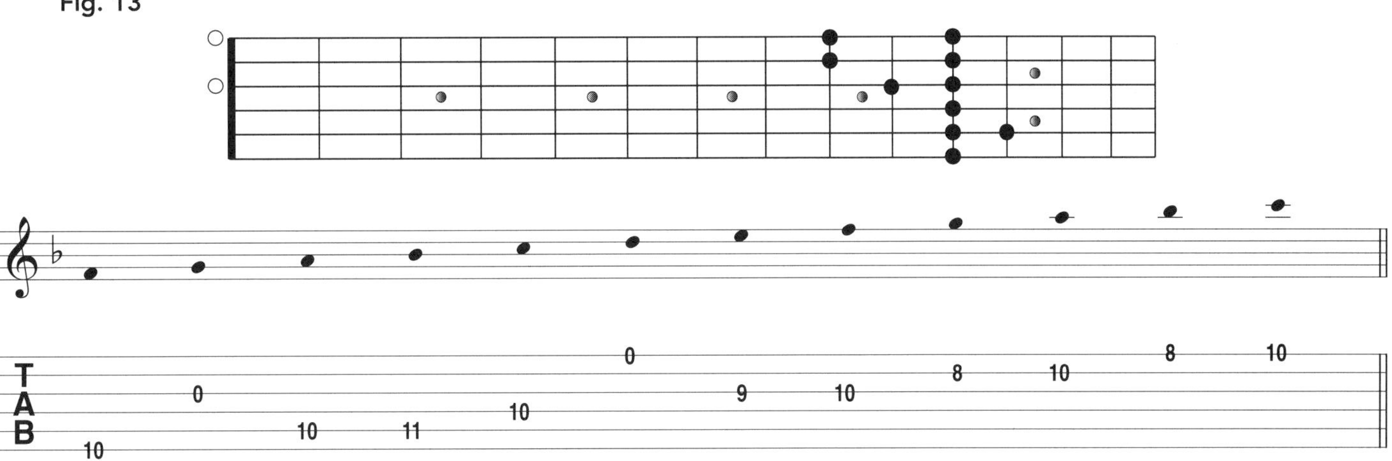

We really only need a handful of these notes for most of what we're going to do. Figure 14 is basically an F major pentatonic scale (R–2–3–5–6), which leaves out the fourth and seventh of the major scale.

Fig. 14

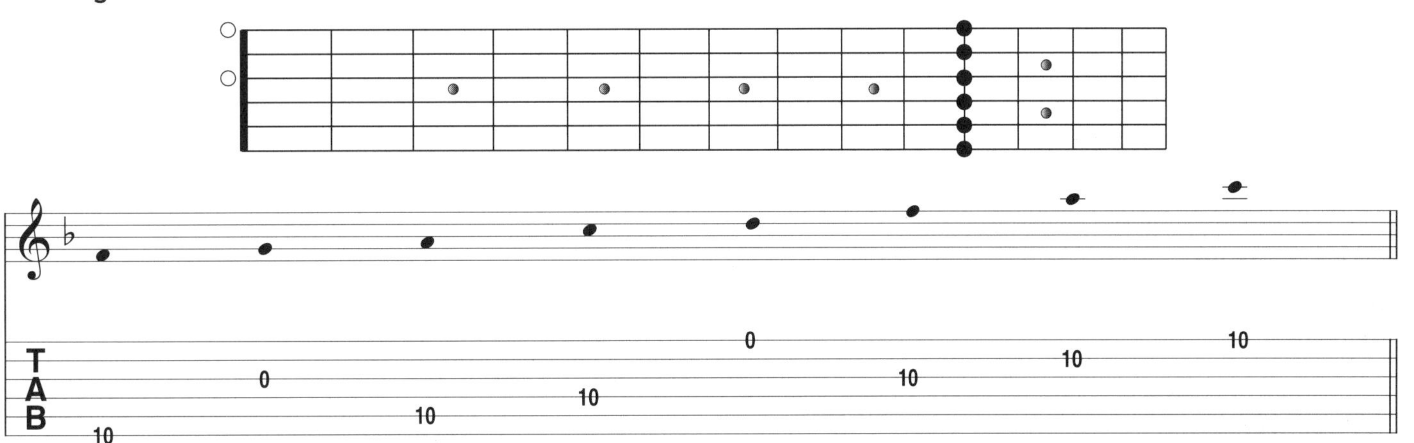

Now we can work out some four-note units. As with C, these are all major and all begin from fretted notes, so they are arranged by what string they begin on, beginning with units starting on the lowest string.

Fig. 15

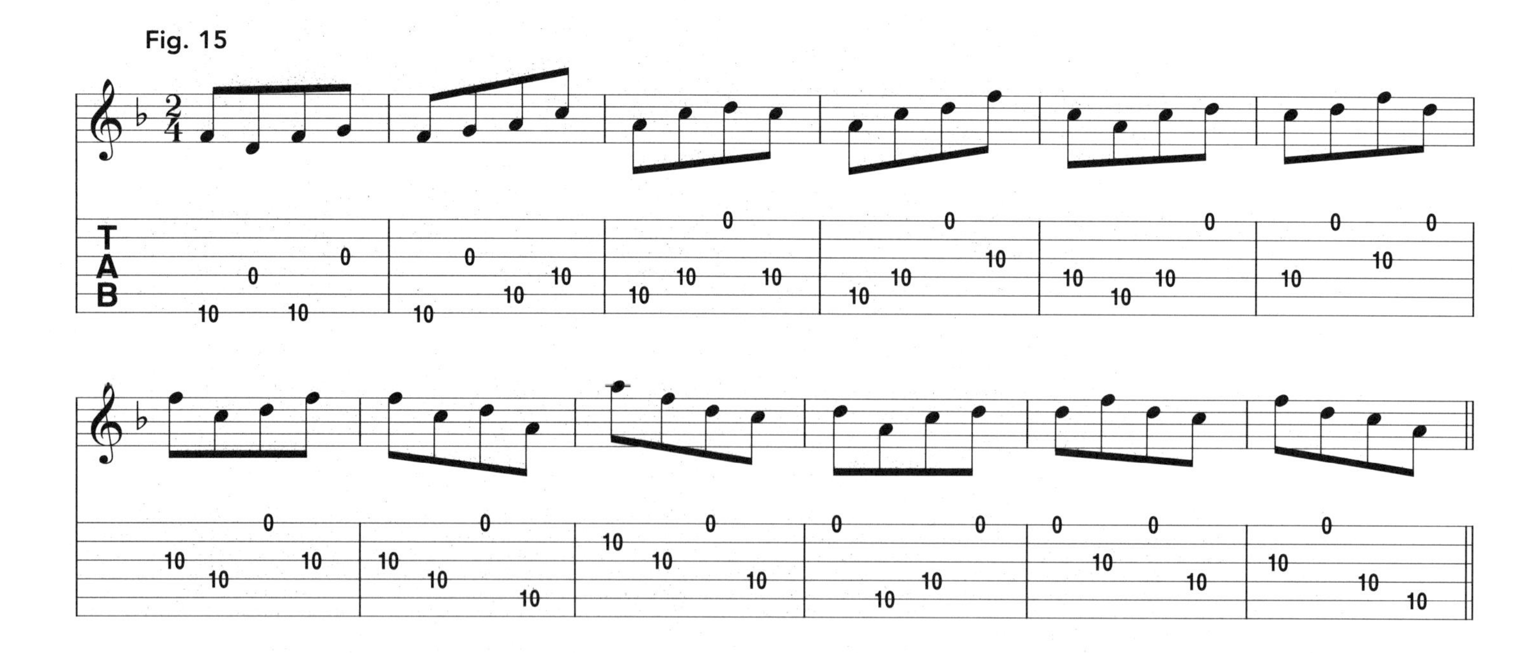

Practice mixing and matching these on the fly with a metronome; Figure 16 gives you a few ideas of what's possible.

62 Fig. 16A Fig. 16B Fig. 16C

Fig. 16D Fig. 16E Fig. 16F Fig. 16G

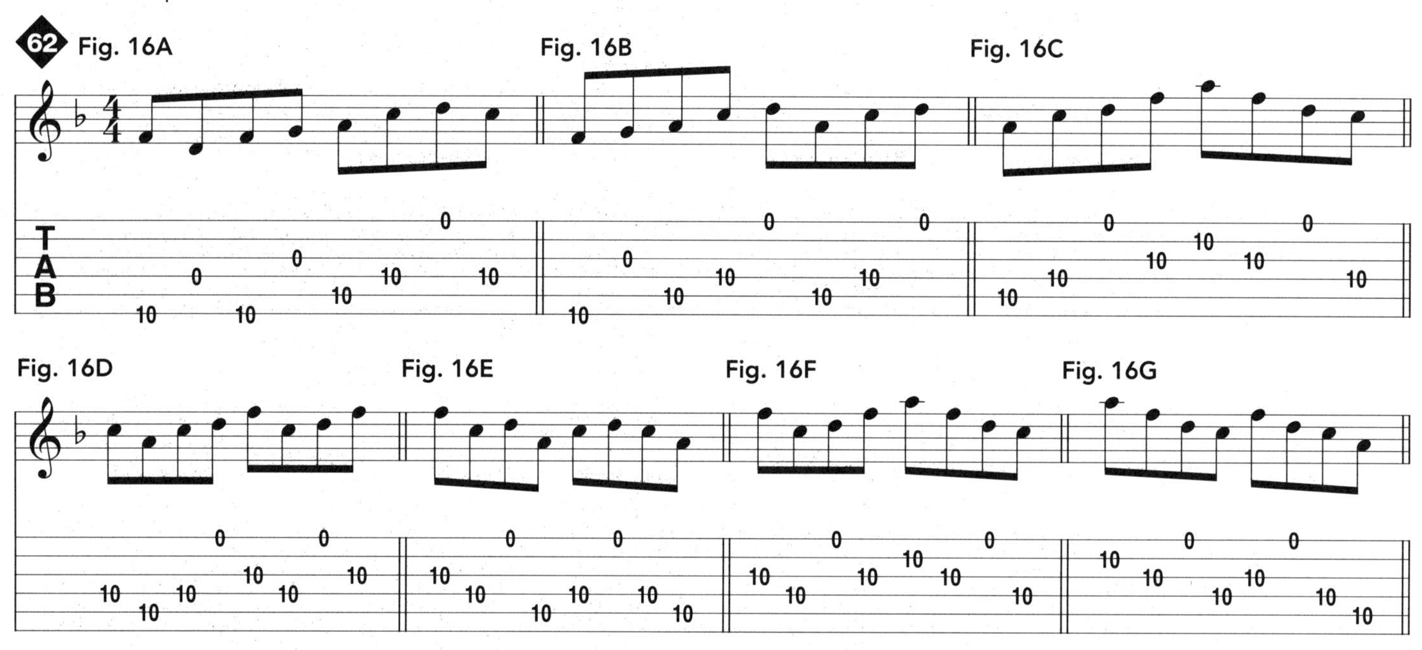

In a two-measure lick, you can create a little breathing room and put a rhythmic charge into things by either anticipating or delaying the first note of the second measure by an eighth note. In Figure 17A, jump on the bluesy slide at the end of measure 1 and hold it into measure 2; in Figure 17B, wait until the "and" of the first beat of measure 2 to land on the funky ♭7 note (E♭), and hold it until the third beat.

63 Fig. 17A

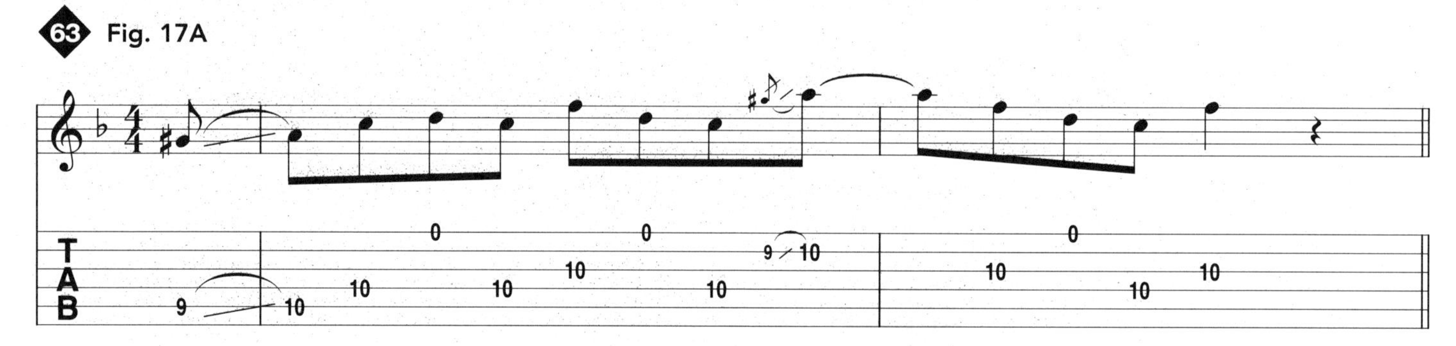

Fig. 17B

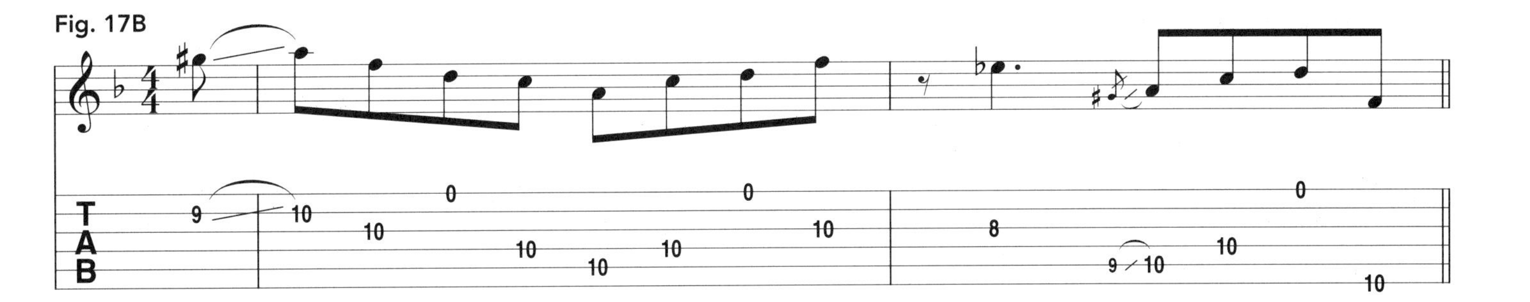

Applications

To warm up for working some of these F licks into a tune, practice switching from two bars of G to two bars of F and back again, all in the melodic style. Figure 18 shows a couple of possibilities using this approach.

64 Fig. 18

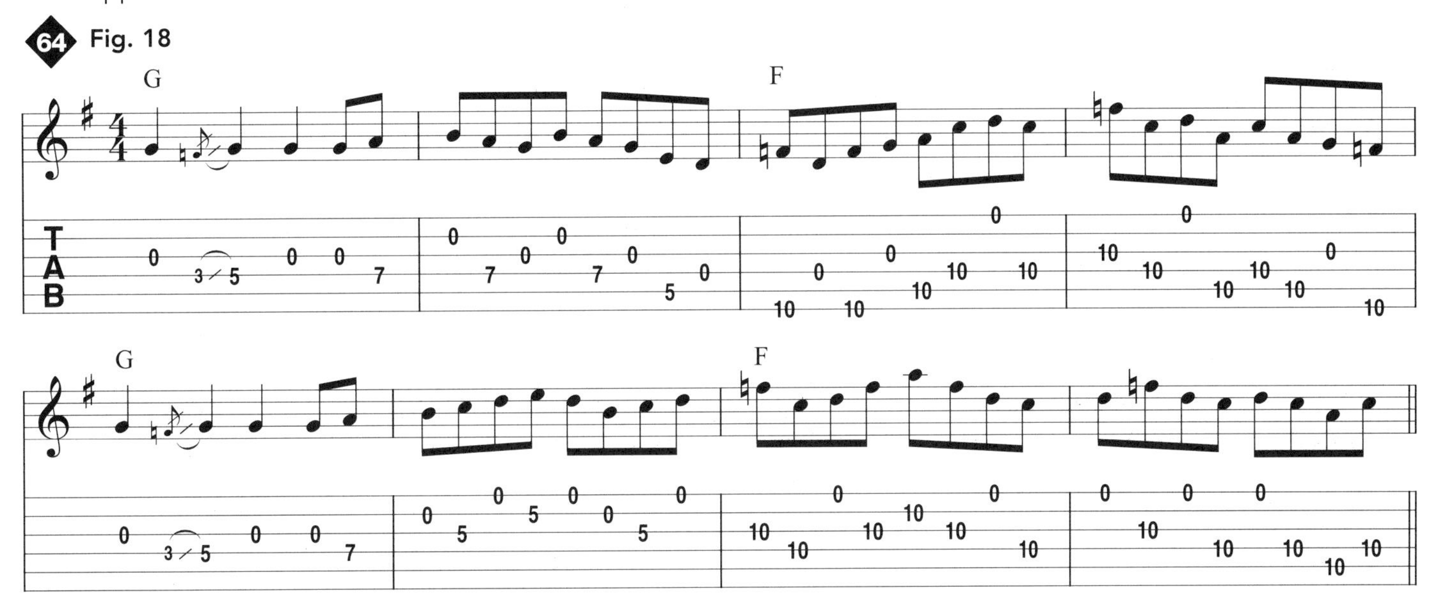

Then there's switching from F to C, which can also come in handy. In Figure 19, the chords change every bar, so the open strings at the start or end of each measure make the shifts in position possible, from the tenth to the fifth fret or vice versa.

65 Fig. 19

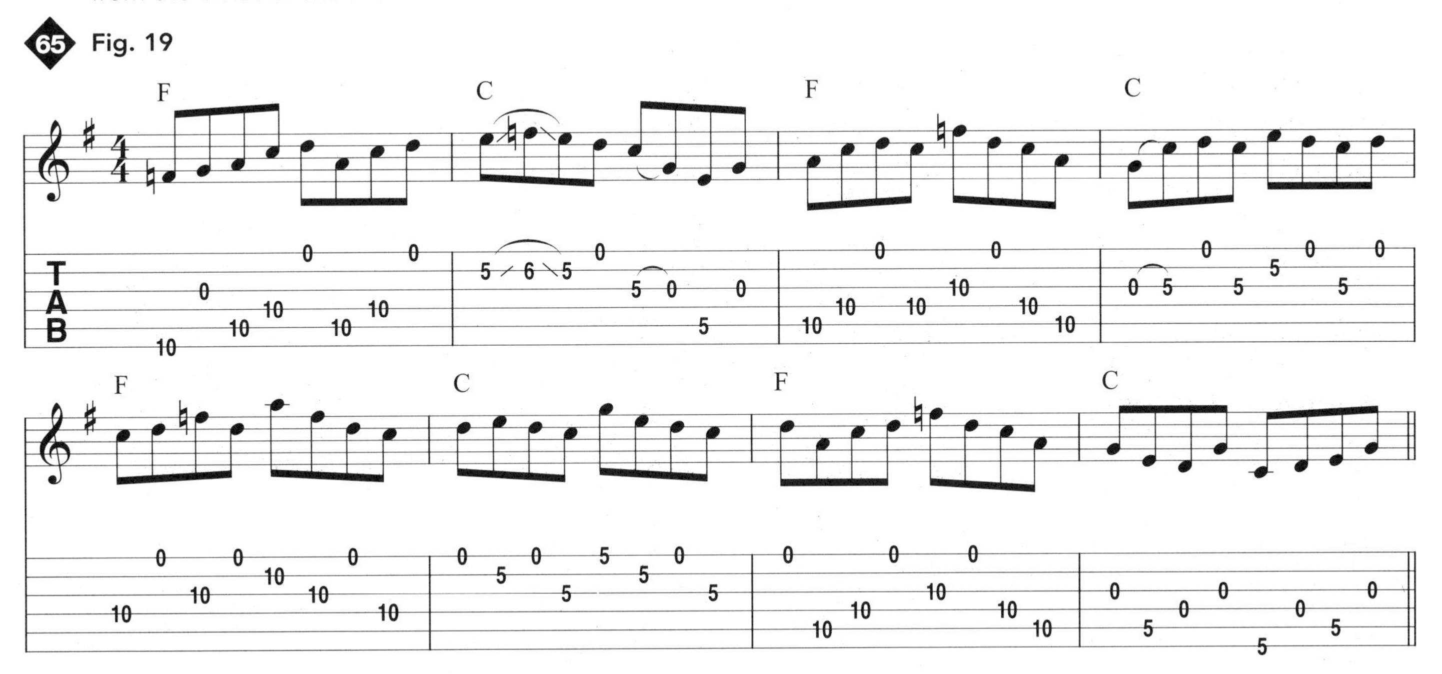

"Red-Haired Boy"

"Red-Haired Boy" is a fiddle tune that I've arranged here in the melodic style. During the tune itself you don't need to leap up to the tenth fret over the F chords; the melody can be found in the general vicinity of the fifth to seventh frets. Stay tuned, however, and we'll look at one idea for playing a break over this tune that will require the use of our new-found chops in both C and F.

> NOTE: Like "Sally Goodin," this tune is usually played in the key of A by real-live fiddlers. Should you encounter such a real-live fiddler in action, don't be intimidated. Simply point over their shoulder, saying, "Hey, isn't that Antonio Vivaldi heading our way?" While he or she is scrambling wildly for a glimpse of the great seventeenth-century baroque composer, calmly slip a capo onto your second fret, and remember that you need to play up at the seventh fret for "C" and the twelfth fret for "F," which are now actually D and G, respectively. When said fiddle player turns back to you, heartbroken at having missed a chance to swap tunes with ol' Antonio himself, just smile sweetly and say, "'Red-Haired Boy'—in the key of A, right?"

66 **Fig. 20**

For a break on the A section, try the call-and-response approach we've been working on: two bars of original melody followed by two bars of improvising. In Figure 21, there are a few liberties taken with the melody itself in measures 5–6, and the figure ends in the open position in measure 8, which is perhaps a good place to begin the next eight measures. You don't have to stay in the melodic style all the time—use it when it seems like a good idea.

67 Fig. 21

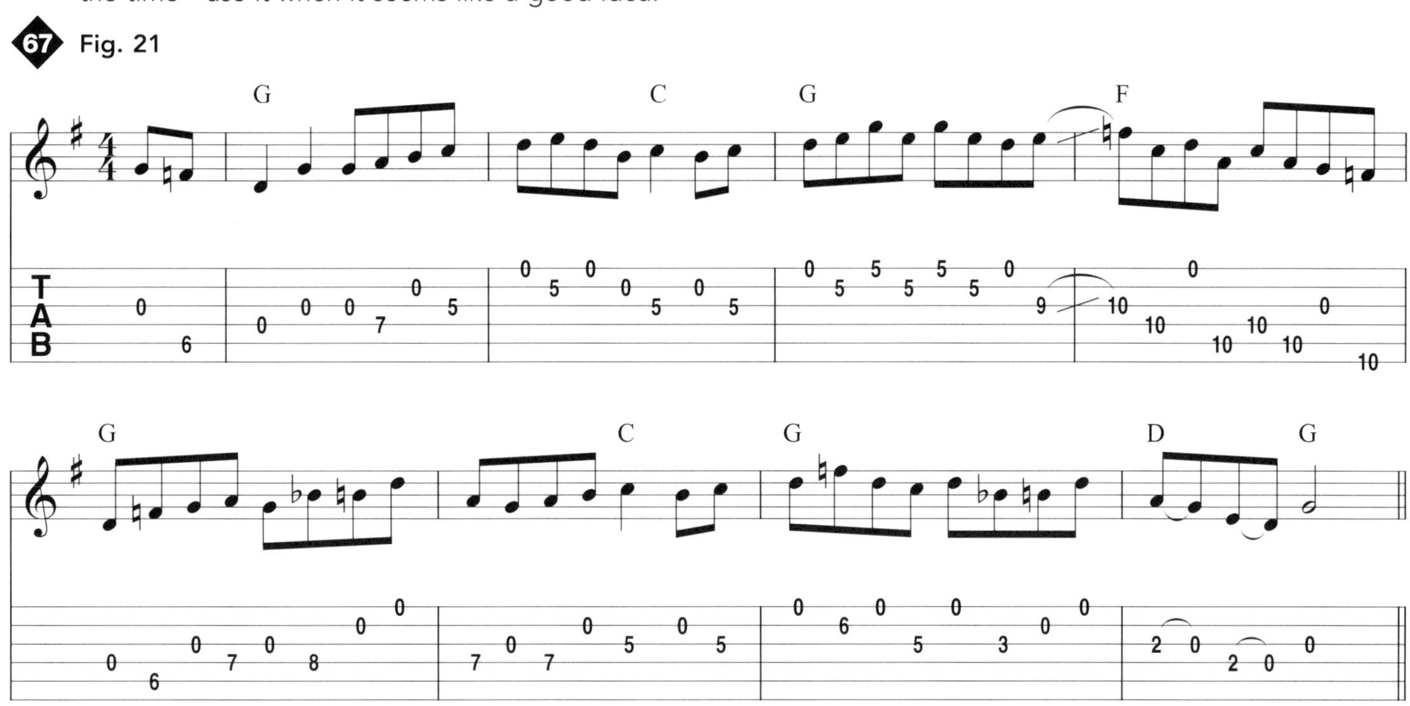

Let's wrap things up with a look at the B section. Figure 22 is done as one of the other kinds of call-and-response schemes we've looked at—four measures of improvisation followed by a return to the melody, slightly embellished, in the last four measures.

68 Fig. 22

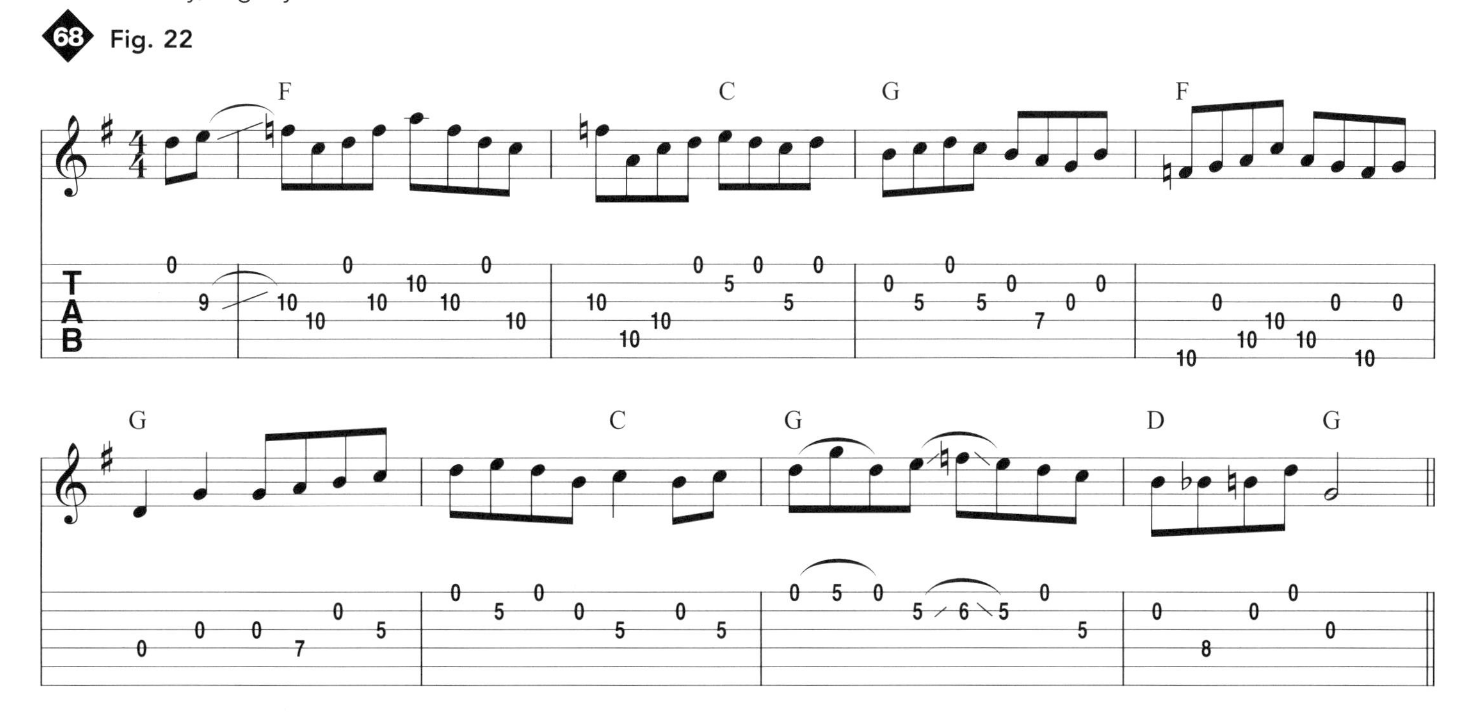

Playing in the Key of D, Open Position

There's no question that lap-style resophonic slide can be played in any key, particularly if you use closed position. Hawaiian and swing players do it all the time, and country and bluegrass players who use a lot of slants or more old-timey double-stops do, too—particularly on ballads and waltzes. But if you want to really tear it up at breakdown tempos, it works best to play in open position or melodic style in the keys of G or D—or to use a capoed version of those keys' shapes. For example, if a song is in A, B♭, or B, you can capo up two, three, or four frets, respectively, and continue to play as if you were in G. If a song is in E or F, you can use the shapes of the open D position and capo up two frets for E or three frets for F. By combining an understanding of how to play in open G and open D with a judicious use of the capo, you can thus play uptempo in G, D, A, E, B♭, F, and B, which is almost every key you're going to run into under ordinary jamming circumstances. For folk songs, bluegrass ballads, country tunes, and the blues, closed position often sounds best anyway, and so there's no great need to hunt for a way to get the open strings involved. But for uptempo tunes, particularly of the bluegrass ilk, a thorough grip on the D and G positions is the best way to get that rippling flow of notes going. Otherwise, you may find yourself gnashing your teeth on the sidelines while a bunch of fleet-fingered mandolinists, flatpickers, and banjo players hog the action. And hey—just because your frets are purely ornamental, why should those other pickers have all the fun?

D Scales

So, D being the other half of the open-position equation, let's get started with a D major scale in open position, played from a fifth below the root to a third above:

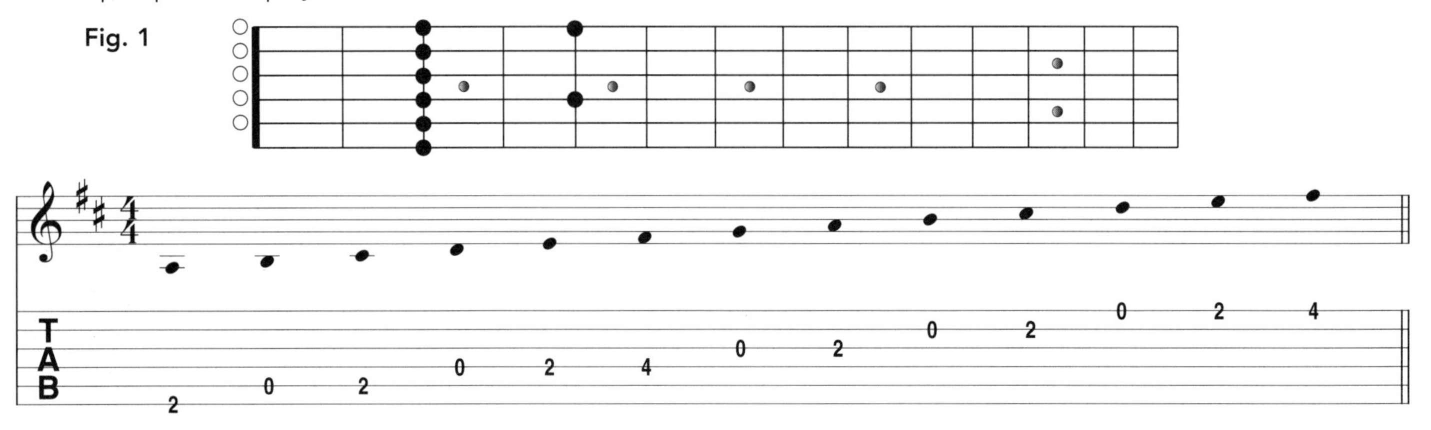

Leaving out the seventh gives us a more neutral sound that's also a little quicker to get around in:

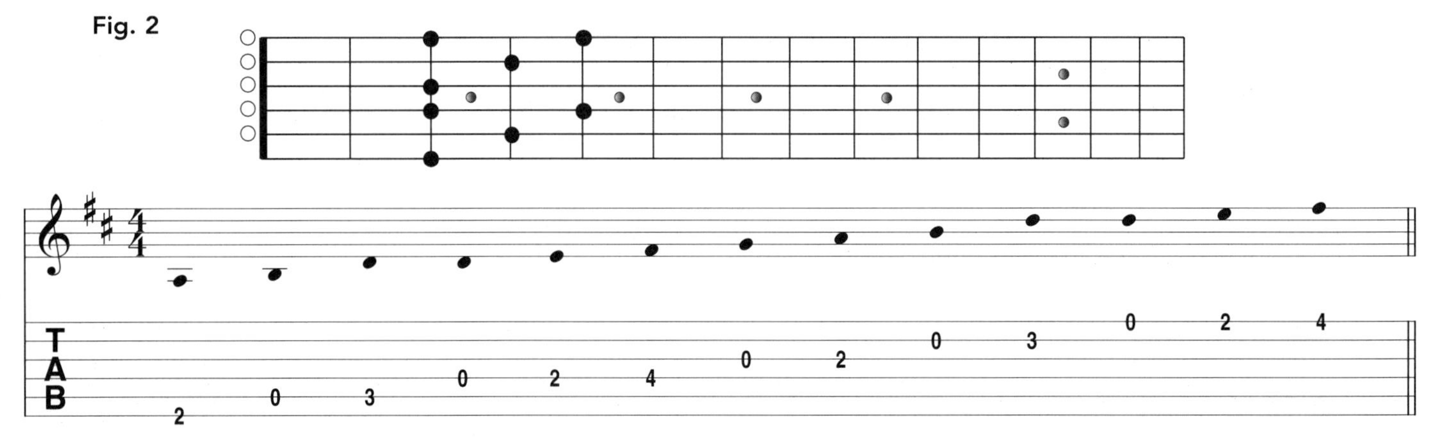

Figure 3 is a D blues scale with the notes R–♭3–4–5–6–♭7. You could think of it as a D minor pentatonic scale with the sixth (B) added. Or, I suppose you could not think about it at all. Either way, here it is:

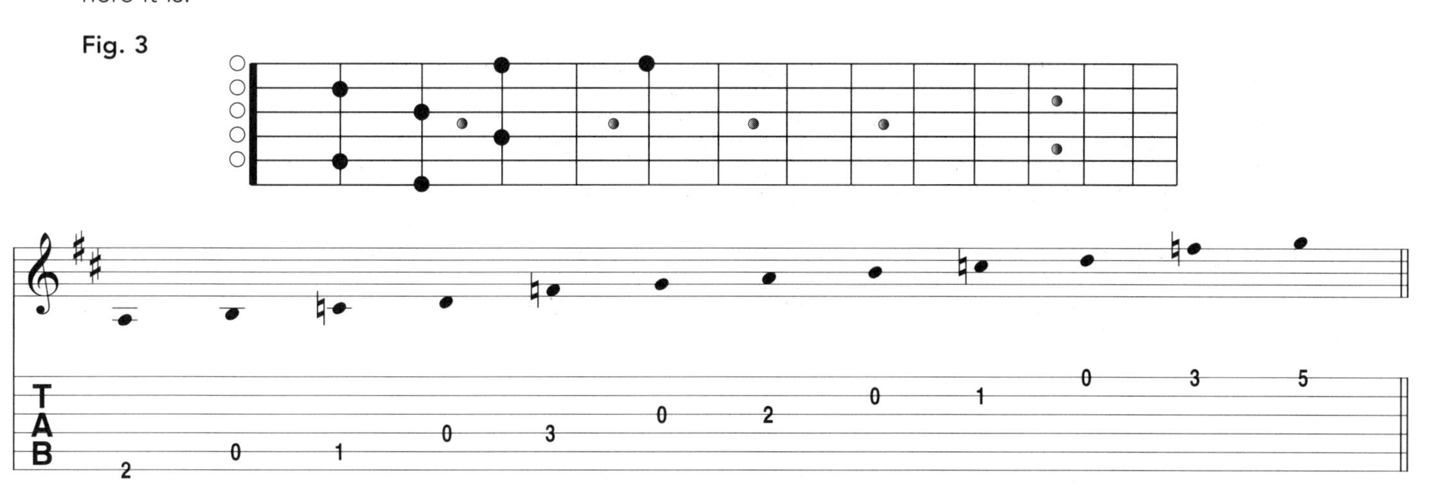

The next few examples are like the warm-ups we did in Chapter 1, but for the key of D. Figure 4, based on pull-offs, is a good review of right-hand finger-alternation. Figure 5 is based on an ascending pattern using both hammer-ons and combined hammer-on/pull-off moves; Figure 6 is a descending pattern using pull-offs and combined hammer-ons/pull-offs.

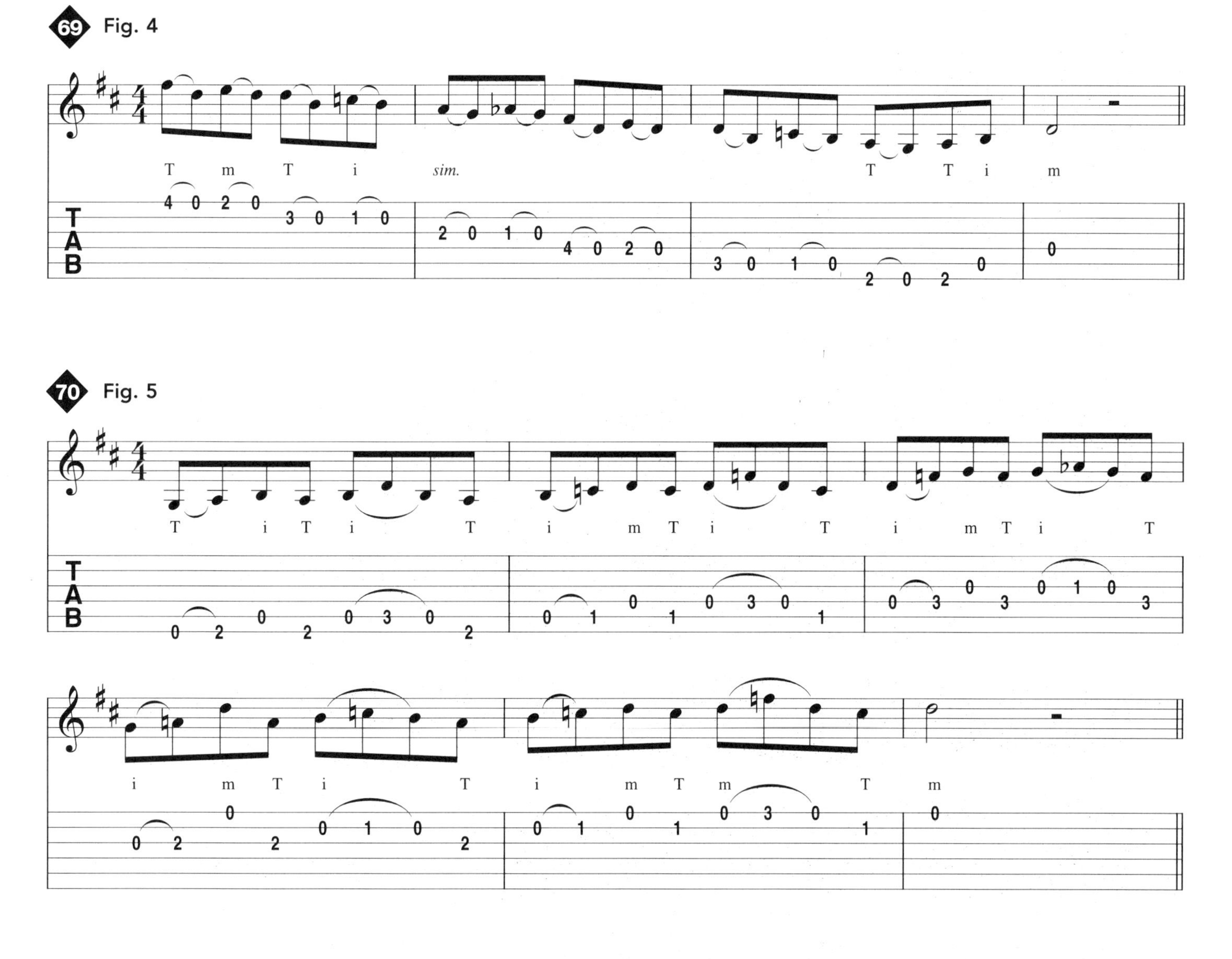

Four-Note Units

Use the above exercises to get familiar with the key of D and to review some of the basic open-position techniques after our melodic-style wanderings up the neck. Then take a look at the four-note units in Figure 7. The units in Figures 7A and 7B are all in D major; those in 7A begin from a fretted note, those in 7B from an open note. The units in 7C and 7D are drawn from the blues scale; the units in 7C start with a fretted note, and those in 7D start from an open note.

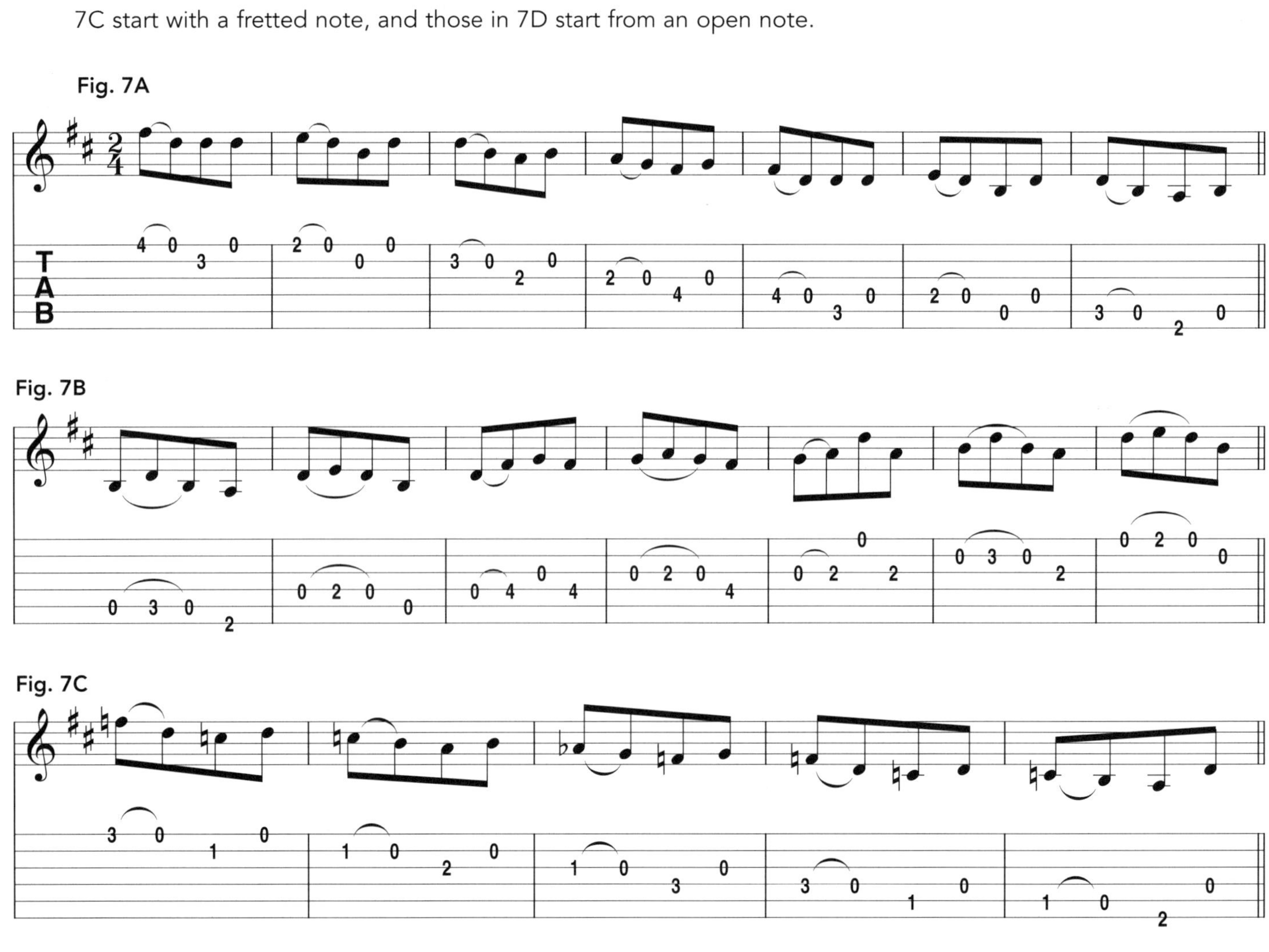

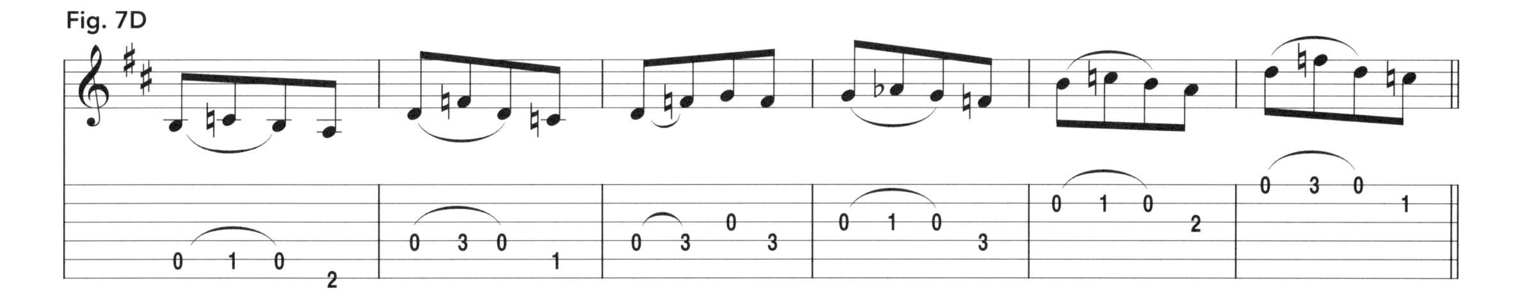

Combining Units to Create Licks

As in G, some of the best moments in open D come from mixing and matching the major sound with the blues sound. I know you are probably already off somewhere with a metronome, furiously combining and recombining these little units on your own, perhaps even jotting down the results you like and adding them to your bag of tricks. However, if you are still with me, or if you should happen to resurface between breakthroughs, you can try out the licks in Figure 8 for an additional taste of what's possible.

Applications

Up until now we've basically been finessing the question of the D chord when it comes up on a tune in G. Not anymore! Take some of these D licks, and practice making the connection from G to D and back again, as in Figure 9. Then go back to some of the earlier tunes, and see where you can work in your ferocious new D vocabulary.

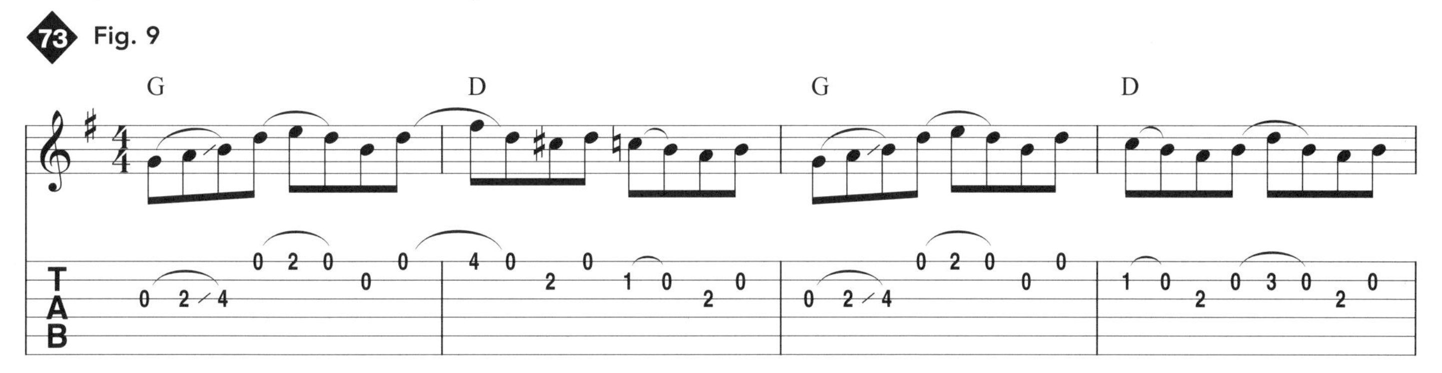

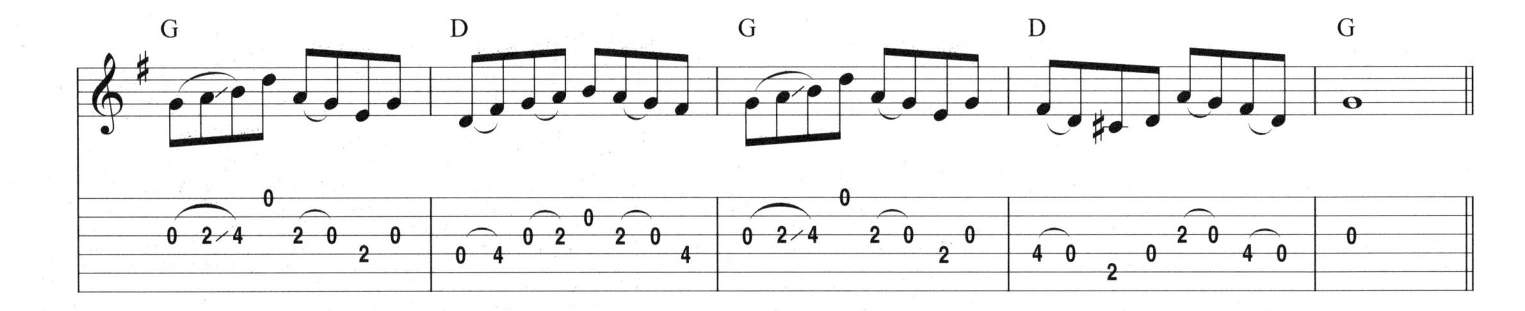

All of this very well and good, but grabbing the V chord in G is just one benefit of our new knowledge. Since we're here to play in D, let's see what we can do with our newfound chops playing "New River Train" in D.

"New River Train"

The melody of the tune is played at the seventh fret, with typical country-style double stops. Since you'd probably be playing backup in this position behind the vocals or someone else's break, this is a convenient place to begin your own break. After each phrase of the original melody, there's room to drop in a fill down in the open position. The hot lick in measure 7 comes from selecting notes from the D major scale that outline the V chord, or A major. The last four measures are a traveling bluesfest, beginning with closed-position slides into the tenth fret and ending in the open position.

74 **Fig. 10**

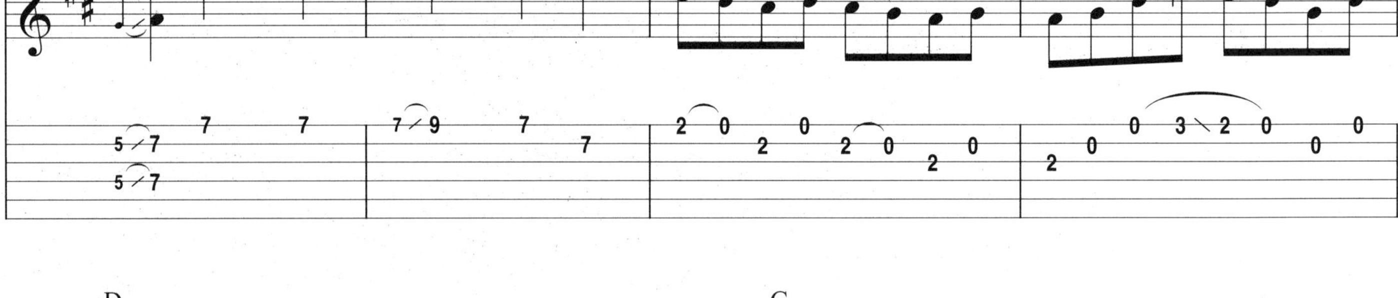

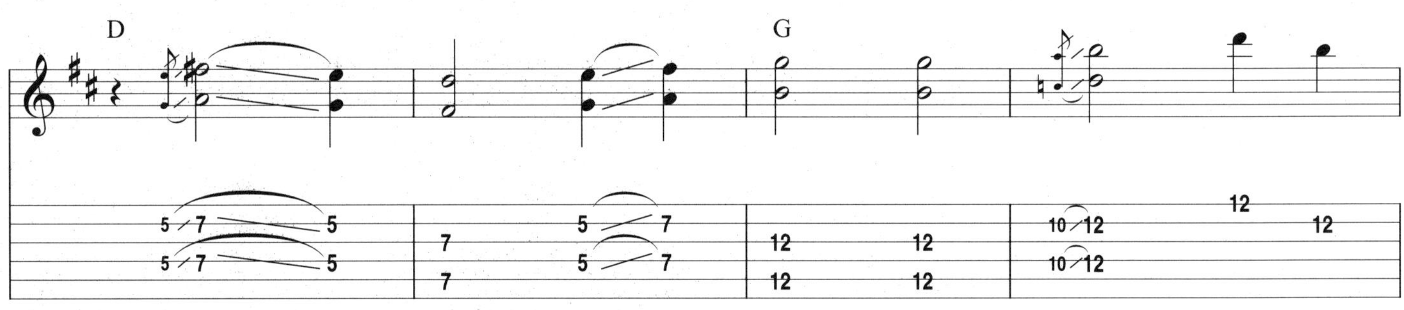

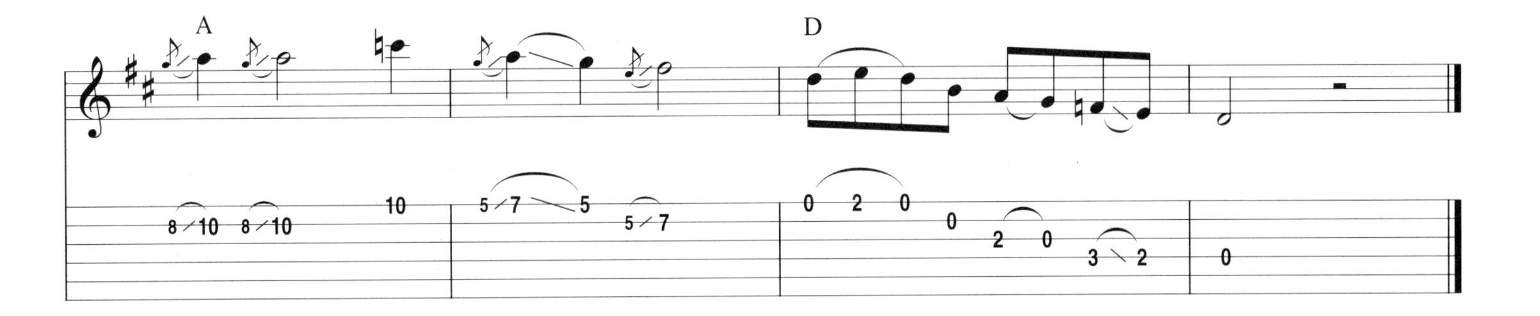

Syncopations in D

Working out syncopations in D is no different from working them out in G. Let's use Figure 11A, a four-note blues unit, as our starting point. 11B is the same unit clipped by one note, which when repeated and rounded off with two more notes, gives us the 3+3+2 lick in Figure 11C. Going back to the original four notes and extending them by two notes gives us the six-note idea in 11D, which when repeated and then completed with four more notes at the end gives us the 6+6+4 lick in Figure 11E.

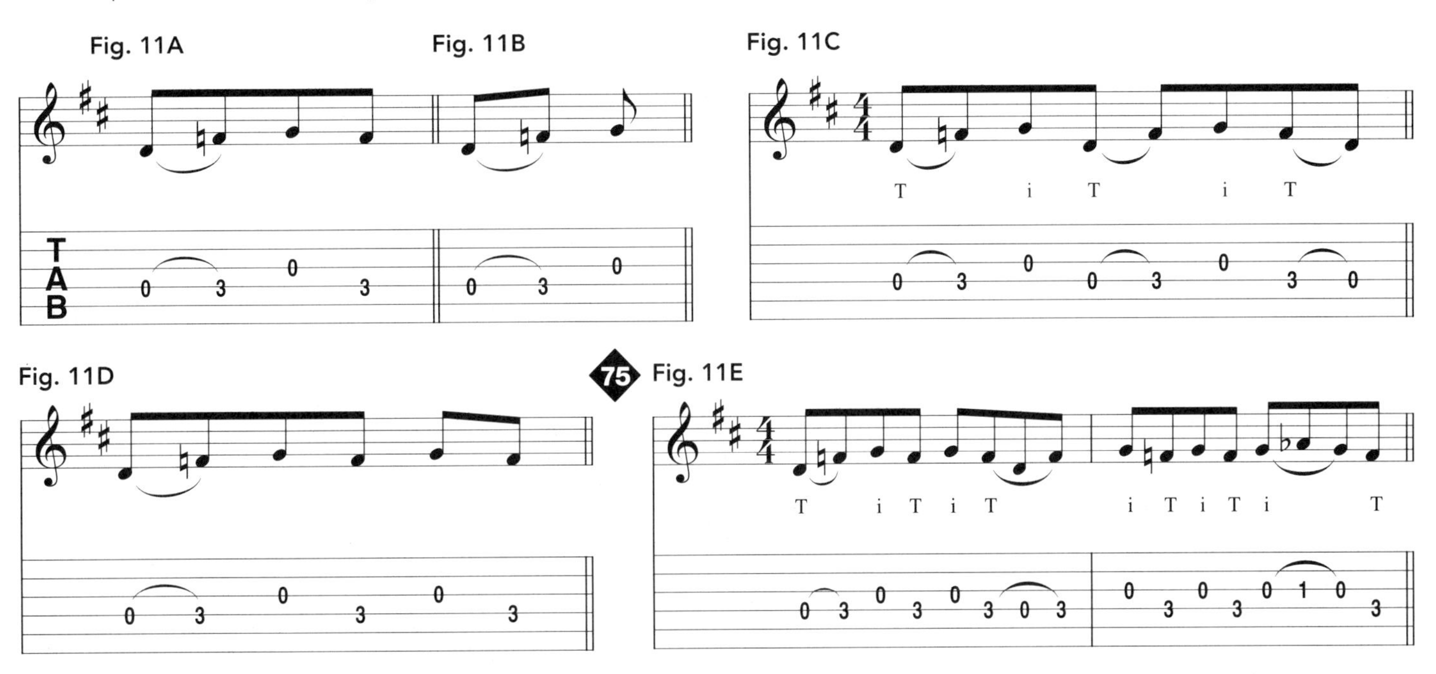

Figure 12 takes you through this process again, starting with the more major-sounding unit in 12A. 12B is the three-note version; 12C is a 3+3+2 syncopated lick. You can extend the original four notes to make the six-note figure in Figure 12D, and then play 12E, a 6+6+4 syncopation.

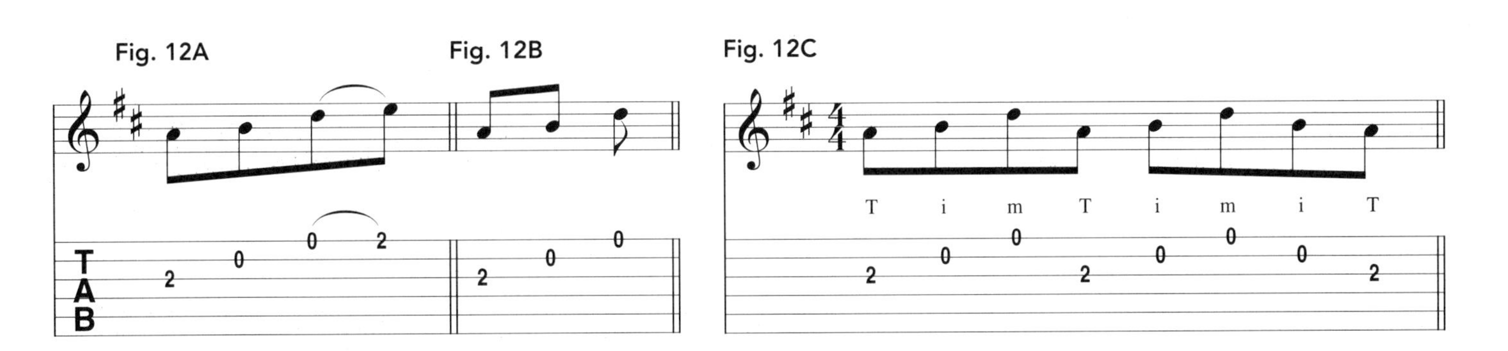

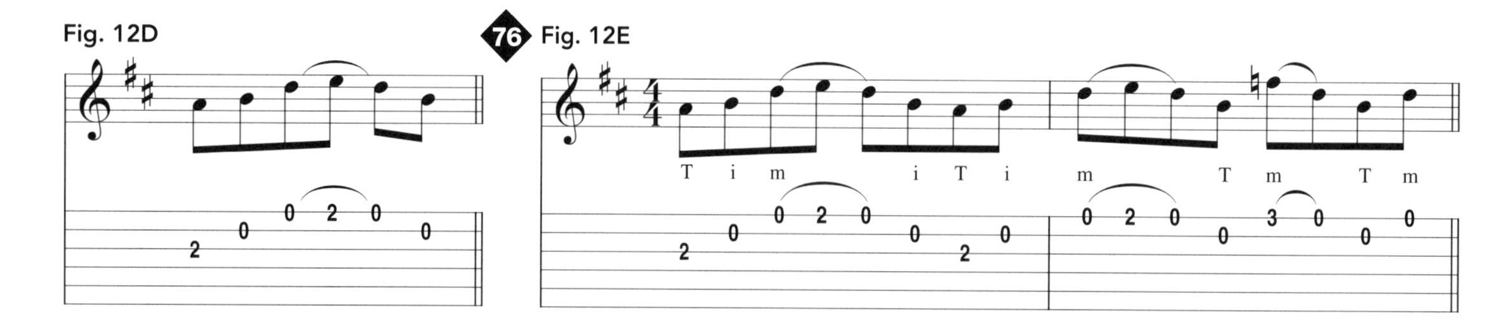

Here are a couple more 6+6+4 licks to add to your stash.

Double Stops in D

With an open D string on top, we can do some cool things with double stops in D. Start with the warm-up in Figure 14A to get used to leading with your index finger, then add in your middle finger, as in 14B.

Next, take a basic blues lick like Figure 15A, and add in the high D whenever you're picking the G string.

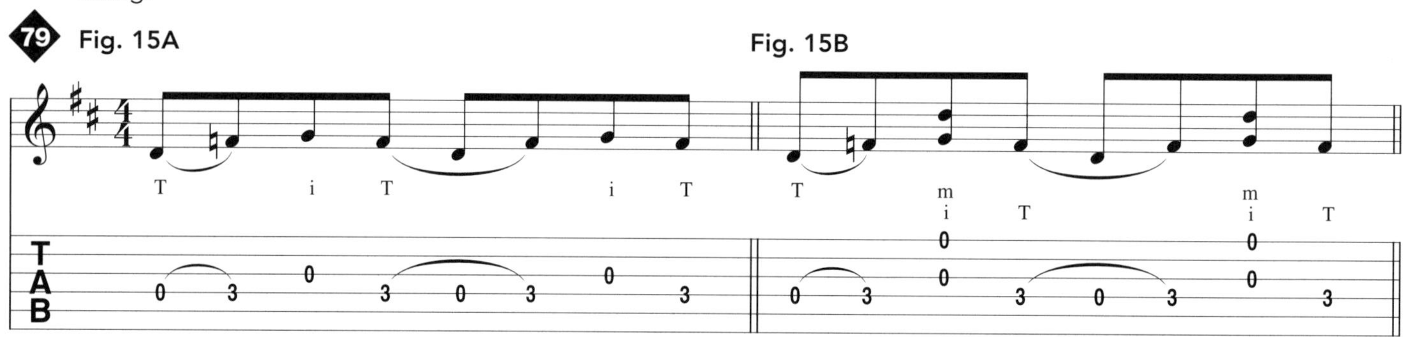

Now try working in the high D string this way on these two syncopated licks. Note the pull-off/hammer-on combination at the end of the first measure of 16A. Figure 16B leads off with the fingers, which may feel a little upside-down until you get used to it.

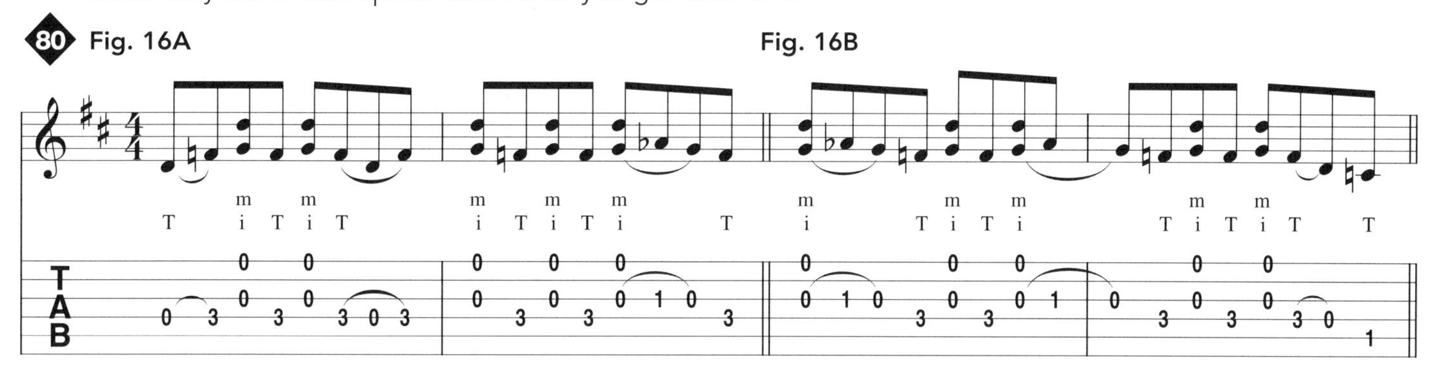

"Reuben"

The bluegrass tune "Reuben" is basically built around one chord and has room for plenty of bluesy maneuvering. As with "New River Train," the plan is to play the melody around the seventh fret—and additionally, up at the tenth fret—and then duck down into the open position to play some fills. We'll be using syncopated double stops, of course—would you have it any other way?

Playing in D, Melodic Style

The melodic approach offers just as much in D as it does in G. Let's work through it in a systematic way and see what we can do with it.

D Scales and Licks

Figure 1 is a D major scale from a fifth below the root to a fifth above the root an octave up, played in the melodic style.

Fig. 1

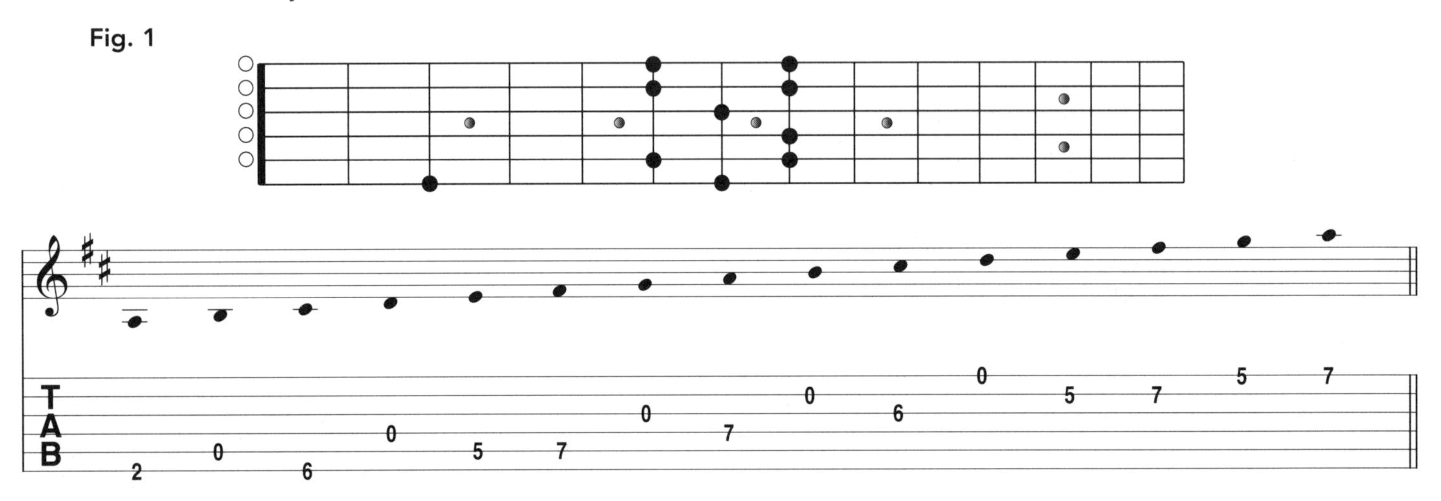

Leaving out the major seventh, the same as we did in the open position, gives us the more fluid set of notes in Figure 2.

Fig. 2

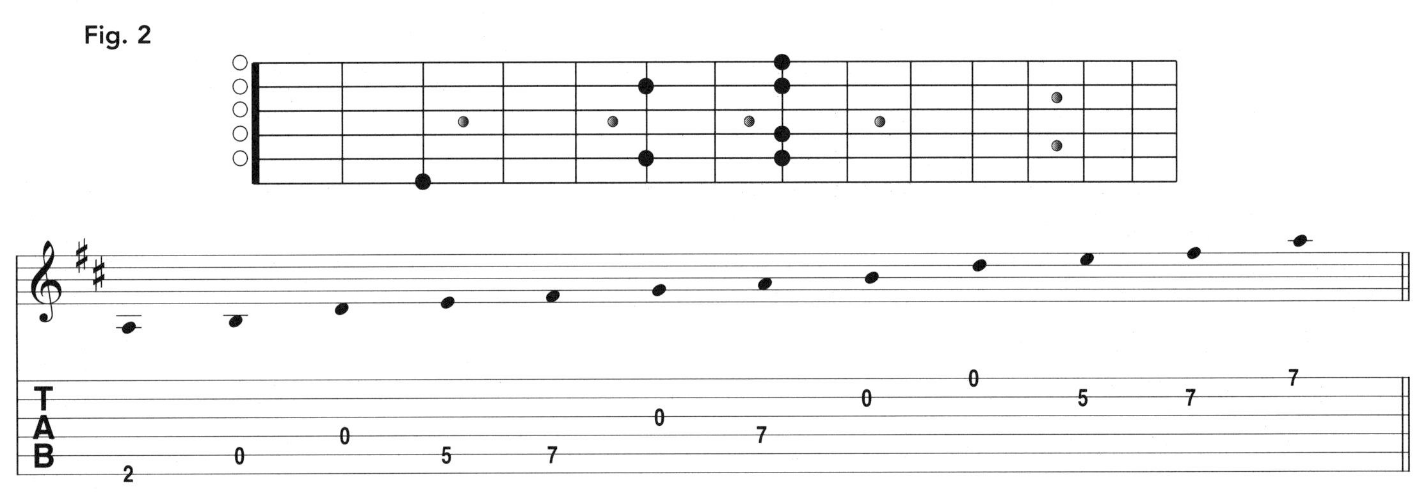

There are two ways to go for the D blues sound using the melodic approach. Figure 3A is the most useful for mixing and matching with the major scale—for instance, if you want to slide from the ♭3 into the 3, use the F at the sixth fret on the fifth string. Figure 3B works better for extended runs in the blues scale, as we'll see in some tune examples later in the chapter.

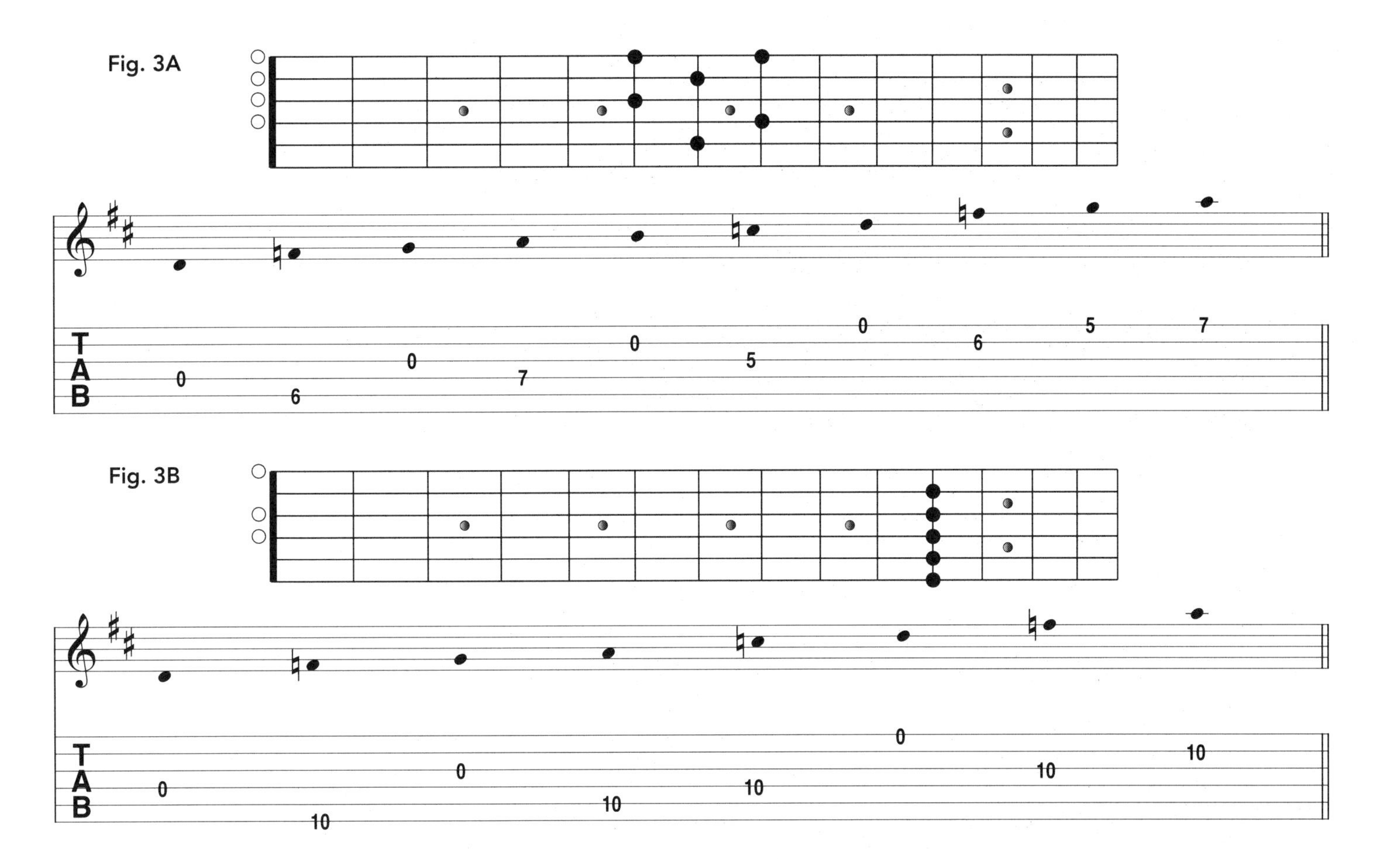

The four-note units in Figure 4A are all created from the D major scale; the units in Figure 4B are created from the blues scale. Most of these units begin from a fretted note, but there are a few that start on an open string.

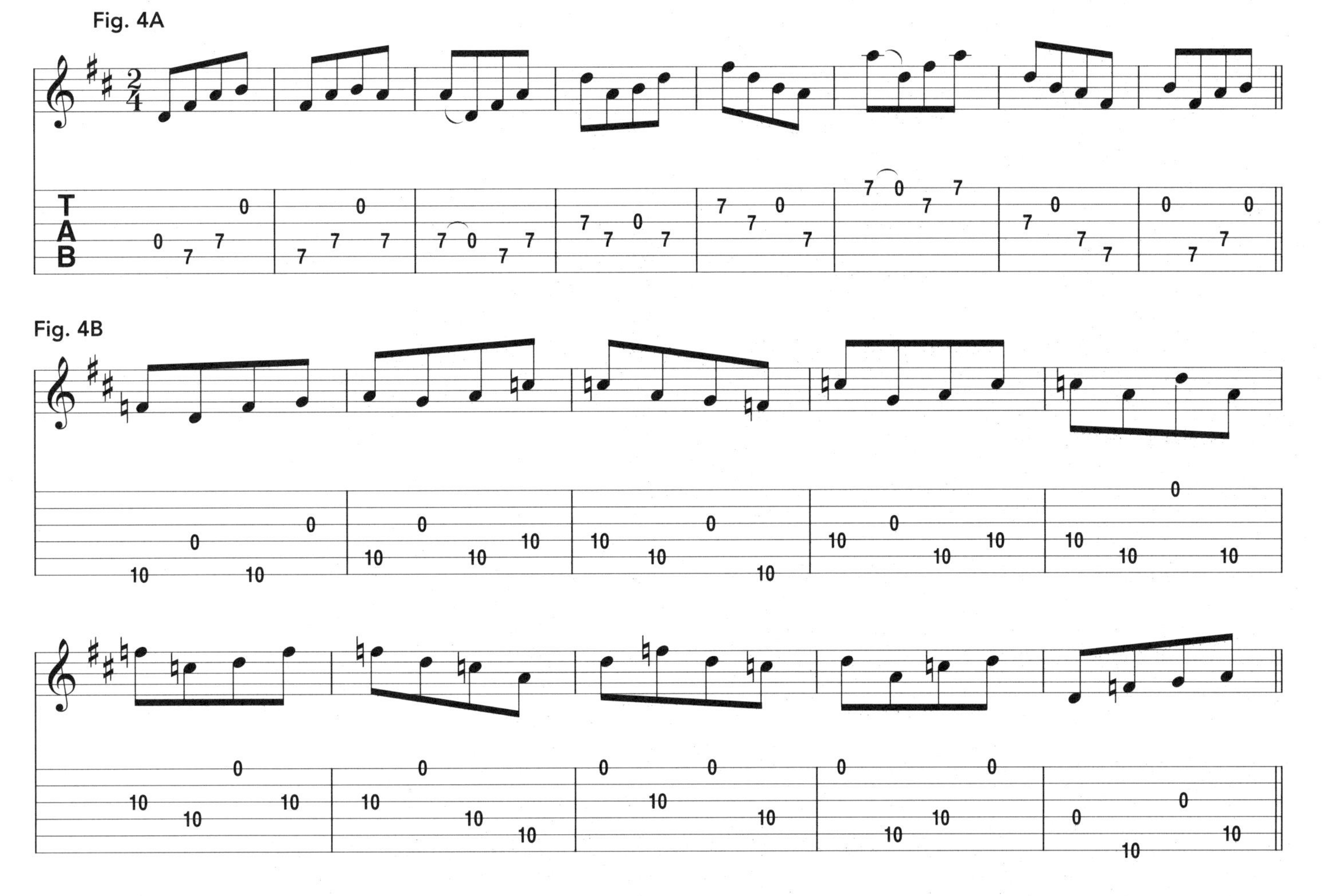

Figure 5A gives you a few one-measure D major licks to try out; the licks in Figure 5B are in D minor.

82 **Fig. 5A**

Fig. 5B

Once you can play each lick in time, experiment with combining them in various ways. Switching between the major and blues sounds is particularly challenging. You might also try moving between open-position and melodic-style licks, one measure at a time, and from G melodic to D melodic, from open G to D melodic, and from open D to G melodic.

"Reuben" Revisited

Let's take another look at the tune "Reuben." This time, we'll play the melody for the first four bars and then swap in some cool melodic moves, beginning with two bars of D blues and ending with a D major lick. Notice how the eighth-note pause on the second beat of measure 5 makes the run that follows that much more effective.

83 **Fig. 6**

"Little Maggie"

"Little Maggie," like "Red-Haired Boy," is a modal tune and includes a ♭VII chord which, in the key of D, would be C major. The first eight measures as played here stick pretty much to the original melody, except for measures 7 and 8. The quarter note C-natural in measure 8, like the rest in measure 5 of "Reuben," keeps the flow of eighth notes in check. Add a little vibrato to emphasize your own bluesy hipness for lingering on this ♭7 note.

84 Fig. 7

Playing over A (in D)

With a little creative selectivity, you can maneuver your way melodically through A, the V chord in the key of D, just by pulling out notes from the D major scale—like A, C♯, and E (the root, third, and fifth of A major). Check out Figure 8 to see what I mean.

Fig. 8

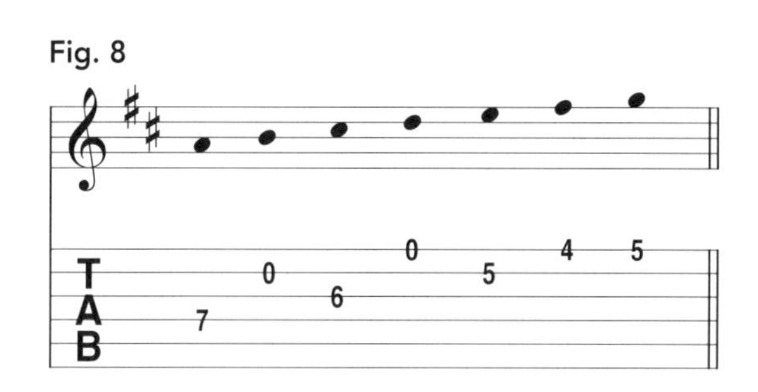

Now try switching from D to A and back with these three two-bar figures.

85 **Fig. 9A**

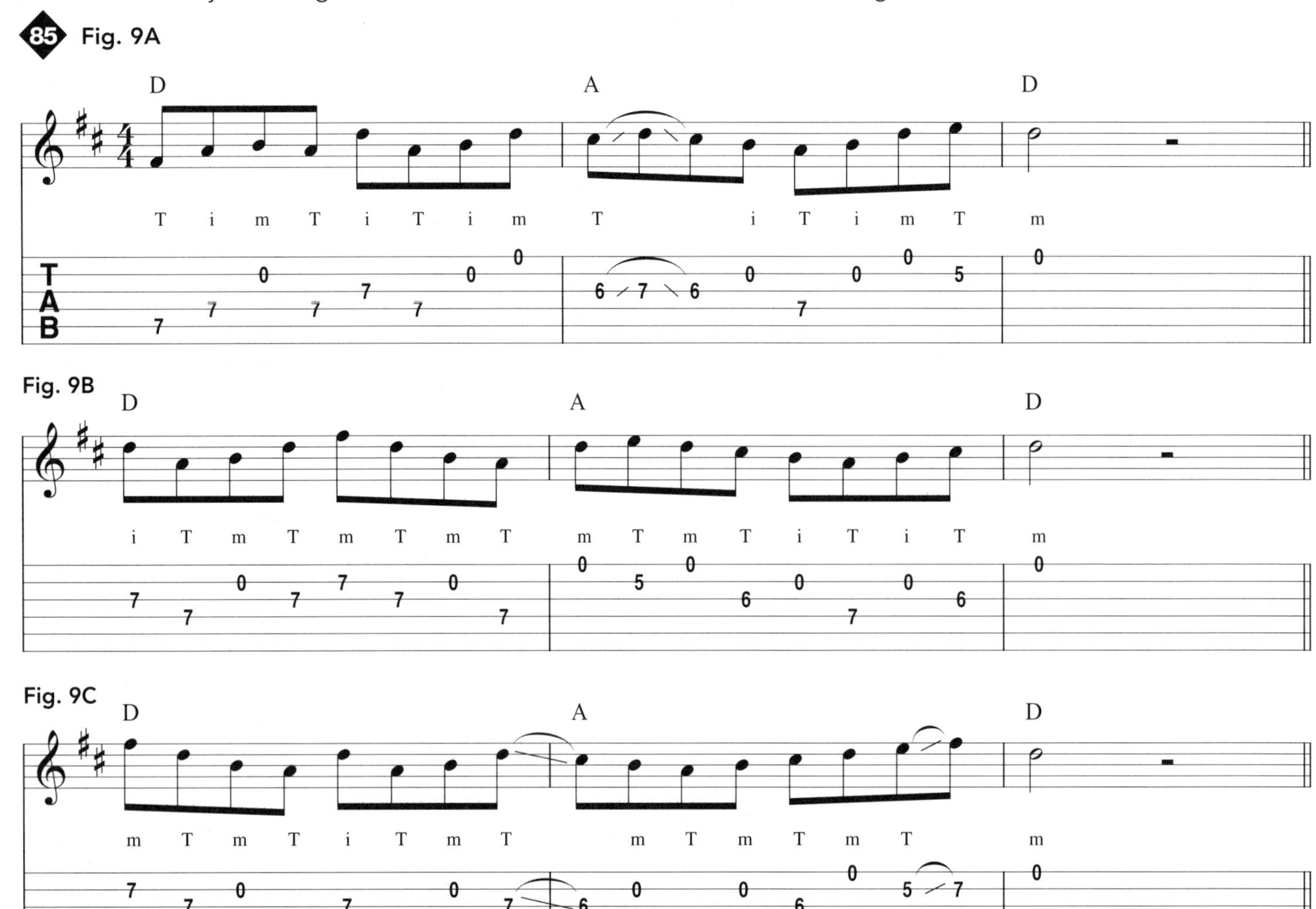

"Soldier's Joy"

Using the whole D major scale in this way—to play off of the V chord as well as the I chord—is very useful in working out more major-sounding (as opposed to modal) tunes in the melodic style. "Soldier's Joy" is a very simple melody in D major that can be and has been embellished in countless ways. Before we start turning it inside out, however, let's get the basic melody together, melodic style, as in Figure 10.

86 **Fig. 10**

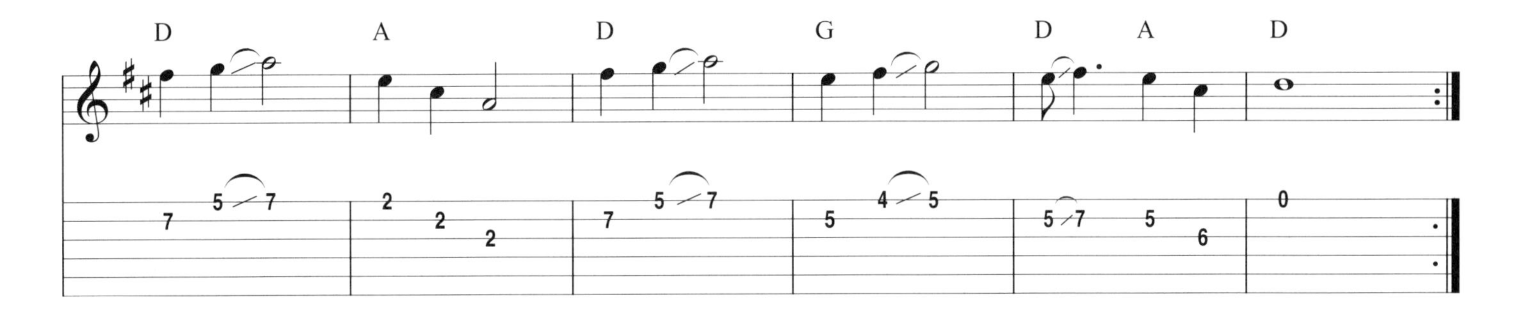

Fiddle versions of tunes like this are often a steady flow of sound in which the key moments of the melody stand out as brief highlights amidst the rush of eighth notes. Figure 11 is a melodically embellished version of "Soldier's Joy" that illustrates one way of providing that steady stream of notes. Pay attention to the trickier right-hand fingerings and the occasional quick bar slides to and from a note. For example, in measure 11, make sure all three notes—the F♯, the G, and the next F♯—all get the same, even length of time. Also, notice the hammer-on from the open high string to the seventh fret in measure 10.

87 **Fig. 11**

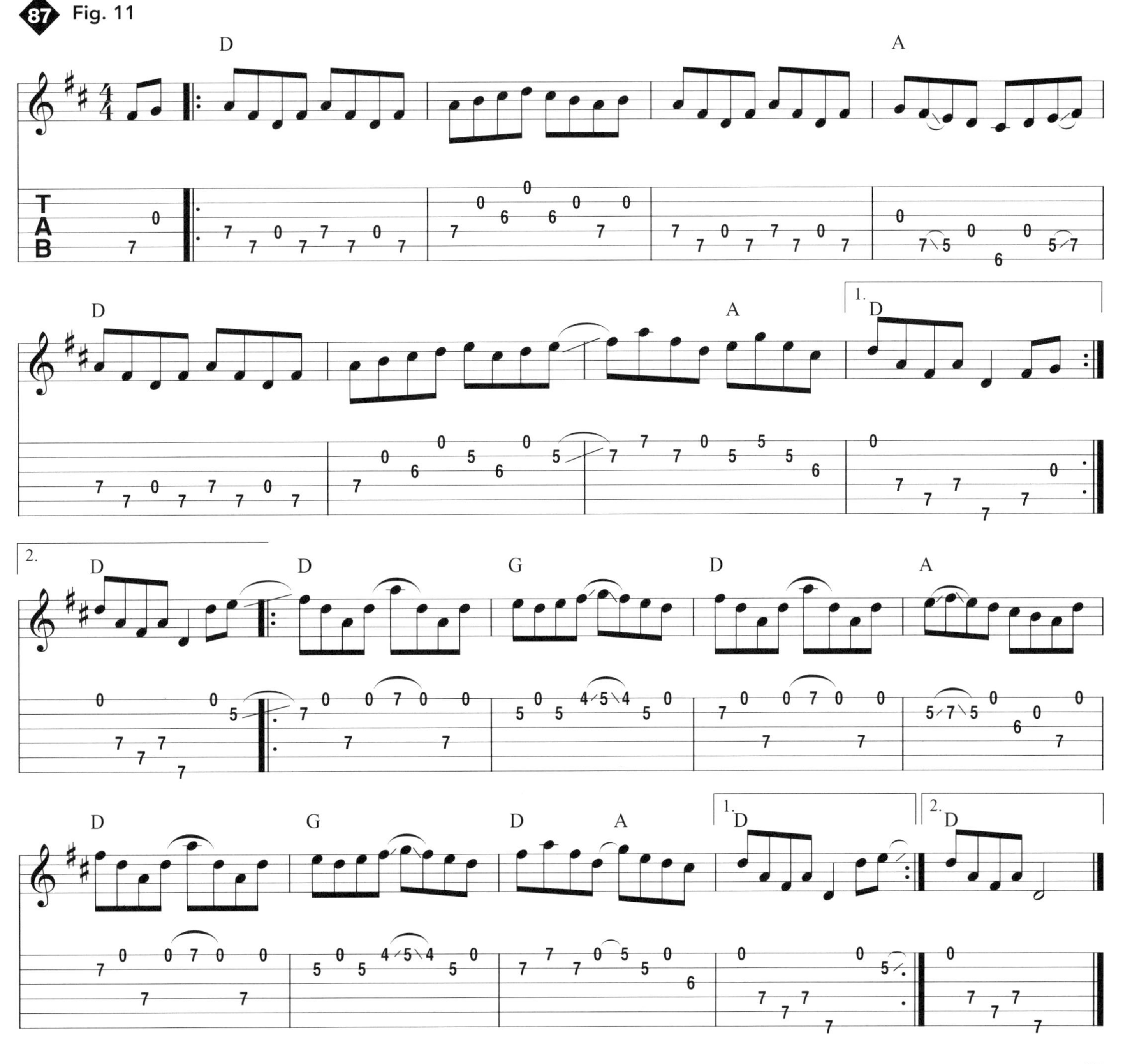

"Whiskey Before Breakfast"

"Whiskey Before Breakfast" is a fairly dense fiddle tune to begin with; the challenge here is to get as close to the fiddle melody as we can playing lap-style slide. The right-hand moves are particularly challenging in places like measures 3 and 4—take it slowly and learn which finger you need when, so you don't end up in a tangle on the floor. Measure 11 has an E minor move that requires you to stretch from your index finger on the fourth string to your middle finger on the second. And the last four measures are a real workout in switching between open and melodic positions. There's a lot going on, but you should begin to feel the flow of the arrangement once you start to get the various parts of it under control.

Fig. 12

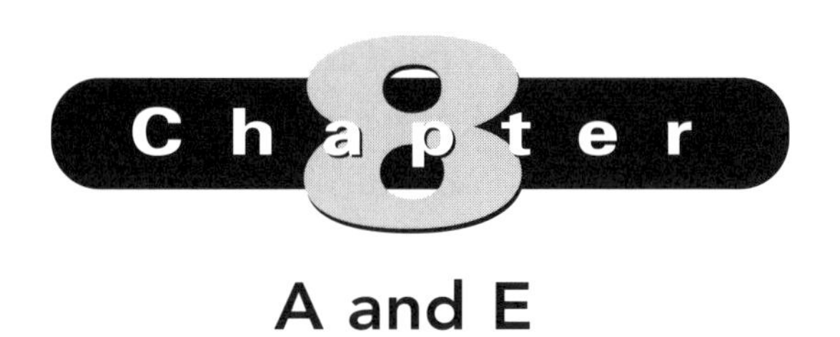

A and E

In this last chapter, we're going to look at some ways to handle A and E chords when they appear, much as we dealt with C and F chords in Chapter 5. Although I have included an uncapoed arrangement of "Old Joe Clark" in the key of A, our primary concern is not playing in the keys of A and E per se. Instead, the focus is on being able to maneuver through the occasional Am, Em, A7, and E7 chord when it turns up in the key of G or D, without losing the flow of what you're doing.

A Minor Scales and Licks

A minor is the ii chord in the key of G. Because of this, playing over an A minor chord is not so much a matter of learning any new notes as it is of learning which ones to emphasize of the ones you already know. For example, here's a two-octave A natural minor scale:

Fig. 1

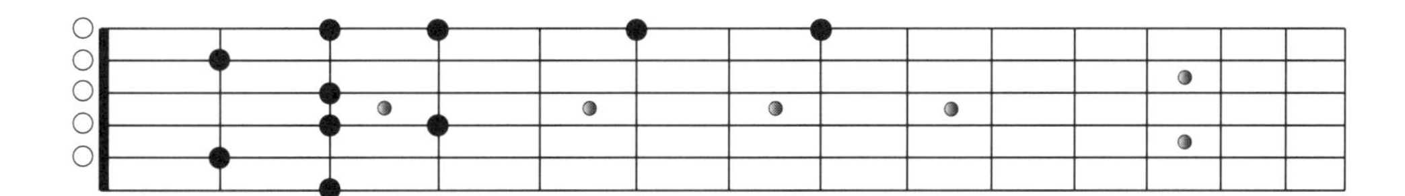

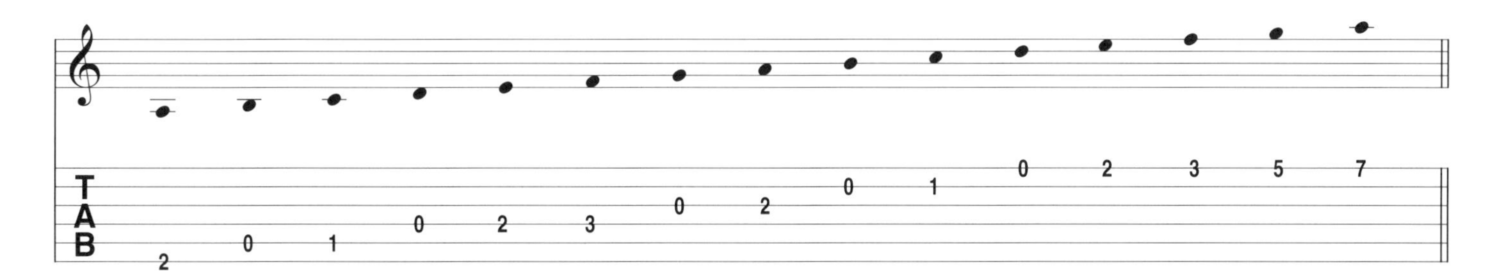

The simple subset of notes to use for A minor licks looks a whole lot like our G major subset from Chapter 1—but starting from the second note of a G scale, which is A:

Fig. 2

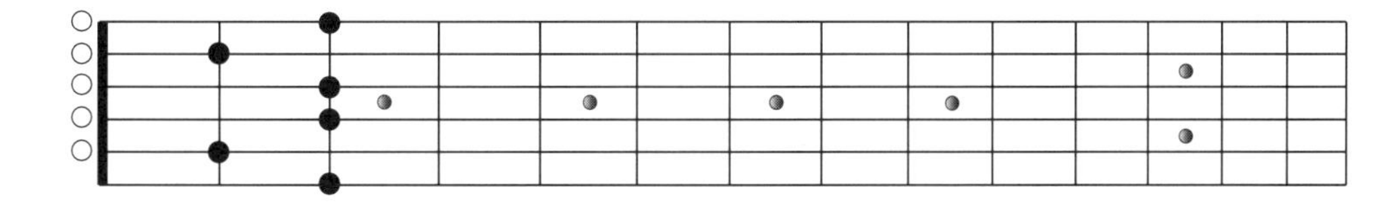

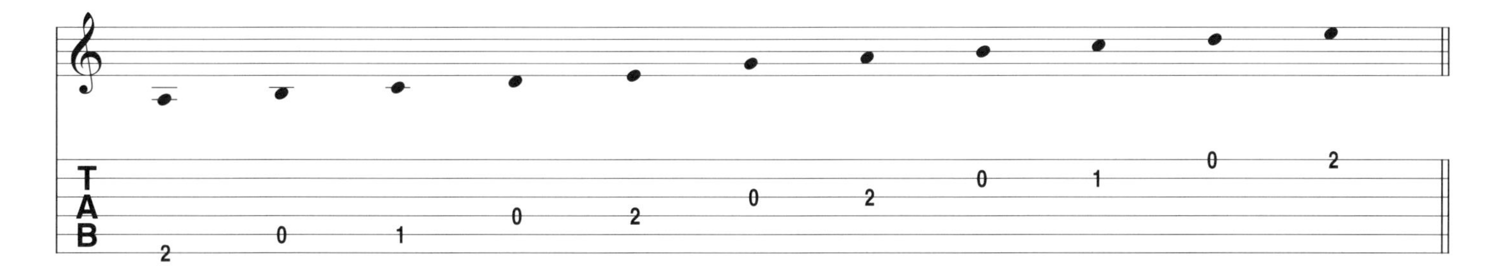

Many of the basic units we've been playing with already will work over A minor—it's a question of where you put the emphasis. Most of the G units we worked with began and/or ended with an open string, which meant you were always starting and/or ending on G, B, or D—the root, third, or fifth of G major. Even the blues licks either started or ended on one of those open-stringed chord tones. Now, we want to place the emphasis on A, C, or E—the root, minor third, or fifth of A minor. In Figure 3A, you always land on a chord tone of A minor. In Figure 3B, you always begin on one.

Fig. 3A

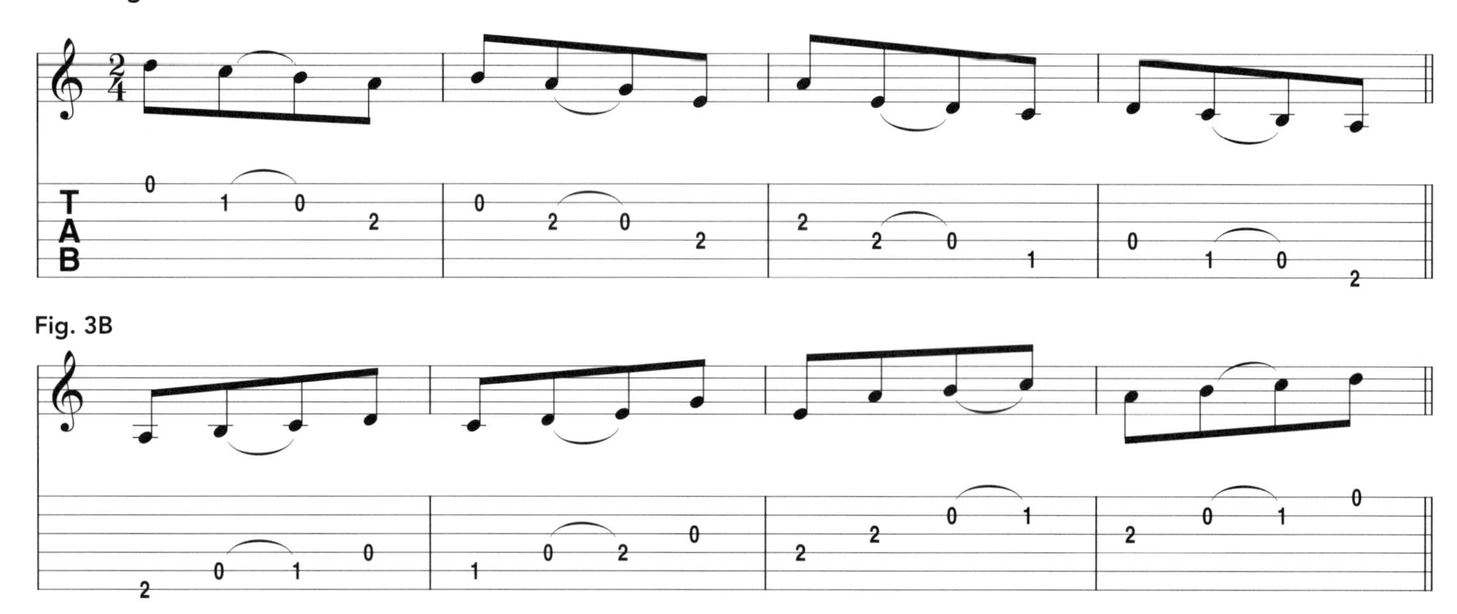

Now we can start to put these units together to get some A minor licks. As long as you emphasize an A minor chord tone—A, C, or E—somewhere in the lick, you can basically draw on the more familiar G vocabulary to round things out.

Fig. 4

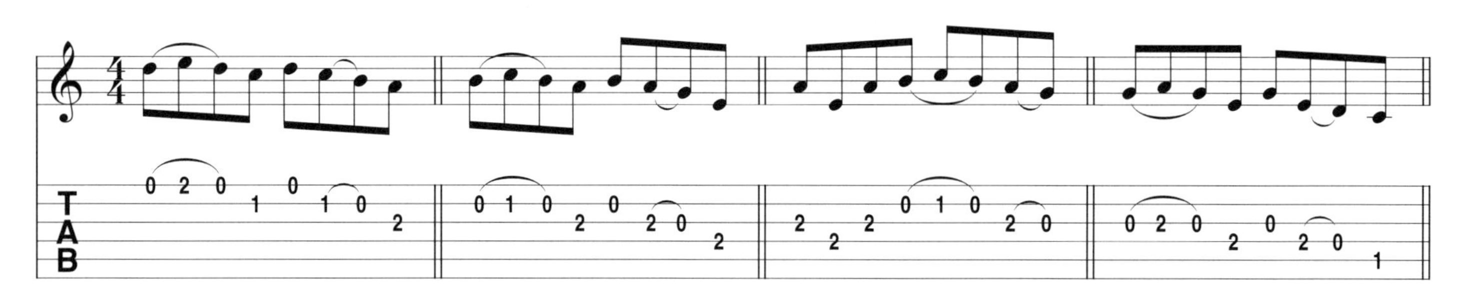

Practice switching in and out of A minor from the various chords you're likely to run into in the vicinity of A minor—G to Am, Am to Dm, Am to C, and so on. Of course, there are tunes in minor keys as well. Figure 5 is an exercise based on a typical minor chord progression of Am–C–Dm–Am.

90 **Fig. 5**

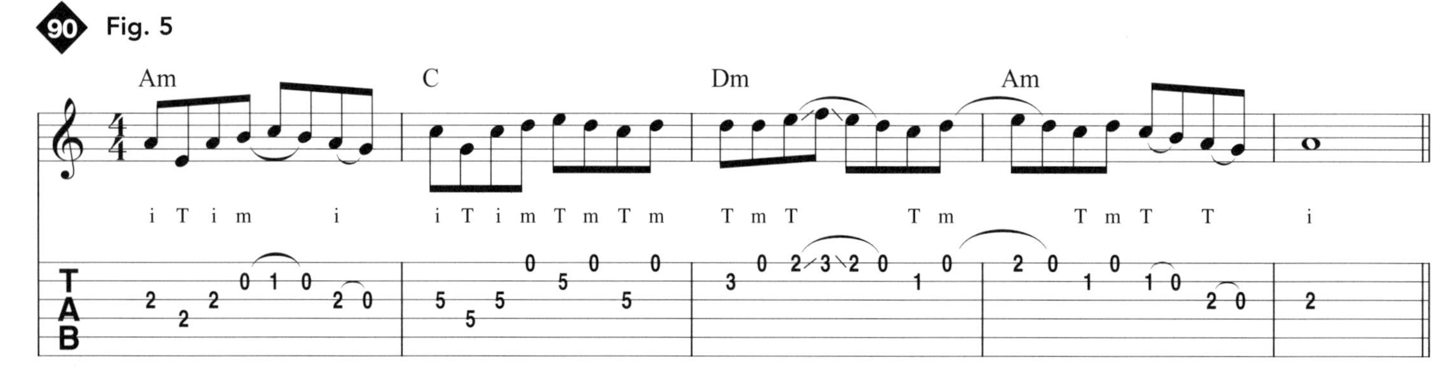

A Major Scales and Licks

Playing in A major, unlike playing in A minor, is distinctly different from playing in G. The basic A major scale is shown in Figure 6.

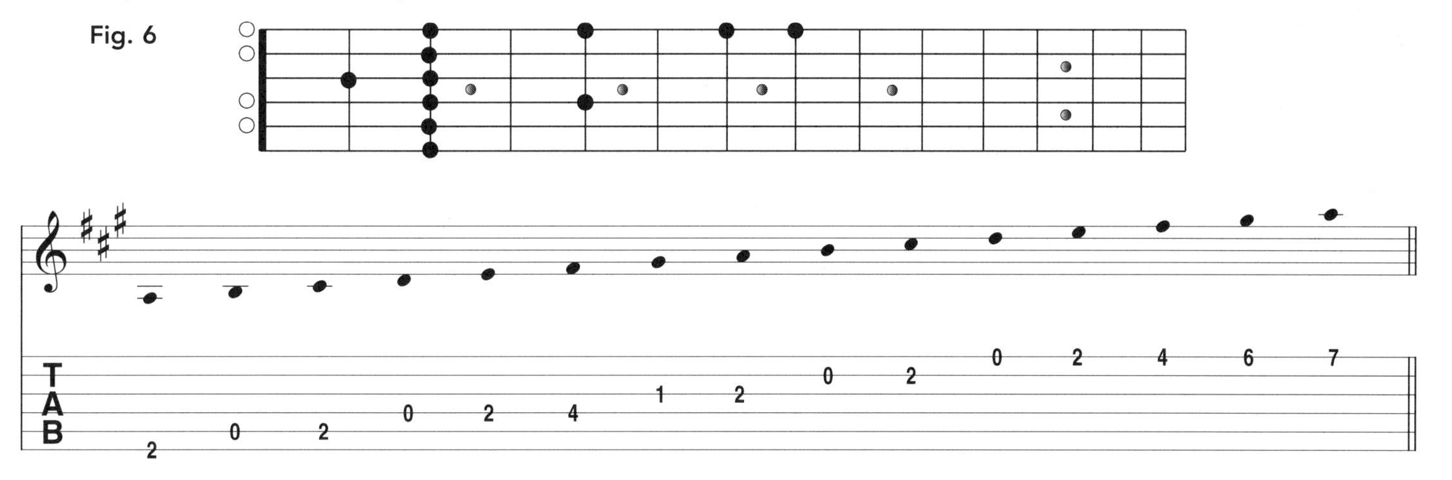

The practical subset of A major is shown in Figure 7.

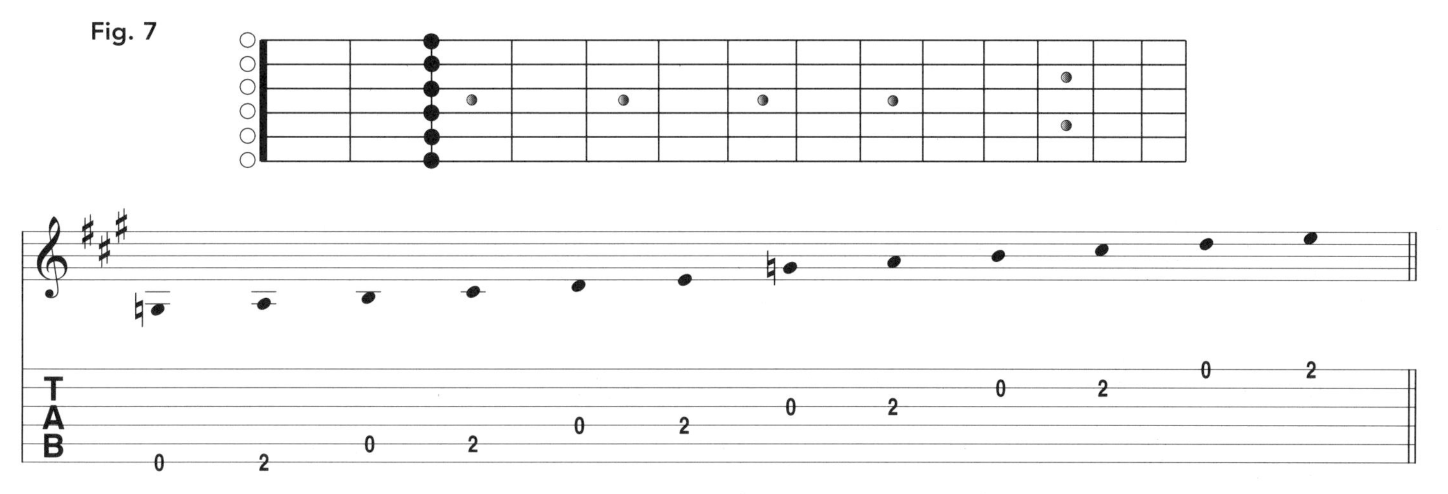

This subset gives you two notes per string, just like our favorite subsets for playing open-position licks in G major and G blues. But it's not really a pure A major sound, because it includes two G♮s. G♮ is the ♭7 in the key of A, which gives this subset of notes an A Mixolydian sound. If you want to keep things sounding purely major, try the units in Figure 8, which all manage to get around the strings without hitting any open Gs.

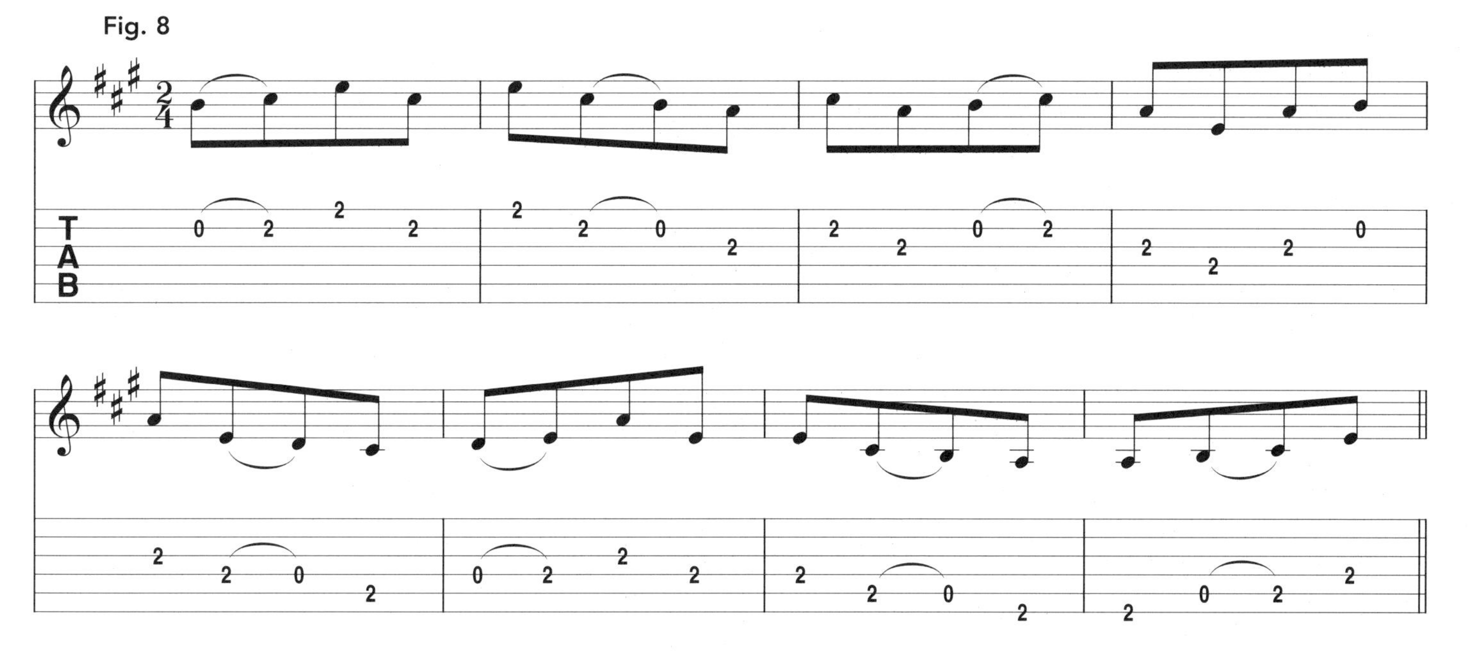

Mixing and matching these, we can create the all-major licks in Figure 9.

Fig. 9

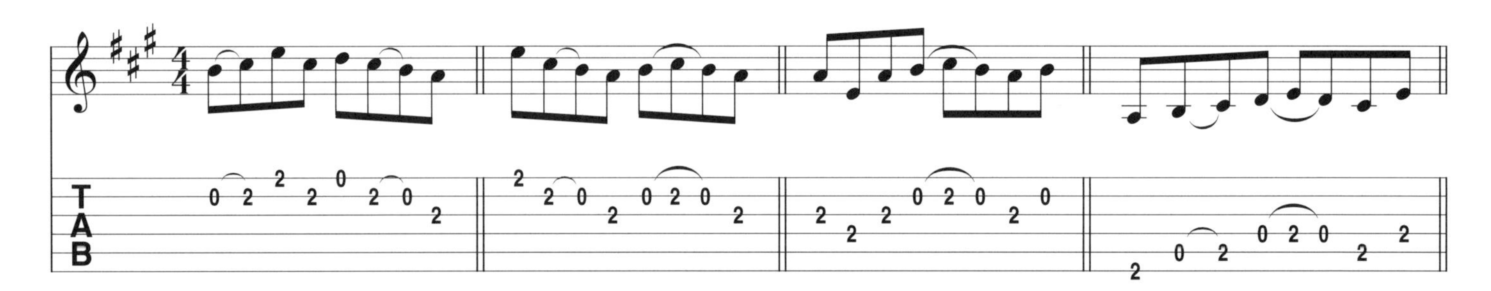

To get the bluesier A Mixolydian sound, just drop in G♮, as in the units in Figure 10.

Fig. 10

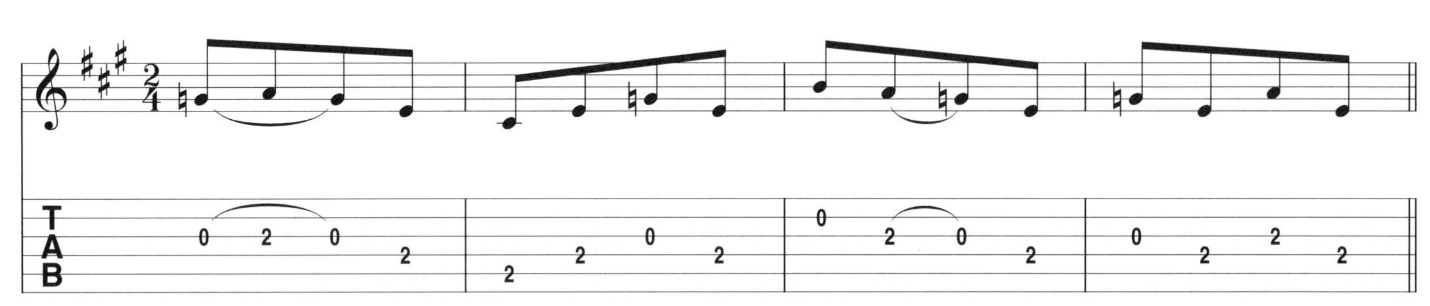

A little G♮ goes a long way: you can combine these Mixolydian units with other purely major units, and the results will have the Mixolydian sound. Check out the licks in Figure 11 to see how this works.

92 Fig. 11

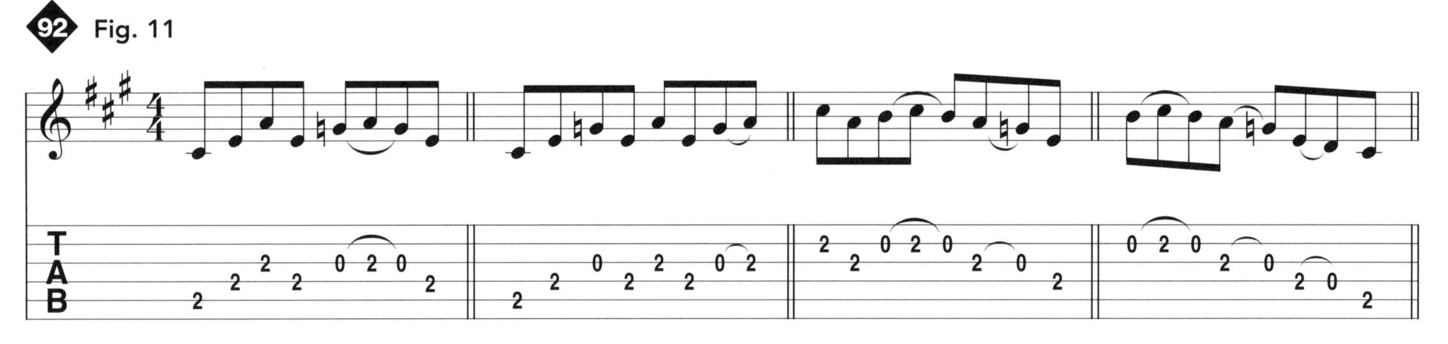

One very typical place for A7 to show up is as the II7 chord in the key of G. Honky-tonk country songs and western swing tunes often employ the chord progression IV–I–II–V, particularly on the chorus or the bridge of a song. In the key of G that would be C–G–A7–D, as in Figure 12.

93 Fig. 12

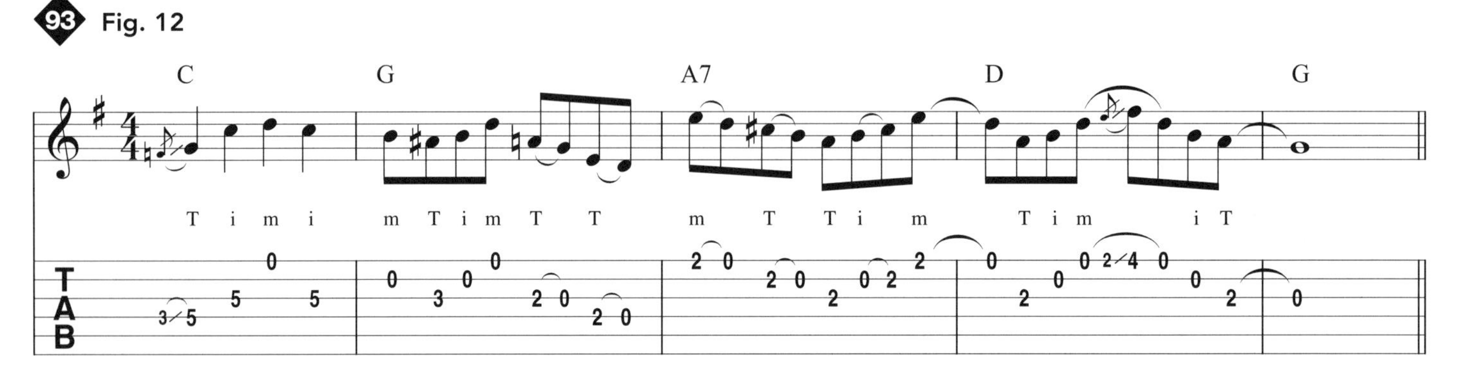

"Old Joe Clark"

Another possibility, of course, is to actually play tunes in the key of A, without using the capo. Figure 12 is an arrangement of the fiddle tune "Old Joe Clark." The A section provides an example of how you might apply the melodic style to the key of A, while the B section, in the open position, gives you practice in switching between A major (and/or A Mixolydian) and G.

94 **Fig. 13**

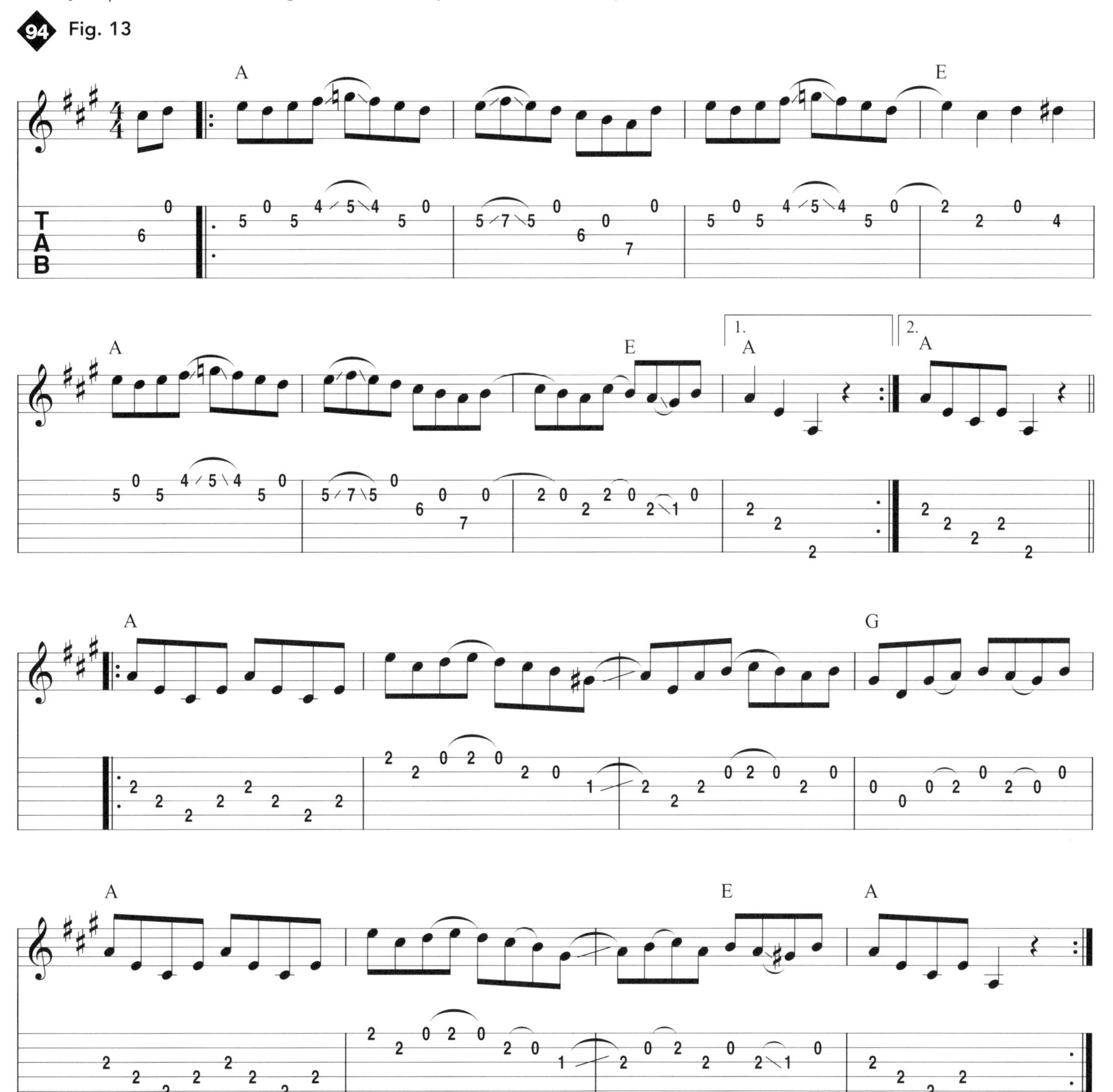

E Minor Scales and Licks

E minor chords often turn up in the keys of G, D, and C. Figure 14 is a full E natural minor scale, starting on the minor third and ending on the root.

Fig. 14

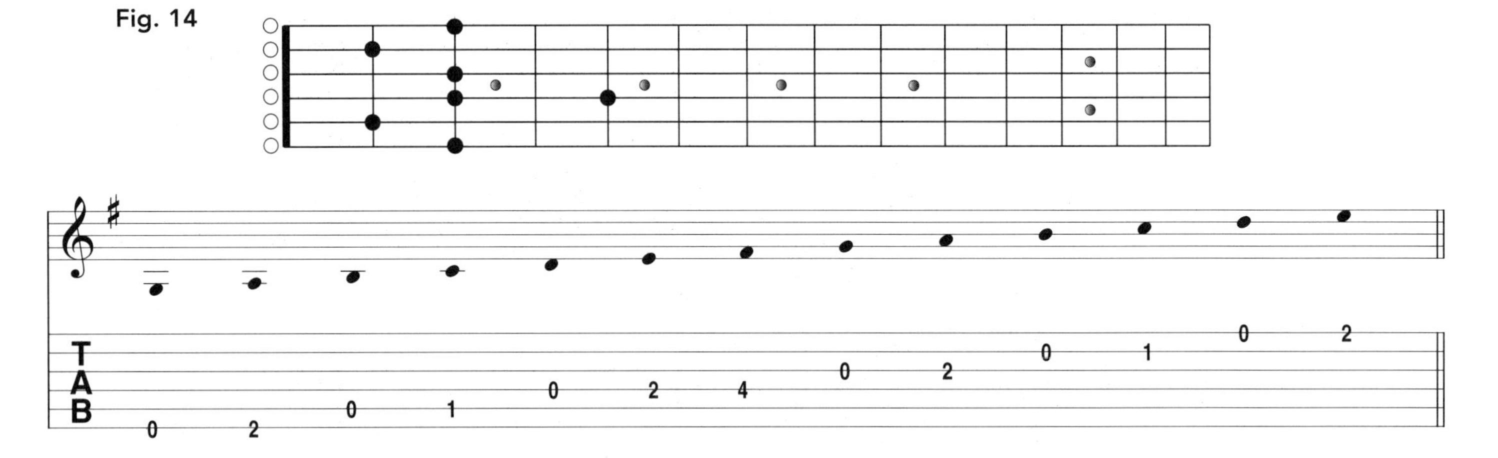

As the relative minor, or vi chord, of the key of G, E minor is closely related to G major. If we simplify the scale in Figure 14, leaving out the second and the sixth, we get the E minor pentatonic scale in Figure 15. This subset of the E minor scale, like the A minor subset of notes in Figure 2, also looks similar to our basic G major subset of notes.

Fig. 15

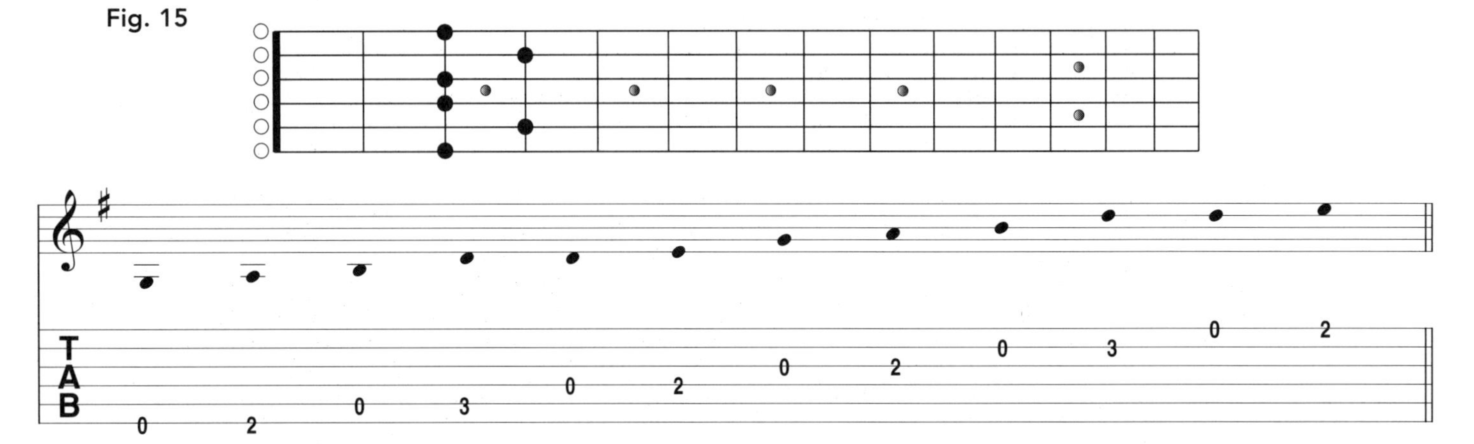

The key to playing over E minor is to know a few units that really emphasize the root, E, like those in Figure 16.

Fig. 16

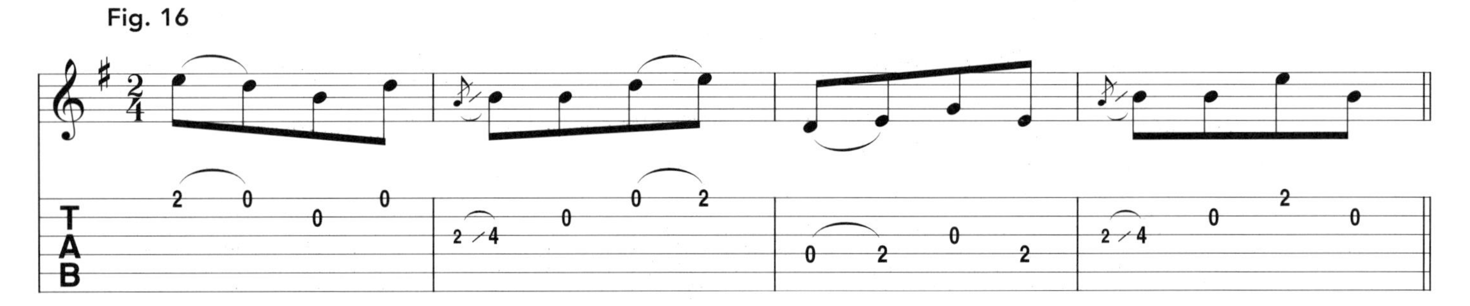

Then you can combine these root-centered units with ones that come more generally from the sound of G major to get licks like the ones in Figure 17.

95 Fig. 17

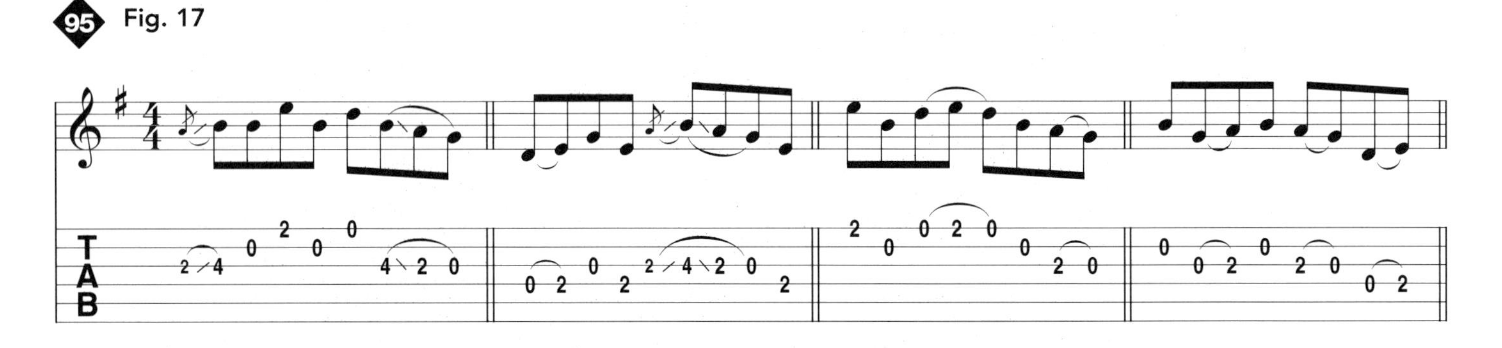

You can practice getting in and out of E minor with various other chords to work on incorporating E minor into the keys of G, C, and D (as the vi, iii, or ii chord, respectively). When you're actually in the key of E minor, the V7 chord is B7. The B sections to fiddle tunes like "Temperance Reel" and "Blackberry Blossom" have this sound. Figure 18 is an exercise in switching between licks in open E minor and playing over B7 (or B major) using the closed position.

Fig. 18

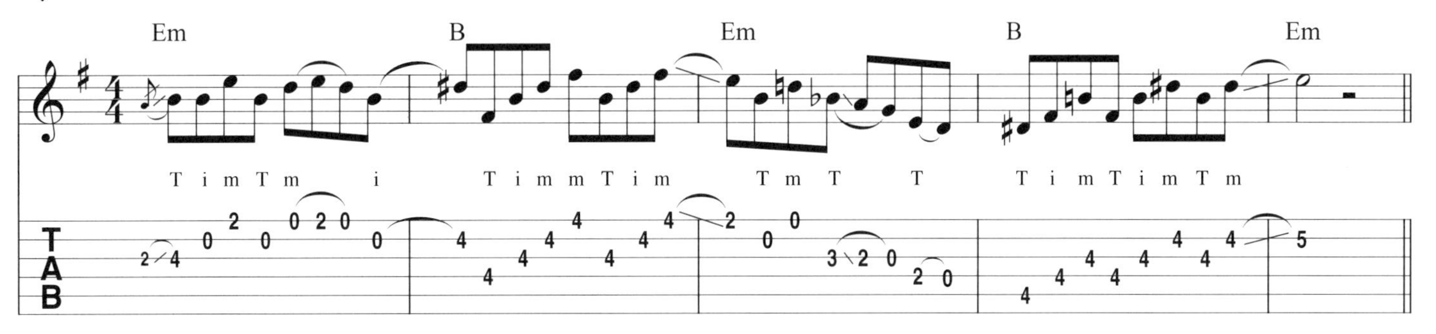

E Major Scales and Licks

With a little tweaking, you can turn some of these E minor licks into E Mixolydian licks, which will work well over an E7 chord. An E Mixolydian scale is the same thing as an E major scale with a flatted seventh, or D♮. Figure 19 is a full E Mixolydian scale in open position, starting on the third and ending on the root.

Fig. 19

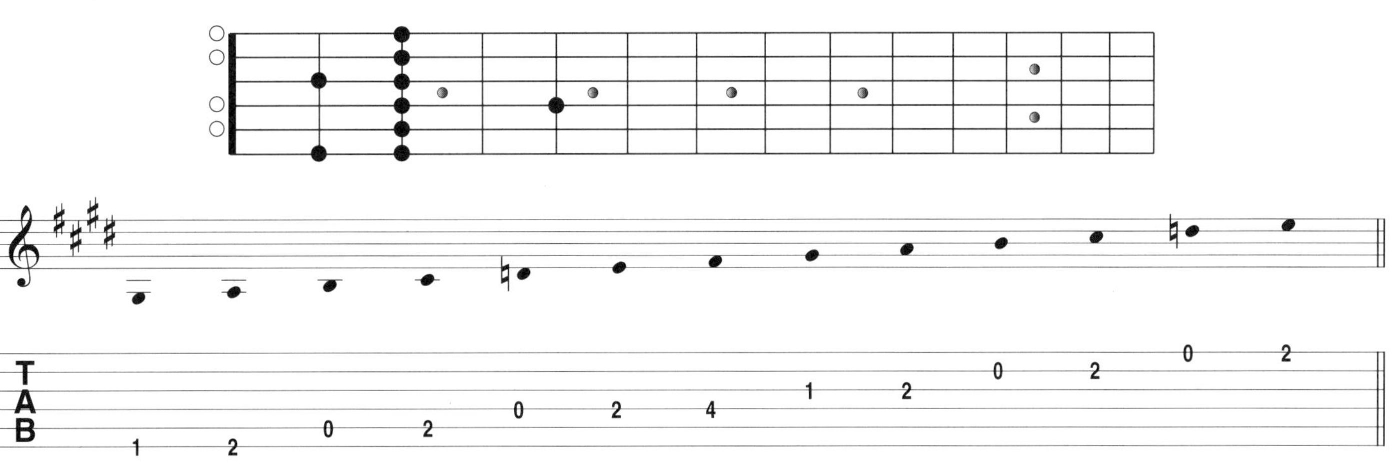

By including the ♭3—as a note from which to hammer on to the major third—and leaving out the second and the fourth, we get the simplified scale in Figure 20.

Fig. 20

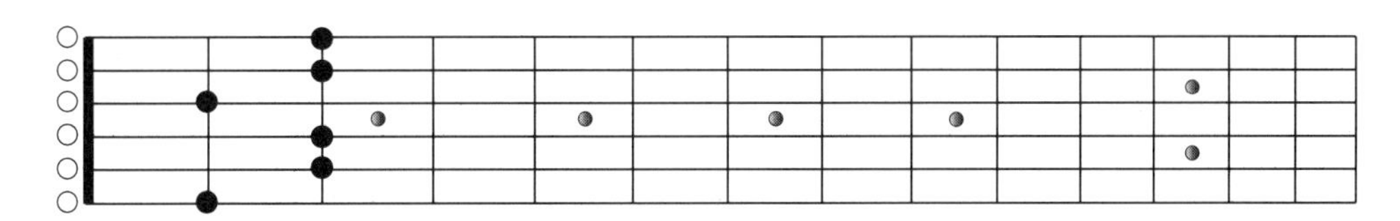

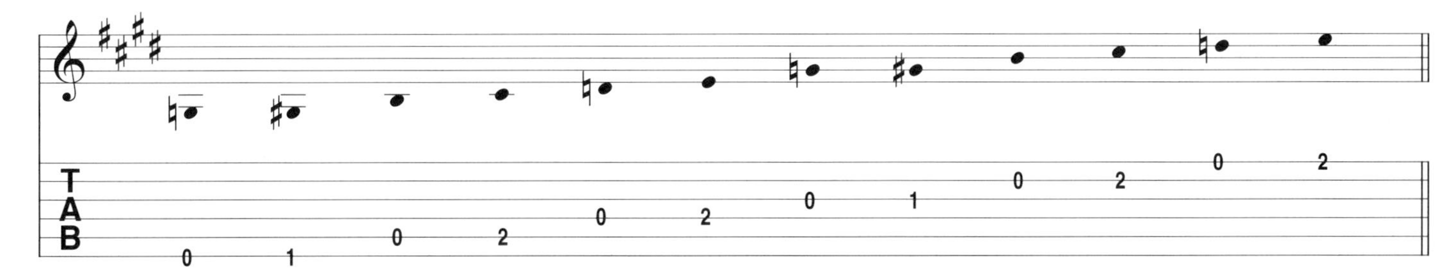

A little major-third and/or major-sixth flavor goes a long way towards creating the Mixolydian sound. The six units in Figure 21 all include either the major third or the major sixth; some have both.

Fig. 21

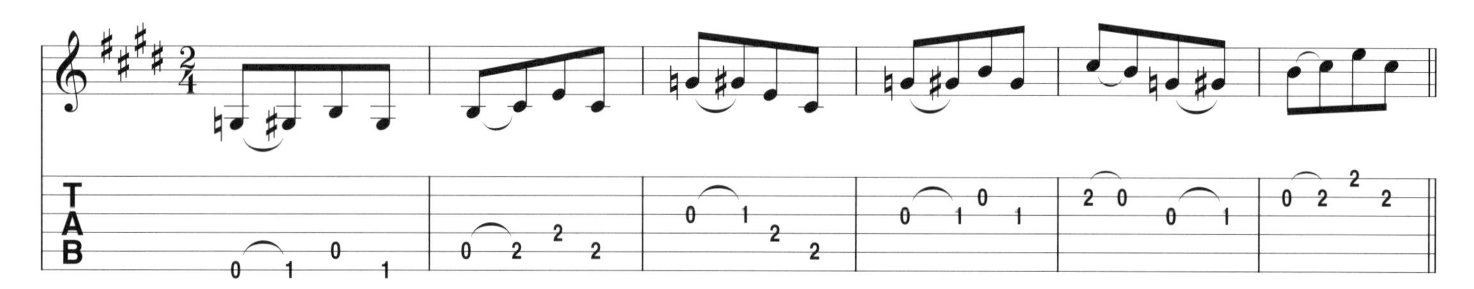

You can combine these with minor pentatonic licks, and as long as you wrap it up by resolving any minor thirds (G♮) to their respective major thirds a half-step up (G♯), it will give you the Mixolydian sound. Try out the four licks in Figure 22.

97 **Fig. 22**

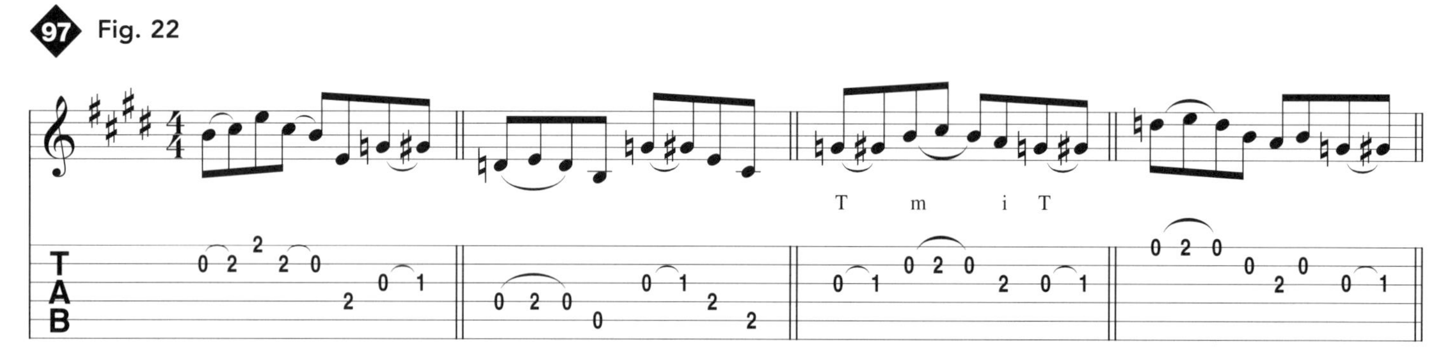

E7 chords appear as the VI7 in the key of G, as the II7 in the key of D, and as the III7 in the key of C, among other places. Tunes like "Salty Dog," "Don't Let Your Deal Go Down," and many tunes from the swing repertoire include *cycles* of dominant chords that take you in a big circle that resolves to the I. For example, in "Don't Let Your Deal Go Down," the verse would begin by walking from G down to E7. E7 is the V chord of A, which is the next chord; A7 is the V chord of D, which comes next in the song; and D7 is the V of G, bringing you back around to the beginning. This kind of progression is therefore called a *circle-of-fifths* chord progression, because each chord is acting as the V of the chord to follow.

"Salty Dog"

For our farewell tune, let's take a look at "Salty Dog." Measures 1–8 are an open-position arrangement of the melody, with a few double stops, unison slides, and syncopated rolls worked in. Measures 9–16 illustrate one kind of break you might take, pulling together E Mixolydian (measure 10), A major and A Mixolydian licks (measures 11 and 12, respectively), a D melodic moment (measures 13 and 14), and some basic open G moves (measures 9 and 15). It's an eighth-note extravaganza, notwithstanding the tasteful quarter-note breathing spot on the D chord in measure 13.

98 **Fig. 23**

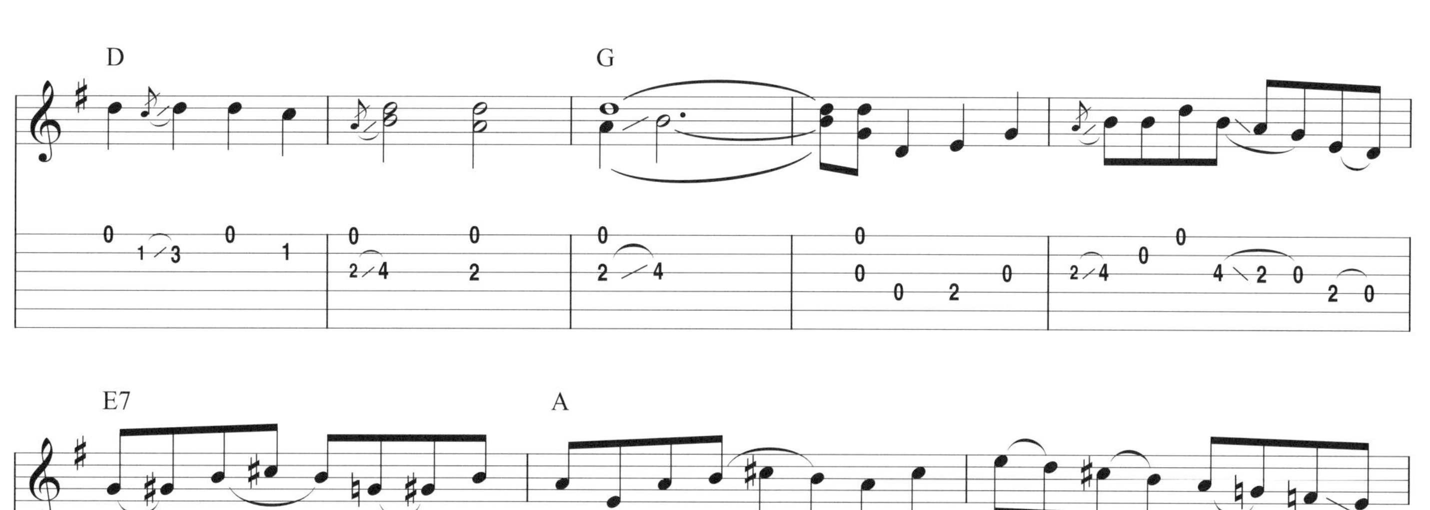
D
G

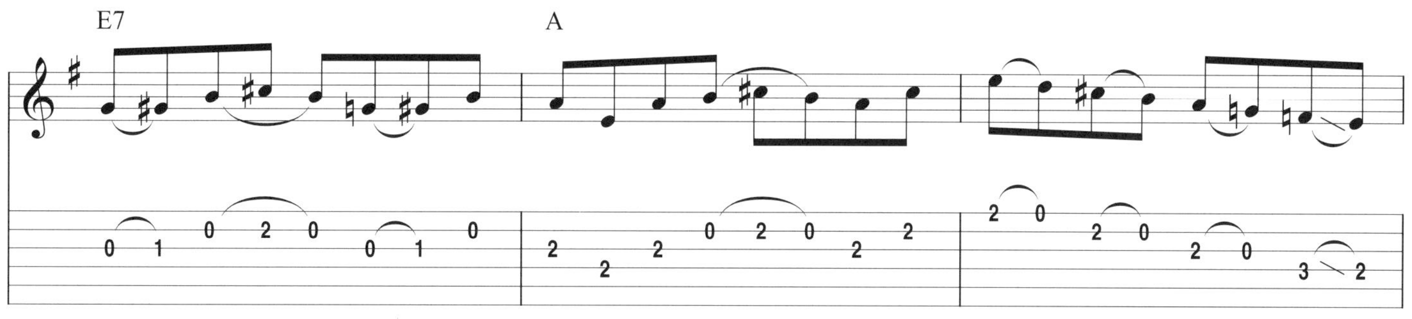
E7
A

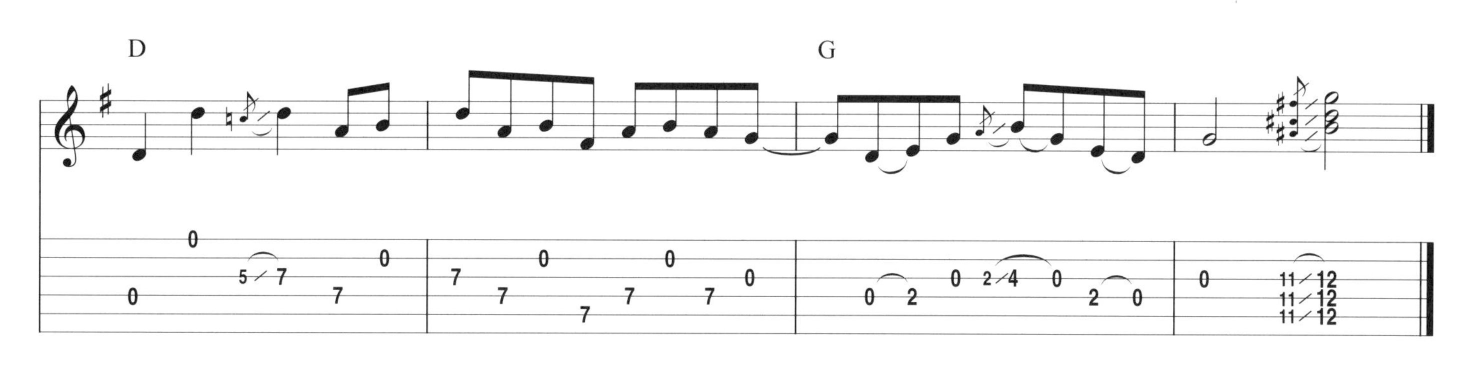
D
G

Appendix
Finding the Notes on the Fingerboard

If you're not familiar with the basic idea of how notes are named and counted in Western music (and when I say "Western music," we're taking the classical music of Western Europe, not Bob Wills or the Sons of the Pioneers), you might want to get hold of a general book on music theory and/or music reading to get oriented. But in the meantime, here is *Dave's E-Z Rundown of What You Need to Know to Not Get Lost in this Book.*

There are seven letters used to name all of the notes you'll ever see: A, B, C, D, E, F, and G. Most of these notes are two frets apart—for example, it's two frets from G to A, two frets from D to E, and so on. In real life, this means that, for example, if you play the open third string, or G, you can then find the note A two frets up—at the second fret on the third string. Likewise, if you play the open first string, D, you can then find the note E two frets up, at the second fret on the first string. The more general musical term for this distance of two frets is a *whole step.* (Remember, people who play other instruments like the tuba or the harmonica don't *have* frets, so you need to have another way to explain things besides putting your strings in someone's face and saying, "You know—two frets up. Come on, maaan, lookit!")

Fig. 1

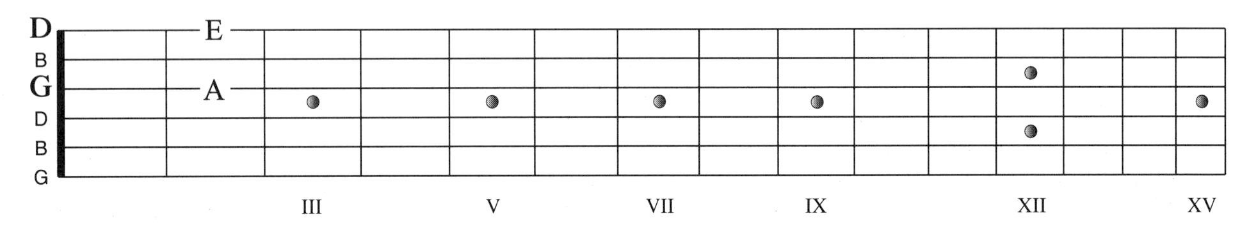

There are two exceptions to this two-frets rule. It is only a one-fret distance from B to C, and a one-fret distance from E to F. For example, if you play the open second string, or B, you can then find the note C at the *first* fret on the second string. Likewise, if you begin at an E, on the second fret of the first string, the note F will be one fret up—at the third fret on the first string. The more general term for a distance of one fret is a *half step.*

Fig. 2

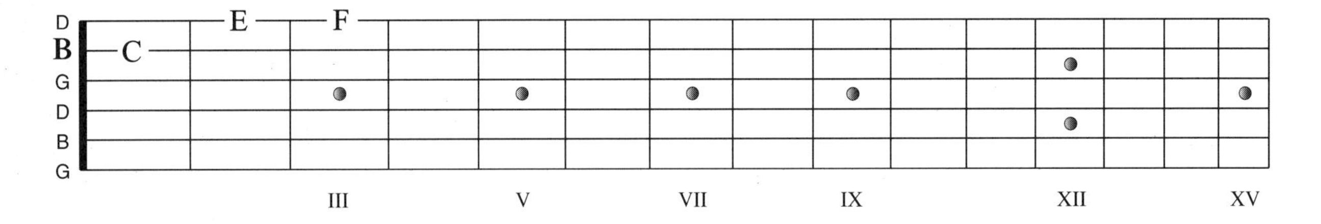

Combining this information with the names of the open strings at the nut in the High G tuning, we can make a diagram of the entire fingerboard up to the twelfth fret:

Fig. 3

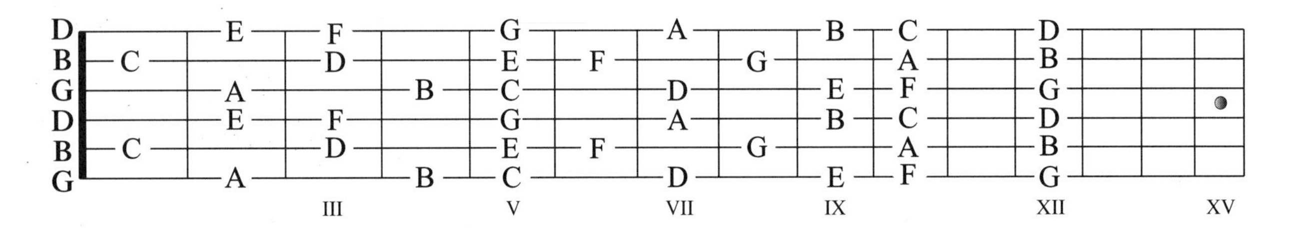

As you can see, this still leaves us with many unnamed notes on the fretboard. These remaining notes are named using *sharps* and/or *flats.* A sharp raises a note by a half step, or one fret; a flat lowers a note a half step, or one fret. For example, the third fret on the first string is the note F; the fourth fret on the first string, or one fret higher, is called F♯. The fourth fret on the third string is B; the third fret on the third string, or one fret lower, is called B♭. Depending on your point of view, a note can have more than one name—you could also call the fourth fret on the first string G♭; you could call the third fret on the third string A♯.

Fig. 4

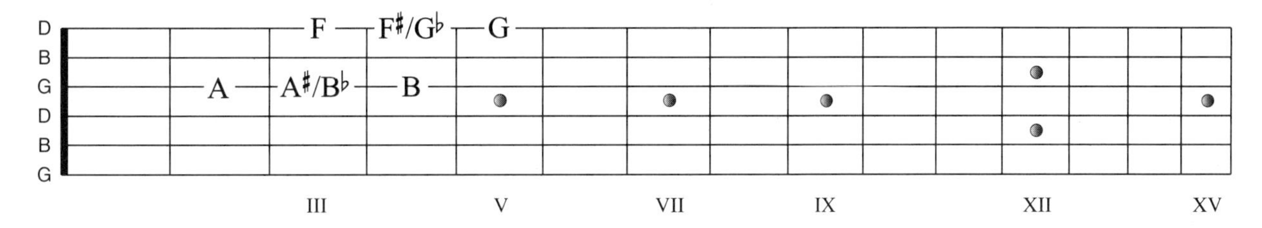

Notes without sharps or flats—the original seven notes we began with—are called *natural.* Here is a diagram of *all* the notes up to the twelfth fret—sharp, flat, and natural:

Fig. 5

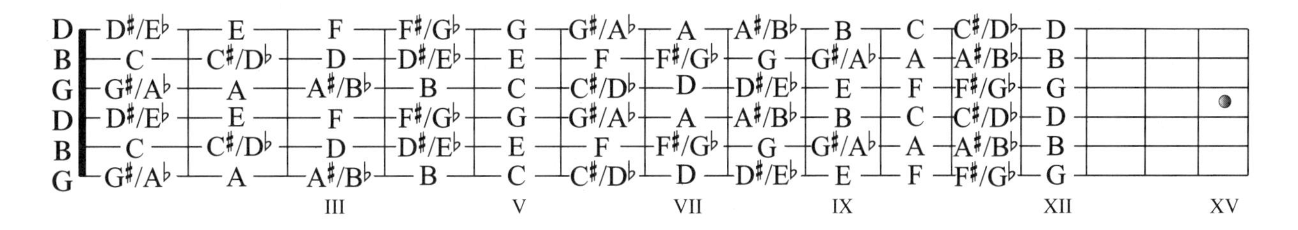

Afterword

I hope this book has provided you with some interesting ideas about practicing and improvising that make it more enjoyable to work on and play your instrument. Here are a few more suggestions on where to go from here:

- Work through this material at your own pace. Try to balance your practice between warm-up exercises, learning repertoire, and practicing your improvisation in some of the ways suggested throughout the book.
- Try to find your own licks, lift other people's ideas off of records, watch people play live, and ask other musicians what they're doing. In addition to working out tunes and licks by other lap-style slide players, there is also plenty to be learned from people who play acoustic and electric bottleneck guitar, electric lap steel, and pedal steel. Meanwhile, if you hear a tune you like and there's no slide involved, or you hear a lick you really like played on another instrument, see if you can work it out anyway.
- If possible, take a few real live lessons with another lap-style guitarist, to see up-close how some of the more technical things are done.
- Finally, get together with other people to play, regardless of the style—you can always learn something from trying to play in any context.

Good luck, and keep on picking.